the
accidental
love
letter

Olivia Beirne is the bestselling author of *The List That Changed My Life* and lives in Buckinghamshire. She has worked as a waitress, a pottery painter and a casting assistant, but being a writer is definitely her favourite job yet.

You can keep in touch with Olivia through her website oliviabeirne.co.uk, or via Olivia_Beirne on Twitter, olivia.beirne on Instagram and /Olivia-Beirne on Facebook.

Also by Olivia Beirne and available from Headline:

The List That Changed My Life

the
accidental
love
letter

olivia beirne

REVIEW

First published in eBook in 2019 by
HEADLINE PUBLISHING GROUP

First published in paperback in 2020 by
HEADLINE PUBLISHING GROUP

3

Cataloguing in Publication Data is available from the British Library

ISBN 978 1 4722 5957 8

Typeset in Bembo Std 11.25/14.75 pt by
Palimpsest Book Production Limited, Falkirk, Stirlingshire

Printed and bound in Great Britain by Clays Ltd, Elcograf S.p.A.

Headline's policy is to use papers that are natural, renewable and recyclable
products and made from wood grown in well-managed forests and other
controlled sources. The logging and manufacturing processes are expected
to conform to the environmental regulations of the country of origin.

HEADLINE PUBLISHING GROUP
An Hachette UK Company
Carmelite House
50 Victoria Embankment
London EC4Y 0DZ

www.headline.co.uk
www.hachette.co.uk

To my mum,
for her continued love and support

I hold my phone close to my ear as I hear the click of the answering machine.

'Hi, Mum.' I smile into the phone. 'It's me. It's not important. I was just calling because my pitch is about to start, and I feel really nervous about it so I wanted to talk to you.' I pause, my fingers tightening around the phone. 'I'm sure it will be fine. I'll call you when it's done. Love you, bye.'

CHAPTER ONE

My eyes scan the room. Faye is leaning back in her seat, her right finger scrolling endlessly on her iPhone. Duncan is pacing in the corner like a dog working out where to sit, and Angela has her head in her hands. I blink, desperate to quell the fizzing anxiety that is brewing in the pit of my stomach.

Why isn't anybody saying anything? This must be the longest they have ever been silent. I take a deep breath and try to look as if I'm completely unfazed by the silence, and not like I'm ready to rip out my fingernails.

I don't usually mind sitting in silence. In fact, I love it. But about one minute ago, I pitched an idea to Duncan (Chief Editorial Something or Other), Faye (colleague) and Angela (my boss. Who is great. Or, at least, I thought she was until she took a vow of silence as soon as I gathered up enough courage to voice my sad pitch. Now I think she's the Devil.)

This is not how today was supposed to go.

It was supposed to go like this.

06.55: Woken up by Emma leaving for work.

07.00: First alarm goes off. Snooze.

07.10: Priya gets in from night shift.

07.15: Priya gets in shower.

07.20: Second alarm goes off. Snooze.

07.25: Priya gets out of shower, leaves bathroom, goes to bed.

07.30: Third alarm goes off. Get out of bed.

07.35: In shower.

07.45: Out of shower.

07.50: Dressed, hair in towel turban. Make breakfast (Weetabix with one spoonful of brown sugar).

08.00: Back in bedroom. Dry hair and apply make-up.

08.15: Check bag and packed lunch.

08.20: Leave for work, wave at neighbour Joy, walk to bus stop.

08.30: Bus arrives. Get on bus. Find seat on middle row, right aisle, corner seat. Go to work.

I glance down at my twitching, slightly damp hands.

That bit all worked out. As always, every minute of this morning went exactly to schedule. Exactly as it has done for the past two years.

08.50: Arrive at work. Walk upstairs, find seat.

08.52: Turn on computer. Check emails.

09.15: Secretly read BuzzFeed articles on nice stories about how cats save their owners, to try to calm burning anxiety.

09.30: Avoid eye contact with Faye as she arrives for work (half an hour late, as always).

09.45: Offer to make Angela coffee in attempt to put her in a good mood.

09.46: Try not to look upset when Angela refuses, and then makes her own.

09.50: Listen to Beyoncé megamix to feel inspired.

09.55: Leave desk and walk to pitching room.

This part of the schedule all went to plan. If I chop up each hour into small segments then nothing seems that scary.

It was the next part that didn't follow order.

10.00: Sit down in pitching room and wait for everyone to arrive.

10.05: Chat to Duncan, Angela and Faye about weekend in attempt to distract them about pitch.

10.15: Start pitch.

10.20: Dazzle co-workers.

10.30: Terrible ordeal over, but discovered new lease of life and am forever seen as serious, top journalist.

10.31: Leave pitching room. Reward myself with morning biscuit and check Facebook.

I glance down at my watch and my stomach lurches.

It's 10.35.

I finished my pitch at 10.29 (one minute sooner than I had planned, another bad sign) and now, six minutes later, we are all still sitting in silence.

And not a single person has offered me a biscuit or told me I can go home.

I shift in my seat.

What are they all thinking about? Surely they have forgotten what I even said twelve hundred years ago, when I originally made this pitch.

I weave my fingers into a ball.

I should have scrapped this whole schedule and just gone with Plan B:

06.55:   Call in sick and avoid entire pitch.

'Right . . .' Angela prises her head from her hands and focuses her eyes back on me. 'So, say it to us again, Bea?'

A rush of heat spins through me.

Say it again?

What? Why? I've already said it once, and everybody clearly hates it.

I open my mouth and take a deep breath.

10.37.

'Erm,' I start, 'so, I just think I'd like to focus on—'

'Oh my God!' Faye squeals from her seat, her eyes still glued to her phone. 'Sorry,' she says quickly, 'just, look at this.'

She angles her phone towards Duncan, who cranes over.

'It's a video of a cat, sat on a washing machine!' Faye cries.

I shut my mouth again, feeling my face burn.

10.38.

'Oh!' Duncan chuckles. 'That is funny. Angela, have you seen this? It's a cat, and it's sat on a washing machine!'

Okay, well this is going well.

Would they even notice if I went home?

I smile back at Duncan as he gestures to Faye's phone.

Duncan is a squat man, with a smattering of bristles that poke out of his scalp like stubborn blades of grass. He has a round stomach that hangs over his belt like a beach ball and large teeth that make me think of individual squares of white chocolate.

He's not a bad guy, he's nice enough. But he's also a total idiot who cries 'slam *dunk!*' every time he finishes a news story and is the cousin of the CEO.

He once asked me how to spell 'successful' and is now convinced I am Carol Vorderman. (Or, as he likes to call me, 'Albus Einstein', which is wrong on so many levels I don't even know where to begin.)

'I just love videos like this,' Duncan chortles. 'They are just so heart-warming. We should add more content like this to the website. Don't you think? I've always wanted a cat.'

His words die in the unbearable silence, and I look back at him.

Yes, welcome to hell, my friend. Where you say things that you think are interesting, and every single person ignores you.

I sink back into my seat.

I work at the local paper, the *Middlesex Herald*, as a junior reporter. I get sent press releases every day, and it's my job to try to make them sound interesting before posting them online. I've been here for two years, and everything was going brilliantly. Until I had my appraisal. Angela said I wasn't 'pushing myself' enough and that I needed to 'broaden my horizons'. I tried to argue that my horizons were fine as they were, but I'm not very good at arguing. She then had the bright idea of me thinking about what I wanted to write about, and pitching a story directly to Duncan.

'Right!' Duncan slaps his hands together. 'I think this calls for a tea break. Who wants to do a Starbucks run? I've heard that the famous pumpkin spiced latte is out today! Exciting times, eh?'

Faye nods at Duncan, who goes to leave, when Angela raises a hand. Angela has cropped, mousey hair and a long neck. She wears her small glasses on a chain round her neck and has a permanent shadow of light pink lipstick on her thin lips.

'Duncan,' she says sternly, 'Bea needs to give us her pitch.'

Duncan swivels his round face towards me, perplexed.

'Really?' he says. 'I thought you'd given it, Bea?'

I stare back at him.

'Go on, Bea,' Angela says kindly. 'Try again.'

10.49.

'Right,' I hear myself say, my voice shaking slightly, 'so, I was thinking that I would really like to try to write some pieces about the community—'

'We're a local newspaper,' Faye laughs, 'everything we publish is about the community.'

I dart a glance over to Faye and then back to Angela, as if she might stop me.

'Yes,' I start again, 'but I mean to really get involved in something that brings the whole community together. Like, I know my friend—'

'What friend?' Duncan chips in, screwing up his face. 'Have I met her? Did she come to the Christmas party?'

What? No! Why would I bring my friends to my work Christmas party? I don't even want to go myself.

'No,' I say, 'well, anyway, at her work they did a Macmillan bake sale and raised loads of money for charity. I think a lot of places do that. So, maybe something like that. I just mean that I'd like to run a story focusing on something good that the community is doing. I—'

'Why?' Duncan interrupts again.

'Well . . .' I flounder. 'I just think that people will like to read about it, and it will make people happy.'

'Our job isn't to make people happy, Bea,' Faye says, pointing her pen at me. 'Our job is to bring people the news.' She adds the last bit and looks straight at Duncan who inflates with joy.

I feel a spark of anger shoot through me.

Duncan high-fives Faye at the casual mention of his meaningless catchphrase.

'Exactly!' Duncan trumpets, thrusting a porky finger in Faye's direction. 'Yes! That's the spirit, Faye!'

Faye beams at him, and I glare at the back of her blonde head.

'Right!' Duncan says again, pulling himself to his feet. 'Are we done here then, Angela?'

Angela looks limply at Duncan. 'If that's all you have to say, Duncan, then yes.'

I watch Duncan flash her a thumbs up and march out of the room, followed by Faye.

10.54.

They didn't even let me finish.

'Don't worry about it, Bea,' Angela says. 'You have to be quite forward with Duncan to be heard. I just think you need to work on your confidence.'

9

I try and smile as Angela walks out of the door, leaving me alone.

Yeah, as if I haven't heard that before.

★

I lean my head back against the bus seat and fight the urge to rest my heavy eyes.

Okay, so today didn't go as planned.

Not that I'm really sure what I thought would happen. I hate public speaking. I hate confrontation, and the idea of 'pitching' in front of three people who are all significantly smarter, louder and better than me makes me want to dig a hole in the ground and stick my head in it.

I knew it would go terribly. I did.

The bus pulls to a halt amongst a smog of traffic and I look out of the window. Steam is crawling up the glass and I rub a spot clean with the back of my sleeve.

Not that I really care. I don't. I don't want to be promoted anyway, or run my own story like Faye. Leave her to show off and flounce around behind the keyboard. I'm happy typing press releases.

I mean, hello? Who spent three hours today trying to think of a pun regarding Mrs Hammond of 42 Hedgeway Drive's record-breaking bush?

(And by think of a pun, I mean think of a pun that wouldn't get me fired. Which was much harder than you'd expect. I mean, I'm not being funny, but 'Mrs Hammond urgently needs her bush trimmed' would almost be worth getting a disciplinary.)

The bus slugs back down the road and my body lurches

forward. I glance down at my phone, which stares back up at me, lifeless. I open my WhatsApp group with Emma and Priya, my housemates, and tap a message.

Hey, either of you in tonight? Could do with some . . .

I pause.

Could do with some what?

Girl time? Does anybody say 'girl time' any more? Did anybody ever say girl time?

I stare down at my phone.

I can't say 'could do with some love' or they'll misunderstand and try to sign me up for Tinder again.

Could do with some . . . fun?

No, definitely not. That will start a whole new conversation that I never want to have with either of them, ever.

Could do with some company?

I type the words into my phone. They stare back up at me.

God, that makes me sound like the saddest person ever. I can't send that.

I quickly delete the last bit and hit send. I look back out of the steamed-up window as the bus waits at the bus stop opposite the park, and I notice an old man slumped on a bench. He has a prominent, square jaw and his hunched body is almost bent in two. His head is hidden under a flat cap, and I spot a pair of glasses that are damp under the rain.

I lean forward to try to see him better. He must be freezing. Why is he sat out in the rain, on his own? Is he okay?

Maybe he's walking his dog and he just needs a break. Or maybe he's run away from something.

I try to look back at the old man as the bus pulls away, but he vanishes behind a sea of cars.

Maybe he just wants to be alone.

My phone vibrates in my hand and I feel a zap shoot through me as I see a message from Emma.

Sorry won't be back until late, out with Margot x

Within seconds, Priya's message pops on to my screen.

Me neither. At work, then seeing Josh.

I stare down at my screen as a weight settles in my stomach.

No worries, I type back, *have fun. See you later.*

I drop the phone back into my bag and make one last attempt to spot the old man, but he's been swallowed up by the swirls of rain.

Does anybody want to be alone?

★

I fumble with my keys as the rain splats on to my head like cold, wet eggs.

Stupid keys. Why do I have one hundred keys when I only ever need one?

As the 'responsible housemate' (a label I never intended) I have been in charge of holding on to the garage key, the PO box key (sorry – *Priya's* PO box key. Why does she need a PO box?), Emma's spare car key (not that I can drive or have had a single lesson), the kitchen window key (?) and, the most useless until last, Emma's girlfriend's flat key. I mean, what the hell am I ever supposed to do with that?

I bought it up with Emma once and she said how I can water the plants if they ever go away together. I'm sorry but: 1) she doesn't own a single plant, and 2) even if she did, I'm not spending my free time flitting around her girlfriend's flat like a creepy, green-fingered Mary Poppins.

I mean, what next? Does she also want me to prance round and do all of her washing while they are sunning themselves in Sardinia? Bake her a casserole that she can heat up when she's back? Organise her bloody post?

I did say all this to Emma but she batted me away and then refused to take the key off my key ring because she said it would 'ruin her nails'.

I finally manage to free the only key I ever use and jab it in the lock as a fresh burst of cold water splashes on to the crown of my head. I kick the door open.

'Hello?' I shout, even though I know that Priya and Emma are both out.

I push my way into the house and drop my sopping bag on to the floor. I glance around at the living room, which looks exactly how I left it this morning, and sink on to our sofa.

I look down at the time.

18.05.

I push my head back against our squashy sofa cushion as my mind pieces together my schedule for the evening.

18.15: Sit on sofa.
18.30: Put colour wash on.
18.40: Start cooking dinner (pasta bake).
19.00: Make lunch for tomorrow.
19.15: Eat dinner.
19.25: Wash up.
19.30: Watch *Hollyoaks*.

20.00: Watch *EastEnders*.

20.30: Put on PJs and get ready for bed.

21.00: Watch *Made in Chelsea*.

22.00: Go to bed and read book.

22.30: Finish reading. Check phone.

22.45: Set alarm. Go to sleep.

As my mind reviews each section I feel myself relax and I sink further into the sofa.

Right, that's what I'll do this evening. Sorted.

I look around the empty house and let my phone drop to my side. The house looks back at me, completely silent, only the slight whir of the heating confirming to me that it's there and not a wild figment of my imagination. I take a deep breath and move my eyes towards the kitchen table. One stale mug is welded to the left-hand corner and a stack of post is slowly towering up on the right. Exactly how I left it this morning, nothing has changed.

Well, one thing has.

I narrow my eyes at the whiteboard propped on the mantelpiece with Priya's latest scribble.

Used the last, of the milk, sorry.

I feel a small laugh tickle my throat as I look at the heart sketched next to the message with another instruction.

P.S. Don't forget it's bin night.

I pull my knees up to my chest.

Sometimes, I think about being alone. I'm sat in the same spot I sit every night. I'm exactly where I'm expected to be.

Nothing changes. I'm always here.

My phone vibrates in my hand and I look down as I spot a

text from Emma. I feel a small leap of hope. Maybe she's coming home tonight after all.

B are you in tomorrow? Me and Priya need to have a chat with you.

My stomach flips over at Emma's message.

They need to have a chat with me, together?

Why? What could I have done?

★

I drum my fingers on my desk, my mind spiralling as my right hand manically turns a small pencil between my fingers.

I look back down to my notepad, covered in neat scribbles. As I stare down at my list, I feel the twitching in my chest begin to ease.

I've made a list of everything I can possibly think of that I may have done to upset Priya and/or Emma. I stare down at the list, my pencil gripped in my hand.

If I know what to expect, then I can manage it. If it isn't a surprise, then it won't be that bad.

Things that I could have done to upset Priya and Emma.

1. They could be mad I turned the heating up (even though neither of them were there and it was so cold in the house that my fingers went blue).
2. They could be mad because I didn't offer to make them any dinner (even though neither of them were here).
3. Emma could be mad that I used her wok last week.
4. Priya could be annoyed that I accidentally woke her up after her night shift last week. (I'm sorry, but I fell down

the stairs in a *towel* so I think I was definitely worse off in that situation.)

5. They could be staging an intervention with me because they don't like my hair and my experimental French plait phase (which they both promised they thought looked great and wildly encouraged).

6. They could both have decided that I am an insufferable, terrible housemate who they can no longer tolerate.

My eyes scan back over the list carefully as a final thought drops into my mind.

They could be asking if both of their partners can move in.

I feel my heart thump.

Please let it not be that.

I like Josh, and I especially like Margot. But I don't want to live with them.

For starters, where would I sit on our three-seater sofa?

I chew on my lip as my hand raps the blunt pencil against my desk.

But how could I say no? I mean, I couldn't, not really anyway. Not if they have both already discussed it and have decided between themselves that they think it's a good idea. I would just look like the jealous spinster, lurking in my ground-floor bedroom like the village troll.

I think the worst part is that they've sat down and decided that they need to speak to me, together. They've pre-planned it. And I have no idea what it could be.

I hate not knowing what is going to happen.

'Bea!'

I jerk out of my reverie and my eyes flit down to the clock.

11.15. Faye's first visit.

Faye is one of the few people who sticks to my schedule almost religiously. Even though she has never seen it and I'd never dream of mentioning it to her. It's one of the only features I like about her.

Maybe she has a schedule of her own.

Faye visits my desk twice a day. When she first started doing it, I happily slotted her into my schedule, thinking that she was trying to befriend me.

But I quickly realised that this wasn't the case as Faye used her five-to-six-minute window to tell me about herself, ask me a question, and then pull out her phone the moment I started replying. I watched her do the same thing with every person in our office (there are fifteen of us - seventeen on the third week of the month, when the finance team come in).

It didn't take me long to work out that Faye does this as a way of wasting over an hour of her morning before doing any work, and then another hour of her afternoon as she asks everybody what they had for lunch (although this conversation tends to only last about three minutes, even for a professional procrastinator like Faye. There are only limited responses you can have to 'I had a tuna sandwich and a bag of cheese and onion crisps').

I look up at Faye as she swans towards me, her eyes flicking over my head to ensure that nobody is going to interrupt her

17

and try to combine morning conversations. She clacks over in her large, chunky boots and I push my notebook under my coffee cup.

Faye has long blonde hair that is usually braided at the back of her head like a horse ready for dressage. Her large brown eyes are always heavily made up and I've caught her taking mirror selfies in the company toilet fourteen times since she started working here.

She's been here three months.

Faye shimmies into a spare seat next to me and glances over at me in acknowledgement as her mouth curves into a smile.

We have a 'cool, fun' hot-desk policy at work, which Duncan started about six months ago and I despise. After four days of hot-seating hell, I started getting to work early enough to ensure that I sit in the same desk every day, in the back corner of the office. That way I can keep an eye on what everyone else is doing, whilst being close enough to the kitchen to sneak myself a cup of tea without having to make one for every single person in the office.

I know that makes me sound like a bad person, but having to remember how fifteen people take their tea – and then having a panic attack about whether you accidentally gave Jane the Vegan full-fat milk instead of soya – is enough to send you into an early grave.

(I never found out if I got the milks the wrong way round, but Jane was off sick the next day. I try not to think about whether that was just a coincidence. Or whether Jane now thinks I'm trying to kill her and wrap her up in pastry like a meat-eating maniac.)

Faye flicks one leg over the other and pulls out her phone. She always does this for about thirty seconds, so I shake my mouse and pretend to look at an email.

I glance back at Faye, and then back to the office clock.

11.17.

I open my mouth to speak when an email from Duncan pings on to the screen. I take a deep breath.

Morning team!!!!!!!!! Here's to another GREAT day at the OfFiCe PaRtAy!!!!! Team meeting on Friday (breakfast me thinks?!!??) Thanks 4 being THE BEST TEAM EVA!!!!! Duncan.

I blink as I feel my eyes shrivel in disgust.

I cannot, and will not ever be able to, fathom how Duncan is our Editor when he goes to such extraordinary lengths to abuse grammar.

We get three emails like this a day. The first arrives mid-morning (to 'rare up the team'), the second just after lunch (which usually involves a novelty picture of Duncan eating a sandwich, with Faye pouting in the background as a funny 'photo bomb' that they'll then laugh about all afternoon) and the last one at about four (to 'spur us on' for the last hour with some dreadful, inspirational quote. This is when Duncan usually asks me how to spell something.)

'How was your evening?'

My eyes dart towards Faye, then quickly back to my computer.

Faye asks me this question every day and it still makes my heart pound like an alarm clock.

I should prepare an answer. Sometimes I do. When I notice

the clock tick over to 11.00, my brain starts storming the possibilities of how I spent my evening.

I went out for dinner with a friend.

I went to the cinema.

I went out for a drink.

But as soon as I fixate on one lie, my brain can't keep up, and suddenly I'm trapped in a hamster wheel.

What if she asks me where I went for a drink? And who with? How did I get there? What did I have to drink? What if she was there too? What if she knew somebody there? What if she finds out I'm lying? What sort of person would lie about what they did on a Monday night because they don't want to admit that they actually sat in on their own until they went to bed, like they do every night?

I look up at Faye as she drops her phone next to her side and raises her large eyes to meet mine. I drag Duncan's email into a folder and flash a small smile in her direction.

'Fine, thank you,' I say, fixing my eyes on my monitor to try to show her how busy I am.

I always hope that if I give Faye lame enough answers then she might leave.

She never does.

'What did you do?' she asks, her eyes wandering around the office.

I pause.

What did I do?

I did exactly what I planned to do. I arrived home at 6 p.m., I got in my pyjamas, made my dinner, watched two and a half hours of TV and went to bed.

I glance over to Faye.

I can't tell Faye that. She's the type of person who seems to go out every night, according to her Instagram, to attend some fabulous party with an effortless low ponytail (which I can never pull off without looking like Will Turner from *Pirates of the Caribbean*).

'Err,' I say, 'you know. This and that.'

That's it. Keep it vague. Like I'm so important that fancy plans mean nothing to me.

'Like what?'

I take a deep breath as I feel my anxiety begin to stir.

Okay, a lie. This is no big deal. I can lie. It's only Faye for goodness' sake, she probably isn't even listening.

'I,' I begin, 'well, I . . .'

I feel my mouth go dry as the pressure sucks every word I know from my brain like a vacuum cleaner.

Just say something, Bea. Say anything.

'I actually ended up . . .' I trail off as I notice Faye's blonde head swivel round.

Jemima from sales walks past and Faye jumps out of her seat.

'Jemima!' Faye oozes. 'How are you?'

I close my mouth, a wave of heat washing over me.

Okay. I survived. It's over. She doesn't care. She never cares.

I watch as Faye totters after Jemima – they swan past my desk and into the kitchen – and then I move my eyes dully back to my computer screen.

If everyone sticks to schedule then I won't be bothered now for another two hours. Unless Duncan is trying to write a pitch and needs help spelling 'astonishing' again.

Two hours until I am spoken to again.

I slip my headphones in and lean forward on my desk.

I can manage that.

21

CHAPTER TWO

I stride up to my front door, my only valuable key firmly in my right hand.

18.00. Arrive home.

I pause, hovering over the lock. Anxiety twists up my windpipe as I imagine the weird intervention that I have no control over with supposed friends Emma and Priya.

My eyes flit over to the neat house next door, and I notice the curtain ruffle slightly.

18.01. Collect post from Joy.

I drop my hand down to my side and walk across the garden path. I see Joy every Tuesday, when I pop round to pick up our post (this visit lasts about six minutes), and Thursday, when I stop by for dinner (this visit lasts about six years).

I slip my phone back into my pocket.

At least one part of this evening will stick to my schedule. At least I know how this next little bit of time is going to go.

I stare at the neat, pale blue door and smile.

Joy has lived in number 3 Runnymede Way for forty years (or something like that, she has told me. I was half listening) and has taken it upon herself to look after our post every day, since she realised that we don't have a letter box. God only knows how she persuades the postman to allow her. I mean, I'm sure it's illegal.

I raise my hand, and as my left knuckle grazes the shiny wood the door swings open.

Joy is a small woman, with neat copper hair (that she has coloured on the first Wednesday of every month) and wide eyes. She is always wearing a perfectly coordinated outfit, in a different shade of pastel. Today she's wearing a pale yellow cardigan and light grey trousers.

Her eyes fix on me and I notice our post, neatly piled on her small table ready for me.

She steps in front of it as if I can't see it. Her body is twitching nervously as her eyes flit across my body.

'Hello, Bea,' Joy beams, 'how are you?'

Her clipped words present themselves as if she's been rehearsing the sentence for the past hour.

'Hi, Joy. I'm fine thanks,' I say, 'how are you?'

I feel my heavy eyes droop as I look back at her.

We go through this every Tuesday. She always acts surprised at me coming round, as if I've just popped round for a chat or to borrow a cup of sugar, even though I come at the same time every week, for the same reason.

'Oh,' Joy leans on the side of her door, 'I'm fine too, thank you. How has your day been?'

'Okay, thank you,' I say. 'How has your day been?'

My eyes flit over to the pile of post behind her. I'm sure

there's a bill on top. Could that be from the electric? Surely my bloody electric bill isn't due again.

'Sorry, you'll have to excuse me,' she laughs as she gestures down at herself, 'I've just taken a quiche out of the oven. Would you like some?' She fixes her shiny brown eyes back on me. 'I'm sure it's too much for one person. You could share it with Priya and Emma. Is she on nights this week? I saw her get in at the crack of dawn this morning.'

She steps back to welcome me into her home and my feet weld themselves to the floor. I take in her immaculate hallway. There isn't a speck of dust on her moss-green carpet, and her oak coat rack proudly holds Joy's single coat on one of its curled arms. The warm, yellow light of her lamp blinks at me and I look away.

I don't have time to go in now.

I've learnt this lesson the hard way. If you go into Joy's house you will never leave. It's like the House of the Living Cats.

'That's okay,' I say quickly. 'I'm fine, thank you. I was actually hoping to grab our post.'

'Oh,' she says, 'of course.' She reaches over and picks up the pile of post. 'Here you are.'

I take it from her. 'Thank you.'

'You've got three letters today,' she says, as if this is a big scoop. 'Bit more than usual, isn't it? I didn't get any post today.'

My eyes quickly scan the post.

Gas? Urgh. What are you doing in there?

'Jenny said that she would send a postcard, but perhaps it got lost in the post,' Joy continues. 'I'm sure it will arrive tomorrow. You know she's in Australia now? She sent me this great picture. Shall I show you?'

She turns back into her house. 'No thank you,' I say hurriedly,

'I mean,' I add, 'I think I've seen it. You showed me a few weeks ago, remember?'

Like I could ever forget. I was stuck in her house for three hours – and two-thirds of that time was spent teaching Joy how to turn the printer on.

'One of the letters is for you,' Joy says. She peers over at the three letters in my hand.

I turn the letters over.

Under the unblinking gaze of Joy, I fan the three letters out to satisfy her curiosity.

My eyes lock on to the third letter. I feel my body twitch.

'See,' Joy says, her voice dancing with excitement, 'that one is for you. You don't usually get handwritten letters, do you?'

I hold the letter in my hands as I look at the scrawled words, etched on the white envelope in slightly smudged biro.

B
3 Runnymede Way
Twickenham
Middlesex
TW2 5BT

As my eyes clock the final letters of my postcode, they sweep to the top and read the address again, my heart pounding in my chest.

Why do I have a letter?

I never receive letters, not handwritten ones. Who has written me a letter?

My eyes scan the top of the letter again and I feel a wave of relief.

Oh. Hang on.

'It's not for me,' I say, looking back up at Joy. 'That's not how you spell my name. It's probably just a random initial.'

I hold the letter up to Joy, who leans forward as if it's written in hieroglyphics.

'Are you sure?' she says. 'It could be for you. That's probably just a mistake. Why don't you open it, just in case?'

I pull the letter away from Joy, feeling a slight niggle of annoyance.

My God she's nosey. She definitely steams open my post and reads it every day.

'No,' I say, putting the letters in my bag. 'It won't be for me. Nobody knows my address. Someone will probably come and pick it up,' I say, closing my bag. 'Or I'll do that return to sender thing,' I add as an afterthought.

I look back at Joy. Her face is fixed in a permanent smile, as if she hasn't heard what I've just said.

I look back at her awkwardly. What does she want?

'Right,' I say eventually, 'well, I'd better go.'

Joy drops her head into a nod, her smile still in place.

'Of course, dear,' she says pleasantly. 'If you change your mind about the quiche, just let me know. You don't have to phone, I'll be in.'

I turn on my heel and walk across the garden path towards my front door.

'Sure,' I say, as I reach my front door, 'have a nice evening, Joy.'

I catch a final glimpse of Joy, still standing in her lit doorway and watching me leave. I click the front door shut and drop the post on the hall table.

I glance down at my watch.

18.13.

'Hello?' I call, as I drop my bag on to the floor.

'Bea!'

I jump as Emma pops out of the downstairs toilet and flings her arms around me. My body is crushed as nerves fizzle in my chest until she lets me go.

Why is Emma treating me as if I'm a long-lost relative she's picked up from the airport?

'Hey,' I say, as she lets me go.

This can't be a good sign.

'Bea?' Priya shouts from upstairs. 'I'm on the toilet. Hang on!'

'Err, okay,' I shout back.

Why is she telling me that?

She's being weird. They're both being weird.

What are they going to tell me?

'How are you?' Emma says as we walk through to the living room. 'How was your weekend? I feel like I barely saw you.'

I sink down on to the sofa and pull my knees up to my chest in an attempt to calm my nerves.

That would be because Emma did barely see me. She popped home briefly on Friday night, to grab some bits, and I'm assuming she's been camped out at Margot's since.

Not that I mind. I'm used to it.

'Good, thank you.' I smile. 'I had my pitch at work yesterday.'

Priya runs through the door, still in her nurse's uniform, with four pens stuck in her hair. 'Sorry!' she cries, settling down on the sofa next to Emma. 'You all right, Bea?'

I frown at her. 'Are you going to work?'

'What?' Priya looks down at herself and then laughs. 'Oh, no. I fell asleep in this and can't be bothered to get changed.'

Emma frowns. 'You slept in your bra?'

Priya bats the question away. 'Listen,' she says, 'I thought I'd make us all dinner tonight.'

'I've just been to Tesco,' Emma chips in. 'Priya's going to make us a chilli.'

'Oh,' I say, 'okay, cool.'

'And,' she adds, 'they had an offer on ice cream, so I bought that too.'

I look back at them as they grin at me.

'Okay,' I say again.

Priya and Emma are still looking at me. Priya's eyes are wide and anxious, and Emma is wringing her hands together like she's squeezing out moisture.

What is going on?

Silence stretches between us as Priya and Emma exchange glances.

Oh God. This is already horrible and they haven't even said anything yet.

What's happening?

'So,' I say, 'there was something you wanted to talk to me about?'

Priya's left eye twitches and her mouth clamps shut.

I try to swallow as anxiety swirls up the back of my throat.

What are they going to say? I feel like they are about to break up with me.

'Yeah,' Emma says, taking a deep breath. 'Right. Yeah. So, I've been talking to Priya and we've realised that we're both in similar situations.'

She looks at Priya who does a small nod, her face flushed.

'And,' Emma continues, 'the thing is, Bea. Margot and I have been getting quite serious, and Priya and Josh have too.'

I feel a rush of heat storm up my chest and I shift my clammy hands under my thighs.

Oh God. I was right. They are going to ask them to move in with us.

What am I going to say to this?

'Okay,' I say slowly.

'And we have both decided that we think that we want to live together,' Emma finishes, the last words tumbling out of her mouth.

I stare back at them blankly.

And here it is. My future. Spread out before me like a big fat carcass of a love life.

I shall be an official fifth wheel for the rest of my life. Clamped to the boot, taken everywhere you go, but essentially useless – and very awkward when you actually need it.

Great.

I'll have to sit on the floor every time we watch the TV. Or (much worse) squash in between them like the child who's come home for the holidays. I'll never be able to stay off Tinder, with them constantly badgering me about how great it is to be in a relationship and how I'm such a catch any guy would be lucky to have me blah, blah, blah.

I mean, God. Talk about unbearable.

'Wow,' I say, trying to contort my face into a smile, 'that's, erm, exciting.'

Yeah, as exciting as clawing my eyes out with rusty safety pins.

I take a deep breath as my smile falters.

Come on, Bea. This is your home too. You have rights! You

have as much right as everyone else to love living here. You need to say how you feel.

You cannot sit in silence!

'I just,' I manage, my face burning, 'I just don't know how we'd all fit here. Like, Margot has a car, right? I know we only have one space and . . .' I trail off feebly as Priya's eyes widen.

'Oh,' Emma's eyes quickly dart towards Priya and then back at me. 'Sorry, Bea. I didn't mean that.'

Priya stares at me, her face practically glowing now.

'Oh?' I manage.

If Emma didn't mean that, then what does she mean?

She takes a deep breath.

'We want to live together, alone,' she says, 'like, me and Margot somewhere, and Priya and Josh somewhere.'

I stare into Emma's blue eyes. My body sags as understanding creeps over me.

Oh.

Why didn't I think of that?

Why didn't I think of that?

They don't want us all to live together. They both want to live without me.

I can't believe I was so stupid.

Priya and Emma both stare back at me, and I realise that I haven't said anything.

'Right,' I manage, the words scratching their way out of my mouth, 'well, that's so exciting. For you guys, I mean. Congratulations.'

'Oh!' Priya squeals, jumping over to my end of the sofa and pulling me into her arms, 'don't be sad, Bea! We'll still see each other all the time! And we won't move for another month at least, so we'll still have loads of fun together!'

I hang limply in her arms.

Oh God, I can't bear this.

'It's fine,' I say quickly, pushing Priya off me. 'I mean, it's more than fine. It's great. Don't worry about me. So,' I add, desperate to erase the sad look in their eyes, 'when did you decide this?'

Priya slouches back against the sofa and Emma smiles.

'Well, Margot and I have been speaking about it for months.'

'And me and Josh are headed in that direction,' Priya says, pulling out her phone. 'We haven't officially spoken about it yet, but it just makes sense.'

I nod as Emma pulls out her phone too.

Well, I guess that's that, then.

I try to swallow the ball that is lodged in the back of my throat.

'Honestly, Bea,' Priya says, 'it will be like nothing has changed.'

I smile weakly.

Like nothing has changed.

I'll be on my own, again.

Nothing has changed at all.

CHAPTER THREE

Faye swans past my desk, her high-pitched giggle following the tail of Duncan's latest knock-knock joke. I avoid her flitting eye contact.

Everything went back to normal after the horrible conversation yesterday evening. Priya went and made dinner, me and Emma watched *Emmerdale*. We spoke about Priya's day at work and Emma's weekend, and I just sat there and listened as anxiety chewed at my insides until there was nothing left to swallow.

I glance down at the handwritten letter, staring up at me from the bottom of my bag. I pick up my mug and walk into the kitchen.

I meant to throw the letter away. I went to sleep last night fully intending to chuck it in the recycling on my way to work. But when I woke up this morning to an empty house, I couldn't let it go.

I'm not even sure what I'm going to do with it. But I can't seem to open it. As soon as I open it and find out that the letter is definitely not for me, I'll feel like I've lost something else.

I take a deep breath as I click the kettle on. I watch it shake into life as thoughts swirl around my mind.

I've never really spoken to Priya or Emma about my anxiety. They wouldn't understand. I don't even know if I understand it.

I've heard stories about people who can't leave their house, or manage a conversation with a stranger. Anxiety, for me, isn't like that.

I imagine it like a creature sleeping in the pit of my stomach. It stays there, untouched and uninterested, as I get on with my day-to-day life. But if I step outside my routine, even for a second, it wakes up.

And then I don't know how to get it back to sleep.

'Bea?'

I look up as Angela sticks her head into the kitchen. She's wearing a long beaded necklace over a fitted suit dress, and flat-heeled, faded shoes.

I feel my face brighten into a smile.

'Hi, Angela,' I say. I gesture to the splattering kettle. 'Would you like a tea?'

'No,' Angela says quickly, 'thank you.'

I feel a flutter of annoyance.

Why doesn't she ever want me to make her a cup of tea?

'How are you getting on with the press releases?' Angela asks. 'I've sent you about four this morning. Did you see them?'

I nod. 'Yes,' I reply.

As if I could miss them. Angela's emails fire into my inbox like bullets. She doesn't use any grammar or any pleasantries, and most of the time they look more like death threats than emails.

Angela nods briskly and strides away from the kitchen. I tip the boiling water into my solitary mug and make my way out of the kitchen.

I like my job. It was my dream to be a journalist. I love writing.

But I don't write - not really, anyway. What I actually do is regurgitate press releases sent by every Tom, Dick and Harry lurking around Twickenham desperate to get a few minutes of fame for their record-sized cucumbers.

That's not a euphemism. I wish it was.

Actually, no I don't. They're all about eighty. Nobody wants to see shrivelled old Dicks from number 84 - in any sense.

I shake my mouse and rearrange the items on my desk, as my screen sparks back to life.

My eyes flit down as another email pops up from Angela: *Press release attached.*

'Ohhhh! What are you doing?'

I jump slightly as Faye reappears, craning her neck over my shoulder.

I try not to frown at her. She's way off schedule. It's 15.15.

'Nothing,' I say, my eyes darting up to my screen and quickly minimising my page.

I don't even know what my screen was on.

'Were you looking at horoscopes?' Faye drops into the seat next to me and leans towards my screen. 'I love horoscopes. I read mine, like, every day.'

She bats her large eyes at me and I pause, unsure of what I'm supposed to do.

'What did yours say?' she probes, gesturing for me to open the screen again.

Faye grabs my mouse and clicks on the *Herald*'s horoscope

page. I watch as little purple stars drift down my screen. It's like a unicorn has thrown up all over it.

'What's your star sign?' Faye says.

'Err,' I say, 'I'm not sure.'

'When's your birthday?'

I feel my face prickle at her quick-fire questions.

Gosh, this is the most interested Faye has ever been in me. Why does she care so much?

'June the fifth,' I reply.

Faye nods. 'Of course you're a Gemini,' she says under her breath.

I look round at her.

What does that mean?

'Okay, here,' she says, gesturing to the screen. My eyes follow her gaze and I read the glittering words swirling on to my screen.

Gemini, this is a big month of change for you. Although things may seem hard at times, you will get through this. And if you ever feel alone, look out for the stars to guide you.

'Oh, wow,' Faye breathes, 'that is so interesting. And I guess it is a hard time, with Duncan not liking your pitch.'

My head snaps back round as I stare at her.

'Oh!' Faye coos. 'Look at mine! It says I am likely to experience an outpouring of love, wealth and happiness.'

Faye beams at me and I force my taut face into a smile.

Of course her horoscope says that. Of course it does.

She gets up and swans off towards the kitchen and I reread the words. I scowl and close the screen decisively as I feel the aftertaste of hot tea at the back of my throat. I glance down at my handbag, which is sitting at my feet.

The letter is practically winking at me.

I watch as Faye props herself casually on Jemima's desk and starts laughing. My fingers curl around my mouse.

Now would actually be the perfect time to read the letter. Faye has had her afternoon visit, she won't talk to me again for at least another hour. Duncan is busy geeing up the sales team and Angela is halfway through her late-afternoon cigarette.

My eyes flit back up to my monitor, and then, as if magnetised, they shoot back down into my open bag.

Nobody will have to know that you read it. If it's not for you (which it won't be) you can drop it in the company shredder. No one will question that. Nobody will even notice.

My hand stretches down and I pull the letter out of my bag.

Okay, Bea. Prepare to be thoroughly disappointed when you read this letter and find it is not an invitation from some far-flung prince, saying that his kingdom is in danger and only you can save them, but it is, in fact, a forwarded letter from your previous landlord asking whether you'd still like to contribute to the village fête.

Immediately, I feel myself fixate on the small smattering of stars, sketched in biro in the right-hand corner.

My heart squirms as the horoscope floats through my mind.

If you ever feel alone, look out for the stars to guide you.

My eyes widen as I stare down at the letter.

Right! It's official. I have a stalker. I have a stalker who works for an online horoscope website, who supplies horoscopes for the *Herald* and then sends creepy follow-up letters. Great. Of course.

I take a slow glug of my tea and glare down at the letter. Before my mind can stop me, my hands reach forward and I peel open the folded seal of the letter. Gently, I pull out a thin piece of paper and smooth it across my desk. I feel my body jolt as my eyes land on the small, scrawled handwriting and I start to read.

Dear B,

It's Nathan. I don't know if you recognised my writing. I can't remember if I ever wrote to you. I know we haven't spoken in years and things weren't left great between us. I know we both said things we probably didn't mean. Well, I know I did. You probably meant yours. I wouldn't blame you. But I hope you're okay now. I hope you still live in this house. I know we had a lot of fun there. I hope you've got that landlord to fix the boiler at least.

I don't know if you know this, you might have read about it somewhere, but I'm in prison. Fuck, it's so horrible having to write that down and send that to you. But there's no point lying. Please don't come and see me, that's not why I'm writing. It's horrible. I don't want you here. I've been here for five months. I'm not going to tell you what it's like, I'm sure you can imagine it. But you spend a lot of time in your own head. It didn't take long for me to start thinking about you. It never does.

I want to say I'm sorry, for everything. I was young and stupid. You think you're fucking invincible when you're young, you never think anything will catch up with you. I lost control of my life and I got caught up in everything, and I pushed you to the sidelines. I was too stupid to think about what I was doing. You were the only person who ever made me feel whole. That feeling has never changed. I still love you, B.

I don't know what you're doing now, you might even have a new bloke. If you do, I'm sorry. And I hope he's better to you than I was. I just hope you're happy.

I still think of you every time I look at the stars. They make me feel less alone in here.

I've included a return envelope, if you want to write back. Whatever you decide I'll respect, but know that I'll never be complete without you. I just needed to say I'm sorry.

I'll always love you, B. You're the other half of me.

Yours always,

Nathan

I feel my throat swell as I read the final words. Fear stirs beneath my skin as my hands stretch across my desk and my eyes lock on to the name scribbled at the bottom.

I take a deep breath and fold the letter in half, trying to keep calm as I place it back inside my bag.

Who is Nathan?

*

I slouch into the sofa as I hear Emma crash through the front door. I pause the TV and move my mug of tea between my hands.

I glance down at my phone. The time blinks back up at me.

18.37.

I've been sat in this exact spot for twenty-three minutes. Almost paralysed as my brain battles against itself.

Do I tell Emma and Priya about the letter?

'Hello?' Emma calls, as she wanders through. 'Oh, hi,' she says, 'you all right? You not out tonight?'

I look back at her and feel my cheeks pinch.

I hate it when Emma asks me this. Mainly because I am always forced to give the same response and I'm worried that she's somehow keeping a tally.

'Err, nope,' I say quietly, 'are you?'

Emma picks up yesterday's post from the kitchen table and turns it over in her hands. 'No. I might see Margot later. Is this gas?'

I watch her pull out a bill. 'It's nothing important,' I say.

Emma nods in acknowledgement as her eyes scan the contents. She looks over at me and notices the letter in my hand.

She frowns. 'What's that?' she asks.

I feel a rush of heat swamp me.

'Oh,' I say, 'it's just a mistake.'

I wave the letter around half-heartedly.

Emma drops her bag on to the kitchen table. 'Something for an old tenant?' she says. 'It's not about a TV licence again, is it?'

'No,' I say, 'it's a letter from someone.'

Emma looks back at me. 'Did you open it?' she says, sitting next to me on the sofa and taking the letter out of my hands. 'You know it's illegal to open someone else's post, Bea?'

I try to smile back at her as nerves begin to spark under my skin.

Why do I feel nervous? It's not like I have anything to do with the letter. It's not for me, that's the whole point.

Emma scans the last few words and looks back at me, her mouth open.

'Wow,' she says, 'that's intense.' She passes the letter back to me and gets to her feet. 'Funny that she's got the same name as you.'

'Yeah,' I say quickly, 'that's why I opened it. It was a mistake.'

Emma grins at me as she starts taking things out of her bag. 'Yeah,' she says, 'sure it was. Are you going to send it back?'

I feel my heart flip. I hadn't thought about it.

'Yeah,' I say, folding the letter back inside the envelope.

'Okay,' she says. 'What did you say you were doing tonight?'

'Nothing.'

Emma pulls out her phone. 'And tomorrow night?'

I look up at her, a tug of annoyance twanging at my chest.

Why does she keep asking this? What does she think I'll be doing?

'Nothing,' I say again, hearing my voice tighten, 'but maybe, if you're here on Sunday, then I could make everyone a roast dinner? Invite Margot.'

Emma scrolls through her phone, and I try not to flinch as I feel my question hang in the silence.

Emma slips her phone back in her pocket and looks up at me, her eyes narrowed.

'Sorry,' she says, 'I was just reading something from Margot. She's back from work early, so wants to have dinner. What did you say?'

I feel my heart twist. She wouldn't want to come anyway.

'Nothing,' I say, my face springing into a smile. 'Have fun. Is Priya with Josh?'

Emma slips her phone in her pocket and smiles. 'Yeah,' she says. 'So you can double-lock the door and - oh,' she turns on the spot and rubs the last message off the whiteboard, 'I almost forgot.'

I watch as she scribbles a new message on the stained board. *We owe Joy sugar.*

I frown. 'Sugar?'

Emma turns to me and nods, clicking the pen lid back on.

'Ah,' I say, 'well, I'm going to go see Joy tomorrow, so I'll take some round.'

'Cool,' Emma says. 'I made some banana bread. It's in the kitchen, help yourself!'

Emma blows me a kiss and I try to keep my smile in place as I wave goodbye.

'Okay,' I say quietly, 'bye then.' But as the words leave my mouth, I hear the front door slam.

CHAPTER FOUR

I drop my phone into my bag and pull out my keys, ready to unlock the door, when I spot a small pool of light flood out of Joy's house as she pulls back the curtain slightly. I turn my head towards her, and she quickly pretends to be rearranging the curtains.

I sigh and click my key in the lock. I know Joy's looking out for me, waiting for my visit. On Thursdays she has an hour of my schedule (from 17.00 to 18.00). Not that she ever sticks to it.

'Hello?' I call, as I push our front door open.

I wait as the silence of our house stretches around me. I click the lights on and step forward. The yellow light fills the hallway and I feel an irrational bolt of fear shoot through my body as my eyes dart around my empty house.

What if Nathan is here? What if he knows that you opened the letter and it was a trap and now he is here to confront you?

I feel my grip on my handbag tighten.

Or what if the police are hiding in the house and are here to arrest you for opening somebody else's post?

Actually, I'm not being irrational because that is illegal! That could actually happen!

'Hello?' I shout again, with more force, as if my single word would frighten an intruder away – even though it sounded more like a teenage boy battling with puberty.

I kick the door shut, trying to shake off the pinpricks of fear sparking up my body.

Come on, Bea. Get a grip. There is no way that Nathan or the police are hanging out in the living room, or hiding behind one of the curtains.

I take a deep breath and walk into the living room, when my eyes fall on the whiteboard. Emma's message about sugar has been rubbed off and I spot Priya's handwriting drawn in big letters across the grey smear.

I blink at the words, my eyes fixating on the message.

Oh no.

Josh broke up with me. Don't want to talk about it. Not going to work. Please leave me alone.

I step closer, my heart thumping as I read the words.

What?

He broke up with her? Why?

I look around the room, trying to spot signs of Priya being in the house. I notice her bag and shoes shoved in a corner, and as I peer into the kitchen, I spot coffee granules scattered across the kitchen surface.

She's here, and if she's had a coffee, then she's awake.

I turn on my heel and carefully make my way up the stairs. As I reach the top, a white light glows from under Priya's door. Instinctively, my hand reaches forward and knocks on the door.

'Pri,' I say quietly, 'it's me.'

I move my ear closer to the door.

I know she's in there.

I lean my weight on the door and push it open. 'Pri,' I say again.

I look around the room and try to find Priya amongst her scattered clothes and mouldy mugs.

My body aches as I spot Priya's curtain of dark hair splayed across her pillow, her small body folded away from me, the place where Josh usually sleeps empty. I take a step forward, and although her eyes are shut, I notice her fists curled into tight balls around the top of her duvet.

She's awake. She's ignoring me.

I'm not leaving her. She can kick me out if she wants, but she'll have a hell of a job trying. I'm the one who takes the bins out every week, my arms are like steel.

Before the thought even enters my mind, I pull back the covers and climb into the space next to her. Priya opens one eye and tries to scowl, and for a second I think she's going to tell me to get out. But her scowl is instantly washed away by a stream of tears. I pull her clammy hand away from the duvet and fold it into mine as she keeps her back turned firmly towards me.

I look at the back of Priya's head, feeling my chest burn.

I never know what you're supposed to say.

'Pri,' I say in a small voice, 'Emma made banana bread.'

CHAPTER FIVE

I lean into my office chair and wince as my burning tea singes my tongue.

Great. That's my day ruined.

I pull open my desk drawer and fish out my small Tupperware full of biscuits. I count them and feel myself scowl. I only have a few biscuits left now, thanks to Faye, who caught me having one mid-afternoon yesterday and insisted on having *four*. Which has thoroughly screwed me in my rationing of the biscuits. Which, obviously, she doesn't care about. I only have three biscuits left, but four days of the week, I guess I could split them into thirds? Is that right? Or halves?

I put the mug back down crossly and reopen another press release.

I start tapping away mindlessly.

It's been five days since Josh broke up with Priya. Emma and I have been on shifts since then, like Priya is a newborn baby. I still don't know what happened, she won't talk about it. So I've gone for a new tactic and decided to distract her instead.

I feel a quell of excitement in the pit of my stomach as I flip open my notepad and beam at my ideas for the coming weekend, all swirled together with my fancy fountain pen. Everything I've wanted to do with Priya and Emma for weeks.

I thwack the enter key as Angela walks past, her narrow eyes glancing down at me, as if she's going to catch me on Pornhub.

Honestly, I've been working at the *Middlesex Herald* for two years now and she still doesn't trust me. Not since that one time I joined a Skype meeting from home and didn't realise my camera was on, and I happened to have a towel turban wrapped around my head.

'Hi, Bea.'

My eyes look over to the clock. 11.13. Two minutes early today.

'Hello, Faye,' I say politely, as she flops into the chair next to me, her large plastic sports bottle dangling from her fingers.

'You all right?' she says lazily, looking around the office.

'Yes, thank you,' I say, keeping my eyes on my computer.

I find that the shorter answers I give her, the quicker she moves on to her next target of the day.

My personal best has been twenty-eight seconds, but I can't take all the credit. Angela came over with a stack of press releases halfway through me warbling on about my weekend.

'What did you—'

'Hello, team!'

I jump slightly as Duncan bumbles over, two boxes of dough-nuts stacked in his arms. Faye swings around in her chair, her smile widening.

'Hi, Duncan,' she says.

'I bought you all a little pick-me-up!' Duncan says happily. 'As it's nearly Christmas. Last slog of the year and all that! If anyone wants a doughnut and a chat, my office door is always open.'

He drops the boxes on to the empty desk in the middle of the room and looks round. Half of the staff continue to tap away, but the odd person gives a small nod.

'Wow,' Faye says, 'thanks, Duncan.'

Duncan looks round at Faye, his smile beaming.

'Why don't you have the first one, Faye?' he says, sticking his chest out.

Faye quickly looks away from the box and holds up her bottle, which is filled with a thick green sludge.

'I can't,' she says, 'I'm on a diet.'

For a second, it looks as though Duncan's face drops, but he quickly turns to me, his smile fixed.

'How about you, Bea?' he says. 'I've got a variety but the best ones always go fast!'

My eyes flit to the clock.

Hmm. I am due a snack in ten minutes. I guess I could have it early. It would actually solve my biscuit conundrum.

'Thank you,' I say, as I reach forward and grab a sticky, shimmering doughnut.

Duncan picks up one for himself and holds it towards me in a 'cheers' motion.

'How is everyone?' he asks, his bright blue eyes flitting between me and Faye. 'What did you get up to at the weekend? Did anyone watch *The X Factor*?'

I nod. 'I did.'

'Me too,' Faye says. 'And did you watch the results show the next day? I was so lazy this weekend, I really binged.'

I feel a zap of confusion.

'Weren't you out this weekend?' I say, before I can stop myself. 'At Queens?'

Faye's smile vanishes. 'What?' she says. 'How do you know that?'

I feel my face burn and I drop my doughnut back on to my plate.

'Oh,' I say quietly, 'I just . . . I saw on your Instagram.'

Faye shrugs. 'Oh,' she says, 'yeah, I was. Stalker.'

I open my mouth stupidly.

Urgh. Why did I say anything?

Faye tosses her head. 'Yeah,' she says, 'it was so crazy. I was out all weekend. I caught up on it when I was hung-over.'

I see her face flush as she shoots me a look. She takes a swig of her bottle and I try to smile at her, as an odd sense of guilt swims through me.

'It was good, wasn't it?' Duncan says, oblivious. 'I did fall asleep at the end, though.'

'Was it that boring?' I offer.

Duncan slots the last piece of doughnut into his mouth and smiles. 'Oh no,' he says, 'it was about three a.m. at this point.'

I take a bite of the doughnut.

Three a.m.? He was awake at three a.m.?

He brushes the crumbs off his shirt as Faye pulls herself to standing.

'Right,' he says, 'must get back. Remember,' he adds, looking back at us both, 'any time you want a chat.'

He gives us a weird salute and I smile as Faye slinks back through the office, on the hunt for her next victim.

I slouch back into my chair, my tongue still burning from the hot tea.

I think Duncan would be the last person I would choose to chat with. I mean, what would we even talk about? I don't think I know a single thing about him.

An email from Duncan pops up on my screen.

Gosh, that's really bad, isn't it? Why don't I know anything about him? Why have I never bothered to get to know him? I should really make more effort.

I click on his email.

Albus! Just thinking of this afternoons quote. Can we make outstanding rhyme with Filofax?

Right. No. I take it back. I'm never having a coffee and chat with him.

Never.

Chapter Six

I place my bag on the kitchen table and take a deep breath, the fresh candle I have just lit wafting around the room like a warm vanilla hug.

Priya and Emma are both out, like they usually are, so I can have the house just how I like it. I can make myself some dinner, and watch all of my TV programmes, and then climb into my fresh, clean bed with fresh, clean hair and have a full eight hours' sleep.

I mean, I know a lot of people spend their Friday nights leaning against bars swirling rum and Cokes, but I bought some new pyjamas today *and* I'm planning on smothering my entire body in my fancy strawberry moisturiser. So I think we all know who the real winner is here.

Me. I'm the winner. I'm going to be unbelievably comfortable whilst smelling like a delicious strawberry shortcake.

The dream.

I take off my cardigan.

Also, as it is just me, the house is back to being the perfect temperature. Emma is the Hitler of heating and Priya acts as if we're living in an igloo.

I flick the kettle on.

See? This is what you get for being in a relationship or having a life. You don't have control of the thermo–

'Bea?'

Argh!

I jump towards the bubbling kettle as Priya appears in the door frame. Her long, sleek hair is hanging over her face and she has dark smudges of make-up smeared under her eyes.

I gawp at her, dumbfounded.

What is she doing here? I thought she was going back to her parents.

I try to pull my contorted face into a smile.

She looks like she's just crawled out of a horror film.

Not that I'll tell her that, obviously.

'Bloody hell,' I say weakly, my hand gripping my chest as my thudding heart realises that Priya is not a lurking serial killer.

Priya blinks at me.

'What?' she says sulkily. 'Do you not want me here? I do live here too, Bea.'

She stumbles out of the kitchen and slumps on to the sofa. I resist the urge to roll my eyes.

Great. I've been with her ten seconds and I've already upset her. I'm the worst supportive best friend ever.

'Sorry,' I say, scurrying after her and abandoning my stewing tea. 'You made me jump. I thought you were at your mum's. You're just not usually here.'

Priya pulls her legs up to her chest, her bottom lip fat and shaking.

'Yeah,' she says, 'I'm usually with Josh.'

The word 'Josh' pushes its way through her vocal cords and the strain of it forces her face to crumple.

I watch wordlessly as fat tears roll down her face, coated in black liquid.

Oh God. What have I done?

I hover awkwardly, like a hopeless duck.

How do I make her stop?

I open and close my mouth.

I am really not qualified to deal with this. What am I supposed to say?

I watch Priya cry and bite my lip.

Just say anything, Bea. You can't just watch her cry like some mentalist. You're her best friend. Say something, for goodness' sake.

Say something!

'There, there.'

Oh, for God's sake, not that. Why would you say that? What's wrong with you? You're worse than Joy.

'I'll make you a tea,' I say quickly.

Priya hangs her limp head in her hands as I bustle over to the kitchen.

'What are you doing this weekend?' I call to her as I flick the kettle on. As soon as I say it I want to kick myself.

What is wrong with you? Obviously she won't be doing anything. She spends every weekend with Josh.

'Because!' I babble before Priya can respond. 'I thought we could have a fun weekend together. A girls' weekend.'

I glance over and see Priya has cocked her head towards me.

'Really?' Priya says weakly, wiping her eyes with the back of her hand.

I feel a wave of relief and I nod quickly.

It's working! She's stopped crying!

'Yes!' I say loudly, tipping boiling water into a large mug. 'I'll plan the whole thing. We'll have a great weekend together. I'll create a schedule, and an itinerary!'

My heart races as the words tumble out of my mouth.

Oh my God, I can crack open my new box of highlighters. Yes!

Priya blinks at me.

'Okay,' she says slowly. 'And it will be fun, right?'

I grin at her, holding the steaming mug of tea.

'Trust me, Priya,' I say smugly, 'it will be a blast.'

★

I wrench my eyes open and suck in a loud intake of breath as my dream fades away and I take in my dark room, silent around me.

I move my damp hands on to my chest, trying to calm my racing heart. My T-shirt is wet and sticking to my skin.

I haven't had the dream in months. I'm with Mum, we're doing something ordinary like shopping or having dinner, but then she goes.

I always wake up before she comes back.

I feel my heartbeat start to slow down.

'It was a dream,' I say quietly, 'it's not real. You're fine. You're in your bed, it's a Friday. You're okay.'

I grip my T-shirt tighter, desperate for my heart to return to normal.

'You're okay,' I say again, drawing a deep, slow breath down into my chest, 'you're okay.'

I find my phone, charging on my bedside table, and turn it over. The time flashes up at me.

3.07.

No messages, no missed calls.

I stare at the phone for a second.

There never are.

I drop my phone back on to my bedside table and notice the small circles of moisture swelling on the screen where my clammy fingers have been. I try to swallow, my mouth dry.

Decisively, I pull my duvet off my body and make my way towards the kitchen, my arms stuck out into the darkness. Which seems ridiculous, but I'd rather stub my toe en route to the kitchen than suffer the agony of turning the light on and blinding my poor eyes with rays of white light.

I mean, no wonder babies cry so much when they're born. It's torture.

I turn towards the kitchen, stepping into the pool of light cast across our living-room floor by the street light outside our house. As I glance out of the window, I hear an odd screech.

What is that?

My eyes are frantically trying to focus in the darkness, when I spot a small fox in the middle of Joy's lawn, tearing at the plastic of her bin bags. I move towards the window and see Joy's rubbish, originally neatly organised and ready for recycling, now all strewn across her manicured garden like a dismembered carcass.

I frown. How does she have so much rubbish?

I knock on the window. The fox's orange eyes flash at me as it digs its claws into another plump bin bag and I wince as another mound of food spills out.

I click the living-room window open and flinch as the wet air slaps me across my face.

'Shoo!' I hiss to the fox. 'Go away.'

I lean out of the window slightly and wave my arm in the fox's direction. It doesn't notice me.

I don't want to get too close. Aren't foxes pretty dangerous?

'Shoo,' I mutter again, glancing briefly at Joy's silent home.

I don't want her to wake up to this.

Begrudgingly, I tilt my body further out of the window and cough loudly, squinting under the heavy drops of rain that splash against my bare skin. At the sound of my cough, the fox slinks across the road and slips into a hedge.

As the fox disappears, I pull myself back inside and click the window shut.

I can't clear all this up now, it's too wet. I'll help Joy in the morning.

I go to turn towards the kitchen, when my eyes stray down to the piles of rubbish, now scattered across Joy's garden. I stare at the sea of food in confusion.

Why does she have so much food?

I look down at a large cake, tipped sadly on its side and sagging under the heavy downpour of rain. There's a smattering of scones, pressed into the mud, and I notice a round, golden quiche, still intact, sitting proudly beside a puddle of milk.

There aren't any packets or wrappers. Just piles and piles of untouched food.

Did she make all of this?

I walk into the kitchen and fill a glass with water, the image of Joy's garden stuck in my brain.

What is she doing with so much food?

Maybe she had a party.

As I make my way back to my bedroom, the confusion is swallowed by a ripple of anxiety as I look down at my bed. I take another sip of water and climb in, gripping the covers.

'You won't have the dream again,' I say quietly. 'You're okay.' I close my eyes and take a deep breath. 'You'll be okay.'

CHAPTER SEVEN

I look down at my chart and beam. It really is a thing of beauty.

It is perfectly organised and colour coordinated, and I've even used my Christmas gel pens.

Priya is going to love it.

I sink down into the sofa and suck my pen as my eyes scan the schedule again.

11.00: Breakfast, prepared by me. Fry-up and continental options available.

11.15: Clean kitchen (mainly aimed at me, but I will heavily hint at Priya helping. Spoiler alert: she won't.)

11.30: Thirty minutes of getting ready time (we can try on cute outfits for each other and do fashion shows like we used to do at uni, and fake fight over who owns what top).

12.00: Country walk.

14.00: Pub lunch with lovely glass of wine and girly chats.

17.00: Head home and straight into PJs and comfy slippers.

18.00: Choose and order takeaway.

18.00: Watch movie marathon or *X Factor*. Eat takeaway
and defrost ice cream.

I smile at the schedule. And then, on Sunday, I'll make us all a roast. We haven't had a roast together in ages.

'Hey.'

I look up as Priya wanders into the room. Her hair is screwed up into a knot above her head and her face is blotchy. She scrunches up her eyes at me in confusion.

'What are you doing?' she asks. 'Are you working today?'

I look back at her and try to contain a laugh.

Please, like I'd ever work on a Saturday.

'No,' I say, following her into the kitchen, trying to stop my voice squeaking with excitement. 'It's our schedule for today.'

My eyes follow her wildly as Priya starts opening cupboards. What is she doing?

She can't eat breakfast now. I had her scheduled to be asleep until eleven. I haven't warmed up any of the pastries!

'Why don't you have a seat?' I say, steering her out of the kitchen.

Priya frowns at me.

'What?' she says grumpily. 'Why? What are you doing?'

'I'll get you breakfast,' I say, as she drops on to the sofa.

I click the kettle on. My eyes flick back over to the schedule and I feel a small swell of pride.

Gosh, I really can't get over how beautiful this schedule is. If today goes well with Priya, I might get it framed.

'So,' I say, bustling back into the living room with two mugs of tea, 'are you excited for our day of fun?'

I feel a grin spread across my face as I look back at Priya. Priya's face doesn't move.

'Yeah?' she says half-heartedly.

Okay. Well, that wasn't the opening Disney number reaction I was expecting, but never mind. Maybe it will come after she's had her tea.

Damn. I should have made her a coffee.

'Great,' I say. 'So here is the schedule I made.'

I pull the schedule across our laps and wait for Priya's reaction.

She peers down at it.

'Wow, Bea,' she says quietly, 'did you make all this?'

'Yes,' I say smugly.

Har har. I'm a genius.

There is a silence as Priya's eyes skim over the boxes.

I loiter, trying not to leer at the schedule as she reads.

Why isn't she saying anything? I thought she'd be bouncing off the sofa in excitement. She's acting like I've just given her a maths equation.

I feel my eyeballs strain in frustration as I look back at her.

Calm down, Bea. You do not require constant affection and reassurance.

'Do you like it?' I practically shout, unable to control my desperation for compliments.

All I want is for her to comment on my colour scheme or my impeccable tick box system. Is that too much to ask?

Priya hunches over, closer to the chart, her phone dangling

limply in her hand. My gaze slips down and I notice an Instagram screen shining back up at me.

I frown.

I recognise that irrefutable beard.

'Is that Josh?' I say, my head craning round to get a better look at Priya's phone.

She snatches her phone back to her chest, and to my alarm her eyes fill with tears.

'No,' she says quickly, shoving her phone into her dressing-gown pocket.

I scowl at her. It definitely was Josh.

Why is she looking at his photo?

'What—'

'I think I might have a shower,' she looks back at me, 'if that's okay?'

Without quite meaning to, my eyes glance back at the schedule.

'Of course,' I babble. 'Shall I start making breakfast?'

Priya smiles. 'Yeah, okay. I'm not that hungry, though.'

'Okay,' I nod. 'That's okay.'

More for me.

'Cool,' she says. 'See you in a bit.'

★

I click open the oven door as the smell of warm, fresh pastries swirls around the kitchen.

Bloody hell, these smell incredible.

I place them all on the cooling rack and beam.

I am such a great homemaker. The house smells incredible! And I've already done my Saturday morning hoovering. Look at me go.

I look down at my phone as the time ticks to 11.00.

And look at that, I am sticking to my schedule, to the second! This is going to be a great day.

'Oh, that smells nice.'

I look up at the sound of Priya and do a double-take.

Her mass of hair is twisted up into foam rollers and she has a lurid green mask pasted over her face.

Wow, she's really making an effort for our day of fun.

I wasn't even planning on washing my hair.

'Are those rollers?' I say.

Priya hasn't curled her hair since she first dated Josh.

'Yeah.' Priya hops up on to our kitchen worktop and flicks the kettle on. 'God, I'm glad to have a weekend off work.'

'When's your next shift?' I ask, taking two mugs out of the steaming dishwasher.

Priya passes me the box of tea bags. 'Monday,' she says. 'I'm back on nights.' She pulls a face and drops two tea bags into the mugs. 'Also,' she says, as I glug the bubbling water into our mugs, 'I've got good news.' She shoots me a large grin.

'Oh?' I say, gesturing towards the pastries hopefully.

Priya picks up a pastry and her black tea and walks back into the living room. I slosh some milk into my mug and follow her, pastry in hand.

Priya picks up her phone again and starts tapping as I drop down on to the floor.

'Do you remember Tim?' she says casually.

I shift on the floor. 'No,' I say, 'I don't think so.'

'He's a guy from work.' Priya carries on, her left index finger scrolling through her phone. 'He's really fit.'

I turn the pastry between my hands, wincing slightly as it

singes the tips of my fingers. I feel like this is too hot to eat. I can barely hold it.

But it smells so good.

Screw it! I'm just going to eat it. What's the worst that can happen?

'He's been messaging me,' she says.

My ravenous mouth takes an enormous bite of pastry, which instantly clings to the roof of my mouth like fire.

Oh my God. What have I done?

It's really hot.

Oh my *God*.

'And he wants to go on a date with us.'

Argh, this was a terrible idea! I can barely breathe.

'What?' I cry, a jet of steam puffing out of my mouth as if I'm a hysterical Thomas the Tank Engine.

I stare at Priya who looks back down at her phone.

I somehow swallow the pastry, which slides down my throat like a burning boulder.

I try to focus my streaming eyes on Priya.

Did she just say a date with us?

'Us?' I repeat.

'Yeah,' Priya says casually.

Hang on, what?

A date with us? Us?

Today? But I've scheduled today. We're going on a walk and having a glass of wine.

That's the plan. We both agreed on the plan.

'Err,' I blurt. 'I'm not going on a three-way date.'

Priya flashes me an amused look and she laughs loudly.

I blink back at her pompously.

'No, you idiot,' she grins. 'A double date. Tim's got a friend, it's a set-up. They want to come over tonight. No offence, Bea, but if I was going to have a three-way it wouldn't be with you.'

She grins at me and I feel myself puff out like a peacock.

Oh, well that's nice.

Why not? What's wrong with me?

'I think you'd find you'd be very lucky to have me,' I mutter, my face flaming.

This is all going terribly. There was a reason why 'awkward conversation about threesomes' has never made it on to any schedule of mine.

Priya laughs again and shifts in her seat.

I blink back at her.

A double date? Tonight?

'But,' I say, glancing at the floor, 'the schedule . . .'

I trail off as Priya goes back to her phone.

I don't want to go on a double date with two random boys. I want to go on a nice walk and sit and watch *Mean Girls* with my best friend and a bottle of wine.

I thought Priya would want that too.

'We can do the schedule another time,' Priya snips, and I flinch slightly at her tone.

Following a schedule at a different time completely misses the point of a schedule.

'They just want to come over,' she adds. 'It'll be fun, like when we were at uni.'

I look back at her as she ignores me, but I notice colour rise up her face as she glares at her phone.

Come on, Bea. You have a say in this too. Priya probably doesn't even realise how much you'd hate this. Tell her how you feel. She's your best friend. She'll understand.

I take a deep breath.

'But, Priya,' I say, 'I don't really—'

'Look!' Priya snaps, her eyes burning into her phone. 'I want to do something fun, Bea. I've just been dumped. Tim is a really nice guy and I want to go on a date with him. I don't want to just sit in on a Saturday night.'

My heart thumps.

Right.

'Okay,' I say in a small voice, 'well, it doesn't matter.'

I glance down at my schedule, which is staring optimistically back at me. I feel a burning sense of humiliation and I suddenly wish I'd never made it.

Of course she doesn't want to do the schedule. Who would? What sort of 24-year-old makes a schedule on a Saturday morning filled with things you normally do with your grandparents?

Who would want to do any of this stuff?

With great effort, Priya tears her eyes away from her phone to look at me.

'I'm sorry,' she says grumpily, 'this day sounds fun. I just need to get out there.'

To my alarm I feel my eyes burn as I attempt to hide my bright schedule under my foot.

I nod and pull myself to my feet.

'I'm going to get in the shower,' I say limply.

Stupid Bea. This is why you spend every weekend on your own.

'Bea!' Priya calls after me.

I turn back to look at her.

'Tonight will be fun, okay? I promise.'

I look at her blankly and try to force a smile.

'Yeah,' I say, 'sure.'

CHAPTER EIGHT

I shoot Priya a look as she shimmies past me, anxiety wriggling inside me like a jittery tapeworm.

I can't believe I'm about to have two strangers in my house. Two strange *men* too.

And one of the strangers will be a man that I'm going to have to talk to all night. Will he want to talk about *RuPaul's Drag Race*? Unlikely.

I glance down at my wine glass, wobbling slightly in my hand.

We didn't follow my schedule. Priya said that we didn't have time to do any of it and insisted that she needed all day to get ready.

I glance over at Priya who is glued to her phone, like she has been all day. Her eyes are angry slits and her lips are sucked together like a prune.

I angle my body to face her.

I bet she doesn't really want to go on this date either. I've never even heard of her mentioning this Tim guy before. And a guy from work? You don't want to dip your nib in the office ink, everyone knows that.

I take a sip of wine.

I try to catch Priya's eye and move the wine glass between my hands. It sticks slightly to my clammy fingers.

'Are you okay?' I ask.

She hasn't spoken to me for about two hours. I'm not sure when she is planning on breaking this weird silence. She'd better speak when they arrive. I'm certainly not leading the conversation. I can barely lead a conga.

(Something I discovered courtesy of Duncan, obviously.)

I can almost see my question float in front of Priya's face, before it fades away hopelessly. She doesn't respond.

What is she even doing?

'Pri?' I nudge carefully.

Her head jerks up and I jump.

'Look at this,' she says roughly, shoving her phone under my nose.

I blink at her screen. It's a photo of Josh.

I knew she was looking at his page earlier!

I look down at it blankly. He's standing in a bar with another guy holding a beer. He's smiling.

His beard is indescribable.

Priya glares at me expectantly and I suddenly realise I'm supposed to say something.

My eyes flit back towards her.

Oh God. What does she want me to say?

'Err,' I say, 'goodness. Yeah. Look at him.'

Okay, that's good. Keep it neutral. She can't get mad if you say practically nothing.

I look down and clock the time, and I notice he uploaded the photo last night. Has she been looking at this all day?

'Doesn't he look really proud to you,' Priya says bitterly, 'and happy? Like, why is he so happy? And he's out, in a *bar*. Like, what is he even doing there? Who is he?'

She looks at me as if she's just announced that he's at a foot fetish party.

'He hates bars!' she explodes. 'He never goes to bars! And now he's there, with the lads. He's obviously going there to get with a load of girls.'

I look back down at the photo, trying to source the cryptic clues that Priya is obsessing over.

To me he just looks like a guy standing at a bar.

'He's such a dick,' she mutters, pulling the phone away from me. She shoves it back in her bag aggressively and I feel a tug at my chest as she glugs down an enormous slurp of wine.

'Pri,' I say, 'you don't seem that good. How about we just cancel on these guys and have a fun night in?'

If she says yes then we can almost hop back on to the last items in my schedule. We'd only be twenty minutes behind.

I smile until she whips her head round to face me, her eyes flashing.

'What?' she spits. 'No! We need to go on this date. I can't sit at home watching TV while he's out getting with loads of girls.'

I look back at her blankly.

'You just don't get it, Bea,' she snaps, pushing her body away from me.

I feel a weight sink down my throat.

Great. Now she's mad at me.

Priya slumps back against the sofa and stares at her phone screen. I open and close my mouth.

Okay. So that went well.

I stand up and turn to tell Priya where I'm going, but she hasn't even noticed my movement. I make my way to my bedroom and shut the door behind me. I take a deep breath as the icy claws of panic grip me.

I put the glass of wine on my bedside table and sink down on to my bed.

It will be fine. It will be over soon. Everything will be fine.

I pull my phone out of my pocket and quickly find Mum's number and hold the phone to my ear. As always, it goes to answerphone.

'Hi, Mum,' I say quietly, 'it's me. I just wanted to call for a chat. I'm not feeling great today, but don't worry. I'll be okay. Hopefully talk to you soon. Love you, bye.'

I click the phone off and run my fingers through my hair. I take in another deep breath, trying to stretch out my twitching muscles as my eyes land on the letter. I pick it up and turn it over between my fingers.

I've never received a letter before. Not a handwritten one.

I pull it out of the envelope and my eyes focus on the jittery handwriting. For some reason, I feel a tug of familiarity.

I wonder if he's found his B.

'Bea!' Priya's strained voice resounds down the hall and I quickly shove the letter under my pillow. 'Where are you? They're here!'

★

I perch on the very corner of our sofa, my back poker straight and my entire body tense as I glance over at Keith, who has cracked his moist feet out from his loafers and propped them on my armrest.

On my armrest.

He'd better not touch me with those horrible trotters or I'll have to set myself on fire.

I mean, who does that? He took off his shoes the moment he got in and has been waving his feet around like he's dancing a revolting Irish jig.

As for Tim, well, I can't for the life of me work out why Priya was so desperate to go on a date with him.

I mean, he's not terrible. He's no Keith. But he did put his beer down without a coaster and then laughed when I flapped about trying to find him one.

'And do you remember,' Tim guffaws to Priya, 'what Stacey did, with the nurses' station photocopier?'

Priya titters, uttering a string of unnatural giggles, and I flinch slightly as Keith looks over at me hopefully, as if I too know all about funny Stacey and the photocopier.

You keep those feet away from me, Keith.

I scowl in Priya's direction as she lightly taps Tim's shoulder.

Priya knows I can't make small talk with strangers. She does the talking and I laugh along, that's our set-up. That's how we always did it at uni.

I glance over at Keith again who is scrolling through his phone.

Right, come on, Bea. Small talk. Talk that is small. You can do this. You've watched enough episodes of *First Dates*.

I feel my heart race as I angle my body towards him.

'So, Keith,' I say, 'what do you do?'

I try to force my face into a relaxed smile. Keith doesn't look up from his phone.

'What?' he grunts.

I blink, slightly affronted. Gosh, that was an aggressive response. How can someone sound so annoyed by that question?

I take a deep breath, using all of my energy to keep my smile from slipping off my face. 'Err,' I start again, 'what do you do? For a job?'

I wait for his answer.

Who knows? Maybe he's some form of writer too.

Although not of something weird. Like porn.

Do porn films have writers? Is that a thing?

Maybe I'll google it later.

Actually, no, I definitely won't do that. Christ.

Keith places his hands around the neck of his beer.

'I'm a surgeon,' he says.

'Oh!' I cry, genuinely impressed.

I never would have thought he was a surgeon.

Well, I guess that's why he's so comfortable with his feet, isn't it? They're just body parts to him, after all. Nothing he hasn't seen plenty of before. I'm sure he's seen hundreds of feet and I am just too uptight and ignorant to appreciate that they are simply functional.

Wow, I really feel like I have been taught a serious lesson here. It was surely meant to be. That Keith, the surgeon—

'Tree,' he adds, and I feel my smile twitch.

What?

'Pardon?' I say.

'Of trees,' he repeats, 'like, a tree surgeon. I'm a tree surgeon.'

71

Of trees? What does that mean? He administers twig replacements and open bark surgery?

Actually, that's quite funny. I should say that out loud.

'So,' I grin, 'do you do open bark—'

'Yeah, it's my dad's business,' Keith continues, and I stifle my brilliant joke back inside of me.

Damn it. That would have been a great joke. I'll have to somehow say it later.

Or maybe I'll tweet it.

'I've done it for years,' he adds, nodding his large head.

'Cool,' I say lamely, taking another gulp of my wine.

What am I supposed to say back to that? I can't think of a single question to ask about tree surgery. I wish Priya was involved, she'd ask something witty and insightful.

I could ask him if he has a lot of experience with wood.

I open my mouth again and then clamp it firmly shut.

No, no, no. Do not say that. Don't you dare.

He could ask me a question, there's a shocking idea. He could ask me what I do for a job, or my opinions on rogue feet, or where I bought my lovely painting from, and yes I did paint it myself, and aren't I so talented, how do I even find the time?

I glance back over at Keith and as we make eye contact I feel my mouth stretch into an awkward smile.

Anything would be better than this terrible silence.

I raise my eyebrows at him and feel the thought bubble into my mind.

Don't say it. Don't say it. Don't say it.

'So, you must have a lot of experience with wood, then?'

Argh! No! Why would you say that?

Keith stares back at me blankly.

What is wrong with you?

'Bea?'

I look round as Priya gestures me into the kitchen.

Did she hear the wood joke? Is she about to give me a stern word?

I follow her in anxiously and she clicks the door shut behind us.

Maybe she's about to confess that she's having a terrible time and we can send these guys home. That would be great.

Priya swings her glass in her left hand and I wince slightly as wine splashes on the kitchen floor.

She locks her inky eyes on to my face and leans in.

'I need you to do me a favour,' she says.

I look back at her.

'I need you to suggest taking some pictures tonight of me and Tim.'

I wait for her to smile, and then realise that she's being serious.

Take some pictures?

'What?' I say. 'What do you mean?'

Priya furrows her brow in concentration.

'I need you to take some pictures of me and Tim and put them on your Instagram. Some of us posing, and some of us laughing. Oh,' she points her glass at me, sloshing her wine around dangerously, 'and definitely one of us touching or something.'

'Touching?' I repeat in alarm.

'Yeah!' Priya cries, curling her free hand around my reluctant arm. 'Okay?'

She tries to drag me out of the kitchen but I feel like my feet are rooted to the spot.

Priya looks back at me. 'What?'

'Can't we call it a night?' I say quietly. 'I want to go to bed and I just feel—'

'No!' Priya's eyes flash at me. 'Don't do this. You're not going to bed, you can't.'

'But I—'

'Just try to have fun, Bea,' Priya whines, 'just for another hour, then they'll go. Look,' her eyes flick down to my empty glass and she grabs another bottle of wine, 'drink more,' she says firmly, 'then you'll feel better. It will help you relax.'

I watch as Priya tips the wine into my glass. She notices my expression and raises her eyebrows.

'Drink it,' she says firmly, 'right now. Down it. You're too uptight.'

I look back at her as I feel the creature sink its nails into my stomach. Before my thoughts catch up, my arm tips the wine towards my mouth and I tilt the warm wine down. It hits the back of my throat and I try not to gag as the acidic taste swirls around my mouth.

Priya grins at me and grabs my hand.

'Okay,' she says, pulling me back out of the kitchen, 'let's go.'

I follow her out nervously and sit back down on the sofa. To my alarm, Keith has crept over slightly in my absence and his feet are now loitering close to mine.

I feel my body tense as the alcohol swirls around, pulling at my snapping muscles.

Okay, right. Some photos. Maybe if I take a good enough picture quickly, then we can go to bed.

★

74

Thirty-five pictures and four glasses of wine down, and I feel like going back in time and aggressively laughing at my optimistic self. I should have known better, Priya used to make Josh take photos of her every time they went out. I never realised how exhausting it was.

I snap a photo listlessly with my wilting fingers and slug another gulp of my drink. My eyes slide over to Keith, who has been steadily creeping closer like a pestering sloth.

He gestures to my phone. 'You should take a picture of us two.'

I look back at him and try to fight the look of horror that spreads across my face.

A photo of us? Why? So I can stick it on our first Christmas card? Or send it to the police to use as evidence when I murder you for skimming your crusty feet all over my freshly hoovered carpet?

I flash him a half-smile and go back to my phone as Priya throws her head back and laughs, flashing me her best 'Look at me, aren't I having such a great time?' smile.

'How old are you?'

Oh, a question. Finally.

I pull my tired eyes away from the phone and look at Keith.

'Twenty-four,' I answer. 'You?'

Keith nods. 'Thirty-one.'

'Cool.'

Great. Look at us. We've both been alive for a period of time.

I shoot him another half-smile to accompany my lame response.

Keith has a tuft of brown hair that quiffs at the top of his forehead and a jagged beard that sticks out of his chin like the bristles of a used toothbrush.

He's not bad-looking, and I'm sure for a female with a foot fetish he'd be the man of her dreams.

'So,' Keith starts again, crossing one leg over the other, 'how long have you been single for?'

I feel a hot flash of anxiety sweep over me.

I hate this question. It's a trick question. Every answer you say back is met with a pity smile, and some dreadful line like 'He's out there somewhere', or 'Good for you'. Or, the worst one, 'You've got plenty of time' like I'm a saggy old hen on the verge of squawking my last cluck.

'About a year,' I mumble, glancing over to Priya to check she's not listening to my lie.

She's not. She's pretending to tell Tim's fortune.

'I've been single about two years now, but it doesn't really matter,' Keith says, resting his elbows on his knees. 'It's different, though, isn't it?'

I force myself to look at Keith. He's swinging his bottle of beer between two fingers, his back arched over.

'Different for who?' I say.

'Girls,' Keith says matter-of-factly, 'women.' He glances at me. 'Chicks. Girls want to settle down and have kids earlier, they need to get married. Not need,' he says quickly, swigging his beer, 'they like it. Every girl wants to get married. My ex was gagging for it.'

I stare down at my phone, Keith's words sinking through my body like a stone.

'Girls need someone,' he says, pulling out his phone.

I nod, my mouth dry.

I don't need someone.

I look at Priya, who is laughing at Tim.

I don't have someone to need.

★

I feel my body twitch as my eyes stare out into the darkness. Anxiety has me paralysed now, as if it has stretched its claws into each of my limbs and pinned me down on to the bed. The only thing I can move is my eyes, which are slowly burning as liquid seeps out of the corners.

I knew I'd hate tonight. I knew it the moment Priya suggested it. Priya should have known too. Maybe she did and didn't care.

I move my hand over to my phone and turn it over.

No missed calls from Mum. No messages from anyone. The time blinks back at me.

1.57.

I scrunch up my face. Anxiety feeds on my insomnia. It sucks every inch of exhaustion from my body like a sponge and leaves me in my own personal hell, with nowhere to go. Nobody is awake at this time. Why would they be? It's just me, alone.

Keith and Tim left shortly after his take on male and female goals. I could barely speak. After Keith had finished giving me his pearls of wisdom, he swiftly pulled out his phone and proceeded to ignore me for the rest of the evening. At one point he even put his shoes on, which triggered the alarming realisation that the display of his feet was just for me.

Priya seemed to get the photo she was after. She then ignored Tim and spent the rest of the evening glued to her phone until they both got the message and left. Priya swept upstairs as soon as the front door clicked shut behind them. I pottered around the house as anxiety popped inside my body like squares of bubble wrap.

I roll on to my back now and stare up at the ceiling.

I've always hated dating. It was different at school. You met boys in English class, fancied them a bit, got your friend to send them a note during Shakespeare and then, poof, you've got yourself a boyfriend.

Even university was better. Me, Priya and Emma would go out together on nights out and be flooded with attention. I never had any problems talking to guys, I didn't really have to think about it.

But I was different then. Everything was.

I take a deep breath in an attempt to relax the creature's harsh grip on my body.

I bloody hope Priya has learnt her lesson from tonight. She kept pretending to laugh at Tim's terrible jokes about the nurses' station printer but I know she can't really have had a good time.

I curl my hands into small fists and push them against my swollen eyes in frustration.

For God's sake, why can't I sleep? What's wrong with me? It's almost two a.m. Everyone should be asleep right now.

I roll back on to my side and exhale.

My eyes open and automatically search for Nathan's letter, which is stashed on my bedside table. I pull it towards me and unfold it.

I've never had anyone write me a letter before.

My eyes scan his jittery handwriting and, somehow, the creature's grip around my heart loosens as a new feeling snakes through my body.

I wonder how long it took him to write this letter. Was it impulsive? Or did he spend weeks thinking about it?

As I read the final line, it's like a magnetic force has gripped my eyeballs, forcing them to read the last line again. And then again.

I'll always love you, B. You're the other half of me.

I pull myself up to sitting as the creature is drowned by a new, powerful feeling.

I'll always love you, B.

My eyes narrow as I stare at the words and before I can stop myself, my hand grabs my notepad and pen, and I start to write.

CHAPTER NINE

Joy pulls her front door open and beams at me.

'Hello, Bea!' she chimes.

I smile back as I notice a stack of post and a small box of Tupperware arranged neatly on her wooden table. All of the rubbish on her lawn had vanished by the time I woke up on Saturday morning. I don't know what time Joy gets up, but I was awake at six a.m. and her lawn was perfect, as if she'd painted it on the day before.

'Hi, Joy,' I say. 'How are you?'

Her bright eyes look up at me and her face creases into a smile.

'I'm fine, thank you, love,' she says. 'Would you like to come in?'

She takes a step back, and I shake my head routinely.

'No thank you,' I say. 'Just the post, please.'

Joy dips her head slightly.

'I have some spare muffins that I made,' she says. 'I'll never be able to eat them all. I don't know why I made so many! I thought you and the girls would like them.'

She hands me the Tupperware.

I'm going to get so fat if I keep collecting the post from Joy.

'Oh, thanks, Joy.'

Maybe it will be good comfort food for Priya.

'Here is your post,' she continues, 'and I popped that letter in the post for you too.'

I look up from the small stack of letters and fix my eyes on Joy as a dart of panic flashes through me.

What?

'What letter?' I say.

I didn't ask Joy to post any letters for me. Priya and Emma never write letters.

I've only written one.

'The one Emma gave me,' Joy says, moving back inside the hallway. 'She must have forgotten to put a stamp on it but I had some spare. I don't mind. I think she was trying to do that "return to sender" thing, but I'm sure you need a stamp for that.' She smiles at me. 'You can never be too careful, can you?'

I look back at Joy's kind eyes as heat storms up my back.

'What . . .' I manage, my mouth dry, 'what letter was it? Did Emma write it? Do you know who it was for?'

Joy's eyes crinkle slightly.

'Oh no, dear,' she says, 'I never read your post.'

My damp hands scrunch the small pile of letters in my hand.

'Right,' I say, 'thanks, Joy. I'll see you later.'

Before I give Joy the chance to answer, I turn on my heel and race back towards the house, scrambling for my keys.

It can't be my letter. It must be a letter that Emma had written, and then asked Joy to send.

It can't be the one I wrote.

I barge through the front door and jump as I almost collide with Emma, who is carrying a plate of food from the kitchen.

'Whoa!' Emma cries, steering her plate out of the way. 'Are you all right? Do you need a wee?'

I flash her a small smile and charge into my room. My eyes dart over my bed, my bedside table, my desk.

It's not there. It's gone. Where has it gone?

'Bea?' Priya calls from the living room. 'Can you come here, please?'

I stare across the room, desperately trying to spot the letter, hiding somewhere in my room.

Where is it? *Where is it?*

'Bea?'

Slowly, my legs move in the direction of Priya's voice until I spot her and Emma, propped up on the living-room sofa. Priya's hair is washed and piled up on top of her head in a bun, and she is smiling.

I blink back at her, panic clawing at my throat as my eyes flash back to Emma. She tries to speak but I get there first.

'Emma,' I say slowly, 'did you give Joy a letter?'

Emma closes her mouth and frowns.

'Yeah,' she says, 'the one from that prison guy. You were sending it back to him, right? I saw it on the table this morning and was going over to see Joy anyway, she had an ASOS parcel for me.'

My heart drops.

Oh my God. She sent it.

Emma frowns at me. 'What?' she says. 'Did you want to keep it?'

I sink down on to the sofa and try to compose my face as Priya starts carving a slice of pizza.

82

It's gone. I can't believe it's gone.

What did I even write? I can't remember.

I can't tell Emma and Priya what I've done. They'll think I'm mad.

'No,' I say quietly, trying to squash the anxiety back down my throat.

What's going to happen when he opens it? What will he do?

Priya examines my face and I quickly shoot her a smile.

What if he's crazy? He could be totally mental, and I've just written him a letter. A really personal letter.

He wasn't meant to read it. Nobody was meant to read it.

I lace my fingers together.

What if he writes back?

Oh God, why did I write him a letter? What's wrong with me?

'Look, Bea,' Priya says, 'I've had a chat with Emma today, and I need to apologise to you. I was a bad friend this weekend and I'm sorry.'

He won't write back. He'll know it's not the right handwriting. He'll throw it away.

I glance up at Priya and twitch as I realise we're sitting in silence. Emma is frowning at me.

'That's okay,' I mumble, my face burning.

Is there a way I can intercept the post? Get the letter back? 'Bea?'

My eyes jerk up and I realise I'm scrunching up the remaining letters like tissue paper. Emma is eyeing me furiously.

'What's wrong?' Priya asks, her smiling eyes quickly changing expression. 'Are you really mad about it all?'

'No,' I say quietly. I look away as I feel my eyes start to burn.

What am I going to do?

Emma looks at the stack of crumpled post clenched in my fingers and frowns.

'Are you mad that I sent off that letter, Bea?' she asks. 'I know it was quite cool, but it wasn't ours to keep.'

I look back at her, trying to control the creature, which has stretched its claws around my face, covering my eyes with a white mist.

'I know,' I say quietly.

It wasn't ours to keep.

It wasn't mine to answer.

Chapter Ten

My eyes dart around the office as I trot towards my desk, like a horse with an insecure bladder.

Okay, nobody is here yet. I'm the first one in, just as planned.

I barely slept last night. Priya and Emma spent the entire evening chatting, while I sat there slowly mapping out every terrible thing that could go wrong now that I have sent my innermost thoughts to 1) a complete stranger, and 2) a complete criminal.

I drop down into my office chair and switch my computer on. It hums faintly in the silence of the office.

Okay, right. All I need to do now is find Nathan in our archives. He must be local to have had a girlfriend who lived in my house, and we report on every news story, no matter how irrelevant (I'm looking at you, Mrs Fig's Figgy Pudding Fiesta).

I shake my mouse impatiently as my computer slowly whirls into life and I quickly pull up the archives. I hunch over my keyboard and lift my fingers to type.

Nathan prison

I pause as I stare at the screen. Argh, why didn't I think this through? What am I supposed to type? I don't even know his surname!

Okay, well, surely there can't be that many men named Nathan who have gone to prison in Middlesex? Right?

I hit enter and feel my eyes widen as hundreds of stories appear on the screen.

What? How are there so many?

Oh God, I hope they aren't all about the same guy and he's actually committed, like, one hundred different murders.

Maybe that's what he's sorry for. Maybe he tried to murder B.

Maybe B is dead.

The thought slices through my brain like a shard of ice and I blink at the screen.

I hadn't thought of that. What if she's dead and I've sent him a letter from beyond the grave? Oh my God. He'll think he's gone insane!

I try to shake off the cold chill that creeps through me as my eyes zoom in on the stories. Randomly, I click on the first one and try not to whimper as the story spills on to my screen.

Man jailed for strangling woman.

Oh Christ.

I'm a woman. I have a neck.

I scroll down madly, overcome by a horrible but irresistible urge to cradle my neck.

Nathan Diamond, 58, of Dunsford Drive has been sent to prison for the murders of Janet Humphries and Flora West on 18 June 2004.

Panic races up and down my body as I read the story.

Oh my God. I've written to a man who strangles women for

fun! I know I was always warned never to talk to strangers, but I always thought Mum was being dramatic! I never knew it could end in *this*.

I pause as my eyes skim the story again.

Hang on, 2004?

My shoulders sag slightly as I feel myself relax.

Nathan said he'd only been in prison for four months. This guy has been there for fourteen years.

I let go of my neck in relief.

Before my spiralling brain can convince me otherwise, I click on the next story.

Local man jailed for several murders of co-workers.

I blink at the news story.

Gosh. I never thought I could relate to a murderer, but here I am.

Several co-workers? More than one? That means that it wasn't just a freak accident where he accidentally poisoned the coffee run or went mental when he was constantly badgered to get onstage and join in at the office party karaoke. He must have planned it all.

I glance around the empty office.

Could anyone at work kill me? Duncan? Angela? Faye?

Actually, Faye could definitely kill me with her big pointy shoes. She could probably slice my head off with one whip of her ridiculous ponytail.

My eyes quickly skim down the news article.

Nathan Turner murdered his co-workers by arriving early –

I stop in my tracks as a cold burst of fear shoots through me. I've arrived early.

– and spiking the coffee machine with acid.

My eyes flick down to my coffee.

Oh no.

I almost fall off my chair in fright when all the office lights suddenly turn on.

I stare frantically around the room, desperate to spot any movement as my fingers curl around the stapler in desperation.

My heartbeat starts to slow as the light reveals an empty office. There is nobody here. It is just me, after all.

I place the stapler back on my desk and feel the urge to laugh.

Christ, for a second there I really thought I—

'Bea?'

Argh!

I brandish the stapler above my head when I spot Duncan making his way over.

I clutch my chest as I lower the stapler.

Oh, thank God. It's only Duncan. What is he doing creeping around the office?

I cower back into my chair, my heart rate returning gradually to normal.

Why is he here so early?

As Duncan comes closer I notice his usual jolly face is sagging. His shirt has a dark stain down the front and his mouth is attempting a half-smile.

As he reaches me, he lifts his expression into a full smile, like an inflating balloon, and I notice he's holding a toothbrush in his left hand.

Does he brush his teeth here?

'Good morning,' he says in his usual, cheery voice. 'What are you doing here at the crack of dawn? You here to get some early work done?'

I look back at Duncan wordlessly.

Does he come in this early every day?

'Err, yeah,' I mumble awkwardly, trying not to look alarmed at Duncan's grey face.

'Good on you,' Duncan says, maintaining a fixed smile. 'You're a hard worker. I'm about to make a cup of Joel, fancy one?'

Does he mean cup of Joe?

'No thank you,' I say, 'I'm fine.'

I gesture down to my sad coffee staring up at me.

'Duncan,' I say, swivelling my chair round to face him, 'I'm trying to find a story in the archives. Do you know if I can filter the search on dates?'

Duncan frowns and leans forward towards my screen.

'Sure,' he says, 'you just filter it here.' He moves the mouse towards a bar. 'Okay?'

'Great,' I say, taking the mouse back off him, 'thank you.'

'Don't you work too hard,' he says jovially as he makes his way back to the kitchen.

I make a half-laughing sound and move my eyes back to my screen.

Right. Nathan. Who are you?

I click on the filtering options and feel my heart squirm as one story appears on my screen.

Nathan Piletto, jailed for three years for investment fraud.

Investment fraud?

As I read the final line of the story, my eyes alight on Nathan's mug shot. He has light hair and pale eyes and a small, crooked mouth.

He looks about thirty. Thirty-five, at a push.

I feel an odd twinge in my chest as I look at his sad face.

He doesn't look guilty.

He looks scared.

My hand hovers over my mouse as the shadow of his letter floats back into my mind.

I lost control of my life and I got caught up in everything, and I pushed you to the sidelines. I was too stupid to think about what I was doing.

My eyes move over to the clock as the numbers change to 08.15.

If Joy used a first-class stamp, the letter might be with him today.

My letter.

Somehow, looking back into his pixelated face, the burning feeling of fear I had at this thought is replaced with a warm sense that I've never felt before.

For some reason, I feel myself hope that he might write back, after all.

CHAPTER ELEVEN

I delve into my bag, wriggle my key free and go to jab it in the door when it flies open. I jump slightly at Priya, who is beaming at me. Her hair is crafted into an enormous plait and she is wearing an apron that is tied around her middle like a *Bake Off* contestant. Her face is flushed and she has a light dusting of icing sugar on her cheek.

I try not to frown at her.

What on earth is she doing? She never beats me home from work.

Her face splits into a grin and I try to ignore her left eye, which is twitching. Unless she's winking at me.

She looks mental.

'Hi!' she practically shouts. 'You're home! How are you? I've been cooking!' she trills, as she steps back so I can walk in.

I blink at Priya in bemusement as each of her high-pitched statements bursts into my ears.

This is not normal. In the six years I have known Priya, she

91

has never baked. Apart from her signature chilli, she can barely turn the oven on.

Unless she's been lying this whole time to trick me into cooking for her whenever she's hung-over, which would be very clever indeed.

I drop my bag on the floor as Priya totters past me like a tightly wound toy. A thick smell swirls through the house and as I follow her into the kitchen I spot stacks of cakes, all neatly lined up on cooling racks, and a fat loaf of bread resting proudly on the window sill.

Did she make all of this?

'Have you been at work?' I ask.

Bloody hell, this looks amazing. Why hasn't Priya done this sooner? I've lived with her for years!

'Took a half-day!' she says, picking up a bowl and whisking happily. 'Would you like some cake? I'm also making a quiche!'

I glance down at her arm, which is spinning manically as she knocks the whisk against the bowl, barely noticing the little splats of batter that fly out on to her skin.

Why is she cooking so much?

'Okay,' I say slowly, 'err, why? Who is all of this food for?'

'For you!' Priya cries. 'For us!'

I blink back at her.

All of this food is for us? She casually decided to take a half-day from work to make hundreds of cakes for me and Emma?

'Really?' I say.

'Yup!' Priya beams as the oven pings. 'Don't they look good?'

'Err,' I say, 'yeah?'

Something definitely isn't right here.

Has she cooked Josh? Has she murdered him and baked him in a pie like Sweeney Todd?

I glance dubiously at a fat cupcake.

Maybe she is winking at me.

'Well,' I say carefully, 'I'm glad that you're feeling better.'

Priya starts humming as she flicks open the oven and pulls out another tray of cakes.

'Are you in tonight?' she asks quickly as I go to walk out of the kitchen. 'Shall we do something? Shall we stay in? Shall we watch something?'

I blink as she fires questions at me like sugar-coated bullets.

'Sure,' I manage, 'that sounds great.'

Priya claps her hands together. 'Yay!'

I back out of the kitchen slowly and keep my strained smile pinned firmly on my face until I am out of sight.

I shut my bedroom door behind me when I feel my phone vibrate in my hand. I look down to see a message from Emma.

Are you in tonight with Priya? Is she okay?

I sink down on to my bed and type a response.

She's fine! Seems really good. I think she's finally feeling a bit better about Josh.

Emma responds almost instantly.

I wouldn't be so sure.

*

I look up in alarm at Priya, who has been marching around our living room for the past four minutes muttering to herself like she's trying to perform a hex. Every now and then I catch a frantic word that zaps out of the corner of Priya's mouth like an enraged wasp.

She prised me out of my room for an 'emergency chat' about ten minutes ago but hasn't once told me what's going on. Her eyes are red and smarting and tears are threatening to spill over like hot water springs. I've tried asking her if she's okay, but she doesn't respond. She hasn't responded to anything, it's like she's in a trance. I sink into the sofa and pull out my phone, trying not to look bored.

She could have at least offered me a piece of cake.

'Priya,' I say carefully, as she swishes past me again, 'what's going on? Did you burn something?'

I pause as the ridiculous question falls out of my mouth and Priya carries on ignoring me.

What was the point of her calling me out of my bedroom if she doesn't want to talk to me? Is this it? Am I supposed to be witnessing something?

I open my mouth to speak again when there is a knock on the door. I look back up at Priya but she doesn't stop pacing, she hasn't even noticed.

I get to my feet and shuffle towards the door.

Oh great. Who is that?

I bet it's some weird guests Priya has inexplicably invited over for some bizarre cake-off. Maybe that's why she's panicking. Maybe she's secretly entered herself on *Come Dine with Me* and is now having a breakdown about her table settings.

I pull open the door and jump at the sight of Joy, who is leaning in so closely it's as if her ear was pressed up against the centre pane.

She steps back quickly and a smile scurries on to her face.

My eyes flit down and I notice a letter in her hand. My heart jolts as I catch sight of the top right-hand corner.

The stars.

'Joy,' I say, my heart racing, 'hi. I was just about to pop round—'

'Hello, Bea,' Joy cries, as if she's been saving these words all day. 'How are you?'

I glance down at the letter again, which is quivering in her hand. He's written back.

'Fine,' I say quickly, 'thanks. You?'

Joy nods at my words, her smile twitching on her face.

'I'm fine too, thank you. How has your day been? Was Priya not at work today?'

She cranes her neck, trying to peer past me and into our house.

'She took a half-day,' I say distractedly, my eyes fixed on the letter.

He's written back. I can't believe he's written back.

What does it say?

'Did she?' Joy says. 'Did she do anything nice? How is she getting on? So sad about that Josh boy. Is she okay?'

Joy's questions bounce around my head like ping-pong balls. I try to focus on her, my mind spinning.

How does she know all of this?

'She's fine,' I say, my hand itching to grab the letter out of Joy's hand. 'Is that my letter?' I add before I can stop myself.

For a second, I see Joy's face drop and she glances down at the letter as if she'd forgotten it existed.

'Oh, yes,' she says. 'It came this morning. Another letter for you, Bea.'

I feel my hand jerk by my side as if I'm about to rip the letter out of her small hands.

I smile and feel my body lean forward to take it from Joy, when she steps backwards and carries on talking.

'You know,' she says, 'I never get handwritten letters any more, but I love receiving them. There is nothing better than waiting for a letter, is there?'

I try to control my head, which feels like it will rocket off my shoulders in frustration any second.

Nothing better than waiting for a letter? Is she mad? This has been *torture*.

Although I guess Joy doesn't usually write fake love letters to men she's never met.

'Nope,' I say tightly, 'not really.'

Without quite meaning to, my hand jerks forward and Joy's eyes clock the sudden movement.

'Oh,' she says, 'here you are.'

She hands the letter to me and I try not to snatch it from her fingers.

It feels thin. Too thin for an actual letter.

Oh God, it's going to be a death threat, isn't it?

'It's from the same gentleman!' Joy quips, pointing her manicured nail at the letter. 'See? The stars are there.'

He's drawn the stars again.

There they are. Five hand-drawn stars in the right-hand corner.

'Is it a love letter?' she asks, her bright eyes blinking up at me.

I feel my face burn as I feel an odd flash of hope.

Do I want it to be a love letter?

Joy reads my expression and smiles.

'How romantic,' she coos, her hand touching her heart.

I look back at her weakly.

I need to open this letter. I need to know what it says.

'Yeah,' I mumble. 'I'd better go, Joy. Thank you for . . .' I trail off and hold the letter up, 'but I'll see you on Thursday?'

Joy's smile flickers. 'Of course!' she says. 'I've got lots to be getting on with,' she adds. 'I can't stand here all evening chatting. See you Thursday. I'll make us something nice.'

I lean on the door and gradually push it shut.

'Sounds great,' I say. 'Bye, then.'

I hold up a non-committal hand as I close the door and stare at the letter.

He's written back. I can't believe he's written back.

I stride towards my bedroom.

What has he said? Did he know it wasn't from B? Does he care? Is he—

'Bea!'

My heart lurches as I collide with Priya who has stormed straight out of the living room and is face to face with me, her eyes flashing.

I quickly whip the letter behind my back and stuff it in my back pocket.

'Was that Joy?' she barks. 'You were at the door for ages.'

I blink at her, all of the blood rushing to my head.

Oh God. Did she hear our conversation? Does she know?

'Yeah,' I say feebly, 'it was Joy.'

Priya skulks back into the living room and my eyes glance desperately towards my bedroom door, hanging open invitingly.

I need to open this letter.

'Come here a sec,' Priya calls from the living room. 'I need to show you something.'

I follow her into the living room, my hand twitching and reaching for my back pocket.

'What is it?' I say, more snappily than I intended, as I drop on to the sofa.

Priya rips her phone out of her pocket and brandishes it towards me.

'*Look*,' she hisses, holding her phone inches away from my face.

I screw up my eyes and try to focus on her flashing screen.

It's Josh's Instagram page. Again.

Why is she back on his page?

'Right,' I say.

Priya's eyes widen at me in frustration.

'Click on his story!' she cries. 'Look!'

Before I can move, she jabs her finger on the flashing circle and a photo of a girl pops up. She has short dark hair and bright blue eyes. She is holding a beer and is laughing at the camera.

For a second, I almost forget about the letter.

'Is that his . . . sister?' I say slowly.

'He doesn't have a sister!' Priya practically shouts, leaping to her feet. 'It's some girl! Who is she? Why is he with her? Do you think it's his new girlfriend?'

I blink back at her.

New girlfriend? He can't have a new girlfriend already, surely?

'No,' I say firmly, 'it's just some girl he's out for a drink with.'

Even as I hear the words fall out of my mouth I know I've said the wrong thing.

'And look!' Priya bursts, throwing herself back down on to the sofa next to me. 'Look at this!'

She clicks on a name and the girl's Instagram page fills her screen, with the name Joanna C in capitals at the top of the page.

How on earth did Priya find her page? Is this what she's been doing all this time? I look up at her blankly, desperately trying to think of something to say to calm her down.

'She's uploading stories too!' Priya shrieks. 'They're together, uploading stories, probably of them *having sex*.'

She spits the words out of her mouth like poison, and I try not to laugh.

Having sex?

Christ, is that what people do these days? Film themselves having sex for thirty seconds of an Instagram story?

I mean, how would they film it?

Surely they wouldn't use a Boomerang.

'That's definitely not what's happening,' I say solemnly.

'Well, what else are they doing?' Priya cries hysterically, glaring at me as if I have morphed into Joanna.

I look back at her feebly.

'I don't know,' I say lamely, 'something really boring like . . . cabbage picking.'

Cabbage picking?

Priya glares at me.

That's not a thing!

'Or cabbage baking.'

For God's sake, get off cabbages!

'Why don't you just watch it and see?' I flail, desperate to distract myself from my sudden fascination with cabbages, the worst vegetable ever.

Are they even a vegetable?

They can't be a fruit, can they?

'I can't watch it!' Priya seethes, as she goes back to storming around the room like an evil overlord. 'She'll see! And then they will laugh together at me watching it all while I'm sat at home baking like some loser.'

The last bit wobbles out of her mouth and she collapses on to the sofa in a big heap.

'I thought you were enjoying baking?' I offer.

'I hate baking!' Priya snaps.

Oh.

Well, she could have fooled me.

'Look,' I say calmly, 'I'm sure her stories are nothing interesting. They probably aren't even of Josh. He's probably nowhere to be seen.'

I pull myself to my feet and give Priya my most reassuring final look as I turn to leave the room. I can almost feel the letter calling out to me from my back pocket.

'Wait!' Priya calls, rooting me to the spot.

Urgh. I'm never going to bloody open it. He might as well have replied using a smoke signal. At least then I could pretend I was on fire so that Priya could leave me alone.

She scurries over to me desperately, waving her phone in her hand. 'You need to watch it!' she cries, her eyes glinting like she's cracked the Da Vinci code, 'then you can tell me what it is!'

I stare back at her.

What?

'No!' I cry. 'Priya, I'm not doing that.'

'Oh, Bea!' Priya whines, clutching her phone to her chest. 'Please!'

'No,' I say firmly, backing out of the living room like I'm escaping a lion. 'You need to let this go, Priya. We can watch *EastEnders* in a bit, okay? Why don't you go have a hot shower and think of something else?'

Priya's large eyes stare back at me like a wild animal. Eventually, she nods.

'Okay,' she says, 'I'll think of something else.'

My body relaxes as my hand reaches to my back pocket to check the letter is still there.

'Good,' I smile, walking towards my room.

★

I push my bedroom door shut behind me and sink to the floor, my back pressed firmly against the door. Slowly, I pull the crumpled letter out from my back pocket and hold it in my hands.

I can't believe he's written back.

As I stare down at the letter I feel my heart pick up its pace.

I said some really personal things in my letter. Some things I only ever say to Mum. He was never supposed to receive it. Nobody was ever supposed to read it.

My eyes fall on the five stars, identical to the dainty ones I drew back to him. Feeling my hands shake slightly, I peel open the back of the envelope and pull out a single sheet of paper. As I unfold the letter my heart recognises his small, crooked handwriting and I feel a swell of emotion at the back of my throat.

He's written back to me.

Dear B,

I can't tell you how much your letter meant to me. I didn't think you'd write back. I wasn't sure if you'd even receive the letter. I'm so glad you still live in the same place. I loved that house. It meant so much to me to hear from you.

I always thought you would be so much happier without

101

me, I never had any idea that you would be feeling this way. I'm sorry I didn't write sooner. I wish I could see you, but remember that I'm always thinking of you. I have been for the past five years. I'm sorry I haven't reached out to you sooner, but I was so stupid and selfishly wrapped up in my own life that I didn't stop to think. Sometimes it takes something huge to make you realise what you need. Feeling alone is the worst feeling, but you're never alone. I'm always here.

Hope this letter brightens your day like yours brightened mine. Write back soon.

Love you always.

Nathan x

My eyes scan the last words and I suddenly notice my face is damp.

He wrote back. He didn't laugh at me. He understood.

I didn't think anybody would understand.

I brush my cheeks with the back of my hand as a warm sense of relief rushes through me.

Before I can think of anything else, I grab my phone and click Mum's number. It goes to answerphone almost immediately, like it always does.

She never answers.

'Hi, Mum,' I feel myself laugh shakily, 'it's me. I just wanted to tell you that he wrote back, that guy I told you about. I told him all the crap I usually only say to you, and he wrote back. It's just made me feel really . . .'

I trail off and I look at my phone, watching the seconds tick away.

'Good,' I say eventually. 'I just wanted to let you know that, but I'll speak to you later. Love you.'

I click the phone off as I feel the door shake behind my head.

'Bea?' Priya's voice calls. 'Are you okay?'

I jump to my feet and shove the letter under my pillow, dabbing my face. I pull the door open and see Priya, rocking back and forth on the balls of her feet like a toddler desperate for a wee.

She hasn't showered. She looks exactly the same as she did half an hour ago. Crazed.

Oh God. Is she going to be like this all the time? I don't think I can handle it!

I see her eyes flick over my face and for a second I think she's going to ask if I've been crying, but she doesn't. She pushes past me and jumps on to my bed.

'Are you okay?' she says, squinting at me.

'Yes,' I say quickly, 'are you?'

Priya nods abruptly. 'Yes,' she says. 'I've thought of something else.'

I smile as I feel a wave of relief.

Praise the Lord.

'Good,' I smile, 'that's really good, Priya. That's just what you need, something to take your mind off everything. Why don't we do something active, like go for a run? That always clears my mind.'

Priya pulls out her phone again, apparently not listening to me, and thrusts it towards my face.

'Meet Florrie Nannoo.'

I frown at Priya as my eyes flit down to a blank Instagram page.

What in fresh hell is this?

Doesn't nannoo mean vagina? Is this Priya's sexual alter ego?

I open my mouth to voice the question and then quickly clamp it shut.

I do *not* want to know the answer to that.

Priya shakes the phone at me, desperate for me to respond. I look back at her blankly.

'Err,' I manage, 'what?'

Priya giggles and gestures for me to sit next to her on my bed. I sink down slowly.

'It's a fake Instagram account!' she cries. 'I read about it in a magazine. Now I can stalk Josh and this Joanna girl without them knowing!'

She stares at me with her feverish, mad eyes.

'Priya,' I say slowly, 'you've made a fake person so that you can, erm . . . stalk your ex-boyfriend?'

I look at her in the hope that my words will snap her out of this mad spiral of insanity. Instead, she nods.

'Yup!'

'I don't think this is healthy,' I mumble.

Priya rolls her eyes at me and flicks her hair off her shoulder.

'We just need to upload some photos,' Priya says, her assertive manner back, 'so I thought I could take one of you.'

I gawp at her.

What?

Take one of me?

'What?' I spout. 'No!'

Priya shoots me a look. 'Why not?'

'Well,' I flounder, 'he'll recognise me!'

I get to my feet and scowl at Priya, who just rolls her eyes at me again. 'We'll take it from behind.'

What?

Take it from behind?

Oh yeah, just the words every girl wants to hear.

'Priya,' I snap, 'I can't believe I have to say this to you but I do not want a picture of my arse on some random Instagram page.'

For God's sake. How did I get here?

'I'll put a filter on it,' Priya mutters, angling her camera towards me.

I leap back in horror.

'No!' I snap. 'Priya, stop it! Just get a photo of some random girl off the internet.'

Bloody hell, this is horrible! Am I going to have to skulk around the house in a balaclava and a bin bag in constant fear of having my arse papped?

'You are such a prude,' Priya snips, getting to her feet. 'It's not like anyone would know it was yours. It could be anyone's arse.'

I blink at her.

Oh, well, thanks very much. It's good to know that my arse is so unmistakably ordinary that it could belong to just anybody.

'I'll take it from the shoulders up,' Priya says. 'Just a candid one of you holding a coffee or something.'

I open my mouth to protest loudly but Priya gets there first.

'Please, Bea!' she cries. 'I'm going through a hard time and this would really help me.'

'This would really help you?' I repeat.

Priya nods, standing up and locking her pleading eyes on to mine.

Urgh.

'Fine,' I grumble, 'just of my shoulders. And this is it, okay?'

Priya nods happily.

'Yes,' she says firmly, 'this is it.'

CHAPTER TWELVE

'Morning.'

I look up as Faye drops into the seat next to me, ready for her morning five-minute chat.

'Hi, Faye,' I say, moving my hands away from my keyboard, 'how are you?'

Faye frowns at me.

'You're in a good mood,' she says suspiciously, tilting her head as if I could be wearing a mask that she's ready to rip off.

'Am I?' I say lightly.

I wrote Nathan another letter last night. I gave it to Joy this morning, and I haven't been able to shake the feeling that I'm floating.

It's almost like Nathan's letter is a safety blanket, wrapped around my body. The creature can't get to me today. I feel safe.

'Yeah,' Faye says slowly, 'what is it? Have you met someone?'

She moves her head to look at my screen and I quickly shake my mouse to break my swirling screensaver.

Okay, I need to shut this down. Regardless of how happy I

am with Nathan's letter, the last thing I want is for Faye to start spreading rumours about me.

'I'm just in a good mood,' I say. 'How are you?'

Faye flicks her hair off her shoulders. Today she has sculpted half of her hair above her head, wound into a bun, with the rest of it shimmering down her back like a sheet of ice.

'I'm good,' she says, looking up as Jemima walks past. 'Oh!' she says, jumping back to her feet. 'Jemima!'

I sag in my seat as an email from Angela pings on to my screen.

Duncan wants meeting with you now.

I blink down at the email.

I glance over at Angela in the hope of gaining a glimmer of more information, but her head is firmly clasped in her hands, her fingers clawing into her scalp.

I pick up my notebook and slowly walk towards Duncan's office.

He's way ahead of schedule for his four o'clock 'quote of the day' inspirational chat. Maybe he's going to ask me to spell something really huge and is giving me a whole day to prepare.

I reach Duncan's office and knock on the door. I never go into Duncan's office – I never need to, he's hardly ever in it. He spends the majority of the day marching around the office like the Town Crier.

'Come in!'

I walk in and see Duncan, seated behind his small desk. He has a large computer and four coffee mugs marooned amongst a sea of several pens and sweet wrappers. He smiles and gestures to the sofa at the other end of his boxy office.

Why does he have a sofa?

I perch awkwardly, my back poker straight, unsure of how to sit. A sofa feels far too casual to have in an office.

Is that a pillow?

'How are you doing?' he beams, his fat teeth glistening at me.

I feel myself smile back at him. It's impossible not to smile at Duncan, he's like a puppy. Very unpredictable, but ultimately harmless.

'Yeah, fine, thank you,' I say, my back already aching at the stiffness of my posture. 'You?'

Duncan nods and starts lining up his pencils.

'All good!' he chortles. 'Now, I want you to know that your hard work hasn't gone unnoticed.'

I nod, feeling my cheeks pinch slightly.

'Thank you,' I mumble.

'And when I saw you here early the other day, I just thought it was about time you were given your own story to work on.'

I look up, feeling a flicker of hope.

Is he going to let me run my story?

'Really?' I say.

Duncan nods, his chuffed face beaming.

'Of course!' he says. 'And I have the story that is perfect for you. I really think you could nail it. And it's about the community, which is what you wanted, isn't it?'

I look back at him, my heart lifting.

Oh my God, he actually listened to me!

'Yes,' I say, 'thank you so much, that's so exciting.'

Maybe it will be a fashion show, or a fun run, or a big campaign to do with saving a local business. I could interview everyone involved and we could raise loads of money for a really important cause.

Duncan grins. 'Do you want to know what it is?'

★

'So, you're the girl with the newsworthy beaver.'

My head jerks up as Faye swans over to my desk, her eyebrows curled into a sceptical formation as she looks down at me.

I shoot her a look and she flounces away.

Great.

It turns out that Duncan did have a story for me to run, about the local community. He said it was something I could really 'get my teeth into', a story that could 'grip the hearts of Middlesex'.

About a beaver. About a local beaver who has returned home after escaping his . . .

His what? His lake? His dam?

Who cares?

He wants me to write a 'heart-warming' piece and run a phone interview with the owners who thought they had lost their prized beaver for ever.

I mean, what? Is this my life now?

Faye is furious about the whole thing and keeps making snide comments, and Jemima asked me very loudly earlier how it felt to 'have my hands on the most famous beaver in town' – which is *not* a rumour I want circulating the office.

I prod my phone and peer down as the screen fills with light. I glare at the Florrie Nannoo Instagram page with its two pictures of me holding mugs of tea. My face is hidden by a book, and there is a glimpse of one bare shoulder as I look out of a window intently.

Priya said it looked 'really authentic', which made me question her sanity. Who uploads pictures of themselves looking out of windows?

I did text Emma my frustrations in the hope of her siding with me and forcing Priya to delete the page, but she just sent a non-committal reply and said that she'd be out with Margot and would see me later.

I reluctantly look away from my phone as an email from Duncan appears on my screen. I click on it irritably.

Right on cue, Duncan's daily round-robin email of rubbish.

Hey DREAM TEAM!

Just wanted to send an email to keep rockin'!! Also pleased to announce that brainiac Bea has taken on her first solo story with some BEAVER FEVER.

I freeze as my eyes lock on that terrible sentence.

Beaver fever?

Remember, in the words of Tony: thou who shall prosper shall deliver.

I glance over at Angela whose face is screwed up into a frown.

Tony? Who is Tony?

Duncan makes up his own inspirational gibberish every day and always insists on claiming they are pearls of wisdom straight from the mind of some random bloke he met in the pub. My phone vibrates next to me as a string of messages from Priya topple into my phone like a digital game of dominos.

I feel my eyes roll before I've even read one.

I don't even want to know what these messages are going to say.

Oh my God. Have stalked Joanna and she's been with Josh ALL DAY. He's not even at work!!!

I read the message slowly.

She is going insane.

He must have called in sick, I'm going to call his work and tell them he's skiving.

I grab my phone and quickly punch a reply.

Don't do that.

This is a terrible idea. I never should have let her create this stupid Instagram page.

I'm going to report her.

I stare at the phone at Priya's latest message.

Just stop looking, I type back wearily, *get off your phone and focus on something else.*

The two little ticks next to my message flicker blue almost immediately and Priya starts typing a message with such force I can almost hear her.

She's probably trying to curse me over WhatsApp for not offering to report Josh to the police for some crime that I will never understand.

Another message from Priya appears

Josh has blocked me.

I feel myself sigh.

Good. Thank God one of them has got some sense. He saw through our Florrie Nannoo ruse, then. How unpredictable.

Oh, I reply.

Priya starts jabbing a message straight away but I get there first.

Pri, I'll talk to you later. I've got a massive beaver to report on.

I hit send and stare at my phone in dismay.

Well, there's a sentence I never thought I'd type.

CHAPTER THIRTEEN

'Okay,' I stare down at my perfectly organised shopping list, 'so we've got cereal, milk and butter. We now need pasta.' I steer the shopping trolley down the next aisle and try to control the smile spreading across my face.

I look down at my shopping list, pinned to the top of my trolley. I take out my pencil and draw a neat line through 'butter' and try to stop myself from ruffling up like a chicken ready to roost.

God, I love doing the weekly food shop.

Or I usually do. When I don't have Priya huffing next to me, glued to her phone like it's sending her the only source of oxygen.

I forced Priya to come. I came home to find her four years deep on Joanna's Instagram page and shoehorned her out of the house. Needless to say, she didn't appreciate my shopping list, or my offer to buy us both a treat to cheer her up. She muttered something about empty calories and has been stomping alongside me like a moody elephant. I mean, she is fresh off a night shift so is highly sleep deprived. But still, I offered to buy her doughnuts.

'Okay,' I say, as we reach the pasta aisle, 'I think I'm going to get this sauce.' I glance at her to see if she's even listening to my narration. 'Do you want any?'

I wait for a response. Her scowling face is glaring at her phone.

Christ! Was I ever this unbearable as a teenager?

She's not even a teenager, she's twenty-four! How have I suddenly turned into her mum? I feel like I've moved in with Tracy Beaker.

'Priya?' I say, using all of my energy to sound carefree and not as if I'm ready to strangle her.

'Priya?' I snap.

Priya's eyes fly up at me. 'What?'

Oh God, this is a nightmare. Next time, I'm going to lock her under the stairs.

'Do you want some pasta sauce?' I say evenly, trying to fight my jaw from locking.

Priya's dull eyes stare into mine as if I'm speaking Dutch.

'What?' she says again.

'Priya,' I say, 'I know you're upset but you don't have to take it out on me, I'm only trying to—'

'Oh my God!' Priya gasps.

She grabs my body like a human shield and ducks behind it. I stagger about madly.

'What are you doing?' I mutter out of the corner of my mouth, trying to ignore the anxious looks of fellow shoppers.

Priya squeals something barely audible behind my shoulder and I crane my neck round to look at her.

'What?'

'Josh!' she cries. 'He just walked past!'

Her desperate fingers grip my arm and for a terrible moment I fear she's going to crawl on to my back like a baby gorilla.

I look around. 'Well,' I say feebly, 'he's gone now.'

She pokes her head up and I feel her grip loosen. She looks down at herself in horror, and then her eyes snap back at me.

'Swap clothes with me,' she orders.

I blink back at her.

What?

'What?' I say. 'No. Priya, this isn't *Parent Trap.*'

'Swap clothes with me!' she hisses, her eyes flashing. 'I look homeless!'

She gestures down to her baggy top desperately.

I blink at her. She can't be serious.

I try to push the trolley forward but Priya grabs hold of it.

'Please!' she cries. 'He can't see me like this. Look at me!'

'You look fine,' I say, pretending to look at pasta.

There is no way I am taking off my top in the middle of Tesco. Absolutely not.

'I don't want to look fine!' she wails, trailing after me. 'I want to look hot! Bea,' she grabs hold of me, 'please! Just hide behind here and swap.'

She points at a large tower of baked beans.

Good Lord.

'I am not hiding behind a mountain of baked beans, Priya,' I say flatly. 'I'm not a sausage casserole.'

'Look,' she grabs hold of my T-shirt and yanks it up, 'you're wearing a top underneath! Nobody would even notice!'

'That's my vest!' I say in alarm, yanking my T-shirt back down. 'I'm not going to walk around Tesco in my *vest.*'

'Bea, please.' Priya grabs my arm and her eyes stare into mine. 'I'm begging you.'

I open my mouth to reply indignantly and then feel a pang of guilt. She looks like she's about to cry.

I look more closely at her jumper. It does look warmer than my T-shirt.

I roll my eyes at her.

'If I do this, will you stop trying to take pictures of me for that stupid Nannoo page?'

Priya nods desperately, her fingers itching towards the hem of my T-shirt.

I glance around to make sure nobody else is in the aisle.

This will have to be the quickest I've ever got changed. Even quicker than the time I was getting dressed and the window cleaner popped up.

'Fine,' I say quickly.

Priya pulls her jumper over her head and throws it at me. I scrabble at the sides of my T-shirt and feel Priya's hands claw it off me.

Oh my God, I hope nobody sees this on CCTV and thinks we're about to have sex. I don't want to be banned from Tesco. I've memorised all of the aisles.

I pull the jumper over my head and gasp as my face pops out of the top like an anxious Jack-in-the-box.

Priya looks down at my top, which is stretched across her large chest and hanging wonkily on her shoulders.

I turn back to my shopping trolley and start to push it down the aisle.

'Okay,' I say, trying to control my erratic breathing as I put a jar of sauce in my trolley. 'Right. So, tomato and basil.'

115

Good Lord, that was intense.

'I don't know if I can stay,' Priya gabbles. 'Are you nearly finished? I might go wait in the car.'

'I just need to grab some garlic,' I say, 'then we can go.'

Priya coils her arm around mine, her head swivelling around as if we are creeping around a horror maze.

'Okay,' she says quietly, 'garlic. Okay.'

I push the trolley towards the vegetable aisle, when I suddenly spot Josh, crouching over the mushrooms. I turn back to warn Priya, but she's leapt back into the cereal aisle.

'Are you okay?' I mutter, abandoning my trolley and skirting round after her.

Priya nods. 'Yeah,' she says. 'Don't talk to him,' she orders.

My head automatically turns in Josh's direction.

'But,' I say feebly, 'he might say hi to me.' Priya and Josh were together for three years. 'He'll recognise me.'

I don't want to be rude. I can't just stalk past a man who has broken the heart of my best friend, like some fabulous older woman.

Priya bites her lip and nods.

'Okay,' she mutters into her sleeve. 'Wait!' she hisses as I go to return to my trolley. 'Okay, talk to him. Tell him I'm great. Tell him I'm . . .' she looks into the air as if all the answers are flying around her, 'tell him I'm seeing someone new. Someone amazing. Like a body builder. Ask him who Joanna is. Pretend you've forgotten his name.'

I blink back at her. That is a lot of orders.

'Right,' I say eventually, 'fine.'

I turn back to my trolley and take a deep breath.

Oh God, this is all going to be horrendous. I can't act! I am a terrible actor.

I notice Josh and stare determinedly at the floor.

Hopefully, he won't even notice me and I won't have to engage in any small talk whatsoever. I can just grab my garlic and leave. Then I can take Priya home and that'll be the end of this—

'Bea?'

I pretend to be surprised as I look up at Josh, who is carrying two boxes of vegetables.

'Oh, hi . . .' I burble madly.

Don't say Josh, don't say Josh, don't say Josh.

'Julian, is it?'

Julian?

Josh blinks at me. 'Josh,' he says slowly, looking at me as if my nose has just fallen off. 'You okay?'

Okay. Rethink and regroup, Bea. You can do this. Priya needs you.

'Yeah, fine,' I say, trying my best to sound aloof and carefree. 'Everything is great. Gravy, actually. Gravy train. All aboard the gravy train. Choo, choo.'

Urgh, God. What are you doing?

'Yeah, I'm just here to do some food shopping for Priya. She's really busy right now, so can't do it herself.' I spout the words quickly, before Josh can respond to my unauthorised train impression.

'Oh really?' Josh says, his face changing. 'Is she okay?'

'Oh yeah!' I say confidently, waving my arm in the air. 'God, yeah. She's fine, never been better actually. She's following her dream now, at last. I always knew she could do it. She's planning on climbing Snowdon.'

I flounder.

That's not impressive! Children climb Snowdon!

'As a warm-up,' I blurt, 'before climbing Kilimanjaro. The mountain, that is. That's not the name of her new boyfriend. His name is Colin.'

I break off as I finally grab hold of the mad words tumbling out of my mouth.

Okay, great. Priya is now dating a fifty-year-old accountant.

Josh stares at me.

'She has a new boyfriend?'

'Yup,' I say, pretending to look over his shoulder, as if Colin could be prowling around the peppers. 'Have you got a boyfriend? Girlfriend!' I correct myself quickly. 'Or, you know, boyfriend. No judgement, obviously. Whatever tickles your . . . err . . . pickle.'

Arghhhhhh.

What am I saying?

Tickle your pickle? Who says that?

Although it's quite topical, as I'm in the vegetable aisle.

'No,' Josh says flatly, 'no girlfriend.'

I look back at him as we sink into silence.

'Well,' I say, 'I'd better go. I've got to get back to Priya. We're going . . .'

What's sexy? What's sexy?

Say something sexy!

'Pole dancing,' I finish.

Pole dancing?

Josh gives a half-smile and nods.

'Cool,' he says. 'Tell Priya I said hi.'

I hold up a hand as my face burns and Josh walks past me. I wait a second before shoving my trolley back into the cereal aisle and spot Priya, glaring at me.

Oh, for God's sake, now what? I've done exactly as she asked and she's still glaring at me! This is hopeless!

'Don't look at me like that,' I mutter crossly as she lopes along next to my trolley. 'I gave you a boyfriend and a cool new hobby *and* I found out that he doesn't have a new girl-friend.'

'Or boyfriend,' Priya mutters.

'Well, yes,' I say, my cheeks flushing, 'or boyfriend.'

★

I push my shoulder against our front door as the splitting carrier bags dig into my fingers. Priya swans past me, holding *one bag of toilet roll* under her arm, her entire focus on her iPhone. Obviously.

I glare at the back of her head as I kick the door shut.

Right. Well, she certainly will not be getting any of my pasta bake.

Priya swans upstairs and I stagger into the living room where I spot Emma, who is curled into the corner of the sofa cradling a huge mug.

I drop the bags on the floor and smile at her. She flashes me a small smile back and turns her attention back to the TV.

Has she been crying?

'Where's Priya?' Emma asks, looking over my shoulder.

Without quite meaning to, I roll my eyes.

'Upstairs,' I say. 'We saw Josh in Tesco.'

Emma moves her mug between her hands and raises her eyebrows.

'Oh,' she says, 'is she okay?'

119

I kick the shopping bags out of the way of the door and drop on to the sofa opposite.

'Think so,' I shrug.

'Good,' Emma mumbles. 'What did you think of the banana bread? I used a new recipe.'

Her eyes flick over to me and I smile.

Emma has always been the baker. Even at university, when I only had £5 in my account, she was able to whip up a tart in seconds.

(Not a euphemism. Mostly.)

'Yeah, really nice, thanks!' I say.

I look up at the clock.

18.05: Unpack shopping.
18.15: Have a cup of tea.
18.30: Make dinner (pasta bake).
19.15: Eat dinner and freeze leftovers.
19.30: Watch *Hollyoaks*.
20.00: Watch *EastEnders*.
20.30: Make lunch and choose outfit for tomorrow.
21.00: Watch *The Only Way Is Essex*.
22.00: Check phone.
22.15: Go to sleep.

Silence stretches over the room and I feel a small scratch at the pit of my stomach.

'Are you in tonight?' I ask.

Emma flinches slightly at my question but she doesn't look at me.

'Think so,' she says quietly.

'Oh, good,' I say, 'that's nice to have you here.'

Emma usually spends every night with Margot. I've never asked why Margot doesn't stay here.

Emma gives a small nod and sips her tea as we fall back into silence.

I haven't seen Emma in days. She doesn't know about Priya, or about my mad beaver stories at work. She barely knows about the date with Keith.

I open my mouth to speak and then shut it slowly as Emma keeps her face turned away from mine.

But if she wanted to know, she'd ask.

I turn my phone over and look down as the lifeless screen stares back up at me. No missed calls, no texts.

Nothing from Mum.

I look up as Priya comes bustling down the stairs. She's taken my T-shirt off now and springs on to the sofa next to me.

'It worked!' she squeals, grabbing my arm. 'Our plan worked!'

I blink at her.

Plan? What plan?

'What?' I say.

'Josh has just requested to follow me on Instagram! He's obviously jealous about my new boyfriend!'

Emma looks round. 'What new boyfriend?'

Priya bats her question away.

'How do I look?' she asks, pulling her face into a neutral expression and then pouting at Emma. I notice how her face is suddenly covered in make-up.

'Are you going to see him?' I ask.

If they get back together then maybe life can go back to normal.

Priya scowls at me. 'No!' she snaps. 'Of course not.'

'You look great, Pri,' Emma says, pulling out her phone.

Priya shoots Emma a smile and then flounces off into the kitchen. My eyes follow her as she pulls out her phone and starts taking pictures of herself.

I turn back to Emma when I hear a knock at the door. I pull myself to my feet and see Joy's shadow, craning forward towards the pane. A zap of excitement shoots through me.

The post.

I open the door and smile at Joy, who moves back slightly. Today she is wearing a pale pink cardigan and matching skirt, and her eyes are wide and shining. My body jerks slightly as I notice a letter clasped between her dainty fingers. I recognise the jagged handwriting immediately.

I quickly look back up and meet Joy's eyes as I realise I haven't spoken.

'Hi, Joy,' I say, trying to focus on her face as heat sparks up my body like small flashes of electricity. 'How are you?'

Joy's wide eyes look back at me. 'Fine, thank you,' she says. 'You didn't come round at your usual time today, so I thought I'd bring your post.'

She extends her hand and my eyes fixate on the small constellation of scribbled stars.

I reach forward and take the letter out of Joy's hand. For a second, I see her body deflate as she lets it go, as if the letter carries her supply of air.

'It's always lovely to receive mail,' she says, darting a look over my shoulder. 'I thought you'd be expecting it.'

I look back down at the letter as my heart swells.

You have no idea.

Joy smiles at me and leans forward on the balls of her feet.

'How are Priya and Emma?'

I open my mouth to reply when Priya charges through the hallway behind me and thunders up the stairs. Moments later, I hear her door slam.

I guess her selfie didn't go well.

'Fine,' I say. 'Priya's got a few days off now and—' I break off as I feel Emma behind me and a dart of panic flashes through me.

She pulls on her coat and spots Joy.

'Hi, Joy,' Emma says, 'have we got post? Sorry,' she adds, 'I'll pick you up some sugar.'

Emma's eyes flick down to Joy's empty hands and I feel a jolt of anxiety. I stuff the letter hastily into my back pocket.

'Just something for me,' I gabble quickly, my eyes flicking towards Joy nervously.

Joy smiles at Emma. 'Oh, not to worry, Bea dropped some round,' she says. 'How did the new recipe turn out?'

Emma grins. 'Good!' she says. 'Not as good as yours.'

Joy lets out a tinkle of laughter. 'Well,' she says, 'if you ever want a lesson.'

Emma shrugs her bag on to her back and juggles her keys in her hand.

'Thanks, Joy,' she laughs, stuffing her shoes on, 'I'll remember that.' She shoves her foot inside her Converse and turns to me. 'I'm going to Margot's,' she says, 'I'll be home tomorrow.'

I feel my heart sink. I haven't had a proper chat with Emma in days.

'I thought you were staying in,' I mumble, and then want to kick myself for how lame I sound.

Emma slides past me, and Joy steps aside.

'Change of plan,' she says as she walks down the path and clicks open her car. 'See you tomorrow. We'll catch up properly then.'

I hold up a hand as Emma's car door slams and the creaking silence of the house stretches around me.

I look back at Joy who is still gazing up at me, her wide eyes blinking. I pull my sagging face into a smile.

'Thank you for this, Joy,' I say, looking down at her. 'I appreciate you bringing it round.'

'That's okay,' Joy says quickly. 'What are you doing for dinner? I'm making a pie, if you'd like some.'

She beams at me and I feel a pang of guilt.

I'd have to change my schedule.

'Actually, that would be really nice,' I say. 'I just need to sort some bits out here first.'

Joy's face lights up. 'Lovely!' she says. 'Shall we say eight? Priya is more than welcome too.'

Hmmm. She wouldn't say that if she knew what mood Priya was in.

'Okay,' I say, 'thank you. I'll see you at eight.'

I smile one last time as I click the door shut and look around at the empty space. I walk into the living room and sink down on to the sofa, carefully pulling the letter out of my back pocket. My heart twitches as I notice the five stars drawn in the top right-hand corner in black biro. I take one look over my shoulder to check there is no sign of Priya, then I open the letter.

Hi B,

Your letters brighten my day. I feel so lucky to receive them. I never sent letters before, apart from when I was a kid, or if I sent postcards. You always text if you want something, but there's something about getting a letter in here. I've read your last one about ten times already. It's like I've got a piece of you here with me.

I always thought of you and wondered what you were doing, but if I'm being honest, I was too lazy to do anything about it. I thought I had time. You always do, don't you? I don't know if you heard this, but we lost our mum a few months back. She was so strong but she finally lost her fight. I wasn't in here when it happened. It's weird, you think you have all the time in the world, until you realise that you don't. I miss her a lot, she was the best part of me. I never thought I'd lose her. I went into a really dark place when it happened, and being in here there isn't a lot to pull you back out of it. Except for your letters.

Everything that happened made me think about it all a lot, and that's when I decided to write to you. Life feels so short and I had to tell you I'm sorry. I'm so grateful that you wrote back to me. I didn't think you would.

I understand if you say no to this, but I wanted to ask you one more thing. I don't know if you remember my nan, Nina. I know you never met her, but hopefully I spoke about her at some point. She's really cool. She's still in the same old people's home, right by your house. Sunfield or something. I wanted to ask if you might go see her. Now Mum has gone, I don't know who does.

I understand if it's too much. You always had such a big heart and she always liked the sound of you. I think Mum bigged you up a lot. She was gutted when we broke up.

Hope you've had a better week.

Love you always.

Nathan x

My eyes fall on the last words and then, like a typewriter, jump straight to the top and scan the letter all over again. I feel my heart swell in my chest and my eyes start to burn.

His nan? He's asked me to go see his nan?

I sink back against the sofa cushions and pull the letter closer to me, my face hot.

It's weird, you think you have all the time in the world, until you realise that you don't.

My left hand scrabbles madly for my phone. I pick it up and jab in Mum's number.

'Hi, Mum,' I say, my breath short, 'it's me.'

★

I scrunch up my stinging eyes as the words of Nathan's letter reverberate through my heart. I fight the image of a fragile old lady, sitting alone in a house that isn't her home.

The bus rolls around another corner. I try to sit upright, as my head flops towards the man next to me.

I barely slept last night. Each time I felt like I was drifting into unconsciousness, my anxiety would rip me back into the darkness and spark me back to life like a set of fizzing Christmas tree lights.

I shouldn't have written back. I never should have written back. If I had ignored the first letter then this wouldn't have happened. He wouldn't have asked me to go visit a family member. He never would have confided in me.

I feel my body ache as the creature inside me rakes its claws down my windpipe.

He trusted me. I just liked his letters. They made me feel . . . wanted?

I wince as embarrassment fizzes through me at my pathetic train of thought.

I never thought it would end like this. I just thought they were letters.

I just liked having someone to talk to.

The bus lurches to a halt and I look up as the doors fold open and two people step off. My eyes move back to the fogged window as I huddle in my seat.

I can't write back now. This has already gone too far. I'll need to bin the letters and forget about the whole thing.

My heart aches as this thought streaks through my mind.

But I don't want to.

I don't want to throw the letters away. I don't want to not write back. I don't want to pretend this never happened.

The opening line of Nathan's letter skims through my mind and I scrunch up my eyes.

Your letters brighten my day. I feel so lucky to receive them.

He'll be waiting for my reply. If I don't write back he'll think something has happened.

I press the backs of my hands against my swollen eye sockets.

I never should have written back.

What have I done?

What if something is wrong with Nina? What if Nathan has told her that B might visit? What if she is expecting me, and then I never come?

The claws of anxiety sharpen as I feel them sink into the back of my throat.

I can't leave her. I can't leave someone grieving, alone. Nathan made it sound like she doesn't have anybody.

My fingers tighten around my phone and I glance down at the blank screen, shining up at me.

I can't abandon someone who doesn't have anybody.

I exhale and feel my body sag as the anxiety snakes through me.

I just wish I knew what I was supposed to do.

The bus moves off slowly through the traffic and I rub the back of my sleeve against the condensation on the window as we stop at a set of traffic lights. My eyes linger on a stretch of green and I notice a man slumped on a park bench. I frown as I take in his dipped head and his square jaw. My body twitches.

I've seen that man before. He's still sitting there, alone. It's like he hasn't moved.

The bus starts to move and I feel my heart burn as he looks up and turns his head in my direction. For a second, I think he catches my eye, but as the bus moves forward his head dips back down to his lap. I twist in my seat and my eyes follow him down the street. The creature clutching my heart is squashed by a new feeling and I suddenly know what I need to do.

I need to go see her.

Chapter Fourteen

'How is your beaver?'

I jump as Faye drops into the seat next to me, her manicured eyebrows raised expectantly.

I look back at my bland press release about the local butcher's sausage contest.

Mr Hugh J. Titmarsh won.

'It's not my beaver,' I say tightly, my eyes flitting about, worried that anyone overhearing will think I'm sat here jabbering about my vagina.

Faye pulls out her phone and starts flicking through Instagram. I glance over her shoulder and see that she is watching a photo of herself while little red notifications pop up in the corner.

'That's a nice photo,' I say conversationally, desperate to stifle this ridiculous beaver chat.

Faye's shoulders twitch as she turns to look at me.

'Do you think?' she asks.

I frown at her. Faye never asks my opinion. She turns her hand slightly so that her phone screen is facing me, and I look down politely. She's standing in her bathroom, smiling at the camera. I look down and notice it was uploaded two hours ago.

Two hours ago? Did she take it this morning?

'Wow!' I say before I can stop myself. 'You've got like, two hundred likes already!'

I don't think I even know two hundred people.

Faye's poised expression drops slightly as she pulls the phone close to her chest.

'That's not that many,' she says, watching my reaction. 'My one yesterday got six hundred.'

I try to control my mouth from dropping open.

Six hundred?

'I might delete it,' she adds quietly.

I frown at her. Why? What's the point in that?

'Duncan asked me to work on a story today,' Faye says.

I try to force a smile. Ah. That's why she's come over.

'Oh yeah?' I say.

'Yeah,' she says, leaning back into the seat, 'something to do with crime. There's some guy on the loose near Whitton, I don't know.'

I feel my body jerk.

What?

'He keeps murdering girls.'

I swivel round to face her.

That's right next to where I live.

'There's a madman on the loose in Whitton?' I say slowly. 'Who keeps murdering girls?'

Faye shrugs and hops to her feet as Jemima totters past.

'Yeah,' she says casually, 'something like that. I don't know.'

I open my mouth to reply when Faye swishes past me.

Oh, great. That's just what I need.

I watch Faye leave and quickly turn back to my emails as my eyes focus on the blank page.

Info@sunfieldscarehome.co.uk

My stomach turns over.

I'm going to go in once, as a volunteer. I can go in for a day, check Nina is okay, and then leave. I can tell Nathan that his nan is fine and then stop writing him letters. That way, everything ends before I get in any deeper.

That is the sensible thing to do.

My fingers hover over the keys.

And to start this sensible plan, I must first send this email.

Argh. Where do I start?

Dear sirs,

I pause.

Sirs? Is that a thing? Why am I addressing it to multiple men?

I hit the delete button.

Dear Sir or Madam,

No, no, no. This is all too formal. I'm asking if I can come in for the day, I'm not writing to my local MP.

Hello there,

I whack the delete button immediately.

Christ, no. I sound like a prowling older man.

Oh God. Why have I forgotten how to write an email? I write emails every day! Why is this so hard?

To everyone at Sunfields Care Home

I blink at the flickering email before pressing the delete button.

I can't say that. That sounds like I'm about to make some unauthorised, dramatic speech.

Bonjour.

No! What are you doing? Why would you even write that? You are not French. You don't even have a GCSE.

Hello Sunfields,

Urgh, God. Delete, delete, delete. You are not Michael McIntyre. Come on, Bea, get a grip.

Hi

I stare at the single word. That seems to be the only greeting I have left. I take a deep breath and hit the enter key as I tap out the rest of the email and click send.

Almost immediately, an email fires into my inbox.

Hi,

> *Come today from 4pm and I will talk to you.*
> *Jakub.*

*

I look down at the text that fires on to my screen from Priya.

Where are you?

I try to stifle the bubble of annoyance that has been brewing since Tuesday.

Out, I reply, *be back later.*

The reply shoots on to my screen within seconds.

When?

I lock my phone determinedly and shove it in my bag. She never asked me where I was when she was with Josh.

I wriggle my toes in an attempt to peel my feet off the pavement and try to ignore the fiery nerves writhing around my body like a worm with no head.

I've been standing on the corner of this pavement for what

feels like hours. As soon as the clock ticked over to 17.00, I walked out of my office and stepped on to the bus like a well-programmed robot. I knew that if I'd stopped for even a second, I wouldn't have gone ahead with the plan. My mind would have got in the way.

I was doing well. Until now. I got the right bus, I got off at the right stop, I found the care home.

But now I can't go inside.

My legs twitch as the icy air sinks through my jeans and nips my prickling skin.

I'm starting to wonder if I've forgotten how to walk.

I take a deep breath and look back up at the home. It is a small red-brick building with dark windows dotted across the face of the building, each smeared slightly with condensation. If I look carefully, I can see the outline of a yellow bulb hanging from the ceiling and flickering dully.

I haven't seen a single shadow of a person. I've been half waiting to see someone walk past the window, or laugh loudly, or stand up and stretch – but nothing.

My knees jerk slightly as if my legs have decided to move, but then thought better of it.

Come on, Bea. Go inside. They're expecting you. You are doing a good deed, there is nothing to be worried about.

I suck in a breath of the icy air. The longer I stand here, the more the creature inside of me stirs. My stillness feeds it.

My fingers scrunch themselves into balls inside my coat pockets. They burn at the sudden movement and I bite my dry lip.

It doesn't look like how I thought it would. I always imagined a care home to be bright and fresh, like a house you see on a children's TV show.

I jump slightly as a young man with a small dog skirts past me, and I realise I'm stood in the middle of the pavement, paralysed.

If you don't want to go in, then don't. You could just go home. You don't owe these people anything. Nobody knows you are here. You could just get on the bus and pretend this whole thing never happened, go back to your routine and go back to your life.

I pause as this possibility floats around my brain. For a moment, my anxiety is stilled. But my legs still don't move, they stay locked to the floor as if in a vice.

Or you could go inside.

My legs twitch again.

But you cannot stay stood on this pavement corner for ever. You have to make a decision.

Come on. Go inside. You can do this. They're expecting you. You only have to go in once, find this Nina woman, and then leave. You could be in and out in ten minutes and then it will all be over.

You used to do things like this all the time.

I take a deep breath and feel my limbs crack out of their concrete state as I finally move off the pavement. The creature inside me thrashes in the pit of my stomach and scrabbles viciously at my throat as if it's about to drown. But my legs keep moving.

I curl my fingers around my phone in my bag and pull it out. The email from Jakub greets me. I approach the door and my hand reaches out.

★

Okay, I'm in. I've made it in.

The perfumed air of the building hangs around my nose like soup and I try not to cough at the stale, hot scent. The carpet is pressed into the ground with light indentations from visitors' feet, and there is a small desk at the end of the room with a sign hanging over it reading 'Reception'.

I puff out my chest and walk towards the desk.

You can do this. You can do this. It will all be fine. It will all be fine.

I feel my shoulders rise up to my ears as I reach the reception and ding the bell in the centre of the desk.

The sound of the bell echoes in the silence and I wait, my smile still fixed. As the sound evaporates, I look around.

Where is everybody? Why can't I hear anything?

I mean, I know these people are old but surely they aren't all mute.

Are they?

Oh God. I hope not. I can only remember one piece of sign language that Emma once taught me to do to an ex-boyfriend in the street – and I don't think that will be appreciated here.

My body rises on the balls of my feet and drops down again. I feel my smile slip and I force it to stay on my face.

Where is everyone? Should I press the bell again? Maybe they didn't hear.

I ding the bell again. It rings out around the reception area before being swallowed up again by the silence.

How long am I supposed to stand here for? At what point should I give up and go home?

What if this is all some big practical joke and they are all laughing at me from another room? Maybe I'm not supposed to press the bell.

I glance around anxiously.

This is getting ridiculous. How many volunteers do they lose by nobody showing up?

My hand whacks the bell again.

This is infuriating. Nina is probably sitting in the next room. I only want to check she's okay. I could be really busy. I could only be here for a flying visit. Or I could be a delivery driver dropping off something really important. They could miss the most important delivery of the *year* because nobody can hear the stupid bell and then they'd be sorry because—

'Hello?'

I jump as a man appears through the door slightly out of breath and his face pinched. He is wearing light blue overalls and has a sharp, angular face that is sculpted into a frown. His hair is light and shaved close to his head, and his eyes are bright blue and piercing. He's young, he doesn't look much older than me.

Although he currently looks like he wants to kill me.

Shit. Maybe he does.

His narrowed eyes flick down to the bell and then back at me.

I flinch. Oh God. I definitely shouldn't have hit that bell so many times. Especially the last time. I mean, I really whacked it.

Why did I do that?

I feel my cheeks burn as I try to keep the smile from slipping off my face.

'Hello!' I say, trying to keep my voice bright and cheery. 'My name is Bea. I emailed Jacob.'

I see a flash of irritation shoot over his face as he clutches a stack of papers in his hands. His eyes flick up and down my body and then back to the papers.

'No,' he says simply.

I blink at his unfamiliar accent.

Where is he from?

'No?' I repeat, my hands starting to sweat.

Why did he say no? Am I in the wrong place? Is this not a care home?

I look around dumbly and grab my phone out of my bag.

'I emailed,' I mumble, my face burning, 'I emailed someone called Jacob, he said to come here. See,' I finally pull up the email and turn it towards his face, 'see, he said to come in.'

I watch as he scans the email and then looks back up at me.

'Yes,' he says, 'that's me.'

I stare back at him, my eyes darting back to the email.

What? Is he mad?

'Jacob?' I say stupidly.

'No,' he says, placing the papers on the reception desk, 'Yakub. My name is Yakub. That is how you say it. Not Jacob.'

I feel heat engulf my face and my smile evaporates entirely.

Well, how the hell was I supposed to know that?

'Right,' I say tightly, 'well, hello. My name is Bea. I'm here to volunteer.'

I meet his eyes and feel my face narrow into a frown. He looks me up and down again.

'I know,' he says, bending his body forward so that he is leaning against the desk and shuffling the papers in front of him.

I glare at him, fighting the urge to throw the bell at his head.

Is that it?

'What do you want?' he asks, not bothering to lift his head to look at me.

I stare at him.

What?

'To volunteer . . .' I say.

'When?' He waves a hand above his head as if plucking the words from the air. 'For how long?'

I open and close my mouth.

For how long? I don't know. I was hoping just to do half an hour now and then be done with it. How long do people usually volunteer for?

'I don't know,' I say, feeling my body burn, 'for a day?'

I cringe as I hear the words and Jakub looks directly at me, his eyebrows raised in a sarcastic formation.

'A day?' he repeats. 'You just want to come here for one day? Why?'

I stare at him, dumbfounded.

'To volunteer,' I repeat stupidly.

What does he want me to say?

Jakub straightens up to his full height and hooks a file of papers under his right arm. He takes a moment to look at me, and then nods.

'No,' he says plainly and turns to walk away.

What?

'Wait!' I cry, scurrying after him. 'No? What do you mean, no?'

Jakub stops walking and turns to face me.

'No,' he repeats, 'we don't need you.'

What?

Is he being serious?

'You can't say no!' I cry incredulously. 'I'm a volunteer. You can't turn away a volunteer.'

I stare up at him, my heart racing.

He can't turn me away. I need to see Nina. I need to check she's okay.

I can't leave her.

Jakub looks down at me blankly. 'Yes I can.'

'But I want to help!' I gabble, as he goes to walk away again.

Jakub stops and looks at me.

'You want to come once and help to feel good about yourself. I don't need that.'

I stare at him.

'What?'

'This isn't a zoo,' he says, 'these are people. You want to help, you come often. You commit to them. I don't need you coming once, that won't help them. Only you.'

I stare back at him, winded by his comments.

I never thought he'd say no.

His pale blue eyes look searchingly at me and for a second the creature inside is silenced by a sharp feeling.

'Okay,' I hear myself say, 'okay, fine. I'll commit. I'll come more than once. I'll do it . . .' I trail off as Jakub continues to stare at me. His face doesn't change.

Eventually, he speaks.

'Okay,' he says simply, 'you can come back tomorrow.'

'Tomorrow?' I repeat. 'Can't I start now?'

It took a half an hour bus to get here!

Jakub pauses. 'No,' he says, 'we don't need you now.'

I try to stifle my annoyance.

Then why did you tell me to come in today, you stupid arse?

'Right,' I say, my voice jumping up four octaves in an attempt to keep myself upbeat. 'Okay, I'll come back tomorrow, after work.'

Jakub nods and steps back towards the door.

'Okay,' he says, as he pushes his way through the door, 'ask for Jakub.'

I open my mouth to reply, when he disappears from view. My hands fly instinctively into the only sign language I know.

Maybe I'll be using that often, after all.

CHAPTER FIFTEEN

I lean my body against the kitchen counter. My eyes throb under my heavy eyelids, which hang over my eyes like a thick, dry dough. I hear the kettle boil and I take a deep breath, trying to silence the noise surrounding me.

I'm not sure if I slept at all last night. By the time I got home, Priya was locked in her room and the house was hidden under a blanket of darkness. Only the gentle twitch of Joy's curtain as I walked down the drive confirmed that there hadn't been an apocalypse.

I could feel the creature limbering up in the pit of my stomach as I opened the front door, stretching its claws ready to spread through me like tar.

I lay in bed, anxiety pinning my heavy muscles to the bed and pressing my itching eyes open, until my clock ticked to 7.00 and my alarm chirped through the room.

I pull open my reluctant eyes now as the kettle spits specks of water over the kitchen counter. I pick it up and start to tip boiling water into my mug, trying to ignore the icy panic that has been simmering under my skin since I left Sunfields. And then realised I'd have to go back.

I pick up a stained spoon and stir my steaming tea.

Sometimes, my anxiety gets so bad that I switch to autopilot and instead of being paralysed by the fear that is ripping through me, my brain mutes all of my emotions and I just move. I don't even really think about what I'm doing. I just survive.

That was what happened yesterday. I took myself to Sunfields without really thinking. It was as if I had made a deal with my anxiety.

You just have to go once, then you can go back to your routine. Just once, you have to get through this, and never again. Just once.

I pour a stream of milk into my mug.

But it didn't work like that. And now that I have to go back, now that the deal has been broken, my brain has switched back on.

And it doesn't like it.

'Ah, did I just miss a round?'

My head jerks up, pulling me back to my surroundings. I'm in the office kitchen, where Duncan is standing in the doorway, his round face stretched into a smile, like it always is.

Automatically, I feel my face copy his, and for a second, the anxiety is silenced.

I look down at my tea.

Yes, you did miss the tea round, Duncan, but it would have been a fantastic achievement if you hadn't missed it, seeing as I didn't tell anyone about it and darted into the kitchen when Faye was telling the entire office about her dinner last night.

'Yeah,' I say, 'sorry.'

Obviously I don't enjoy being the office snake and never

offering anyone else a drink. But there are fifteen people who work for the *Herald*.

Fifteen! I mean, that is just an enormous amount of unnecessary stress.

But yes, I am aware I'll be going straight to British hell.

I expect I'll spend eternity having someone constantly cutting in front of me in a queue and offering me tea the colour of sand.

Duncan leans forward and flicks the kettle back on. It judders back to life obediently.

'That's okay,' he says, 'for a second I thought I'd caught you having a nap!'

He wags a finger playfully in my direction and I smile back at him limply.

'All that spelling keeping you up?'

I pick up my tea and attempt to edge towards the door.

Oh please.

'I'm just looking forward to the weekend,' I say quietly, feeling embarrassment storming up my cheeks.

Please don't ask me what I'm doing.

Duncan spoons instant coffee into his bucket of a mug, followed by two heaped spoonfuls of sugar.

'Yup!' he says cheerfully. 'I know that feeling! Here's to the weekend, eh?'

I give a small nod, taking a gulp of my tea as I go to leave.

How does he always have so much energy?

'Wait a second, Bea,' Duncan says, 'I wanted to ask your opinion on something.'

I hover, my eyebrows creeping up my forehead as my brain sparks back into life.

What? What is he going to ask me?

What I think of his shirt? Whether he should start *Game of Thrones* before season eight starts?

'You're one of the longest-standing members of staff here,' he says, stirring his mug of coffee. 'In terms of the younger crowd, I reckon you've been here the longest.'

Where is he going with this?

'Yeah,' I say, unsure of what else to respond with.

'How do you think office morale is?' He looks at me now, his watery eyes fixing on mine. I fight the urge to look away. 'Do you think everyone is happy?'

I look back at him blankly.

'Err,' I mumble, 'yeah?'

How should I know?

Duncan looks back at me, his smile slipping.

'I want everyone to be happy here,' he says, picking up his mug. 'I want this to be a fun, happy workplace.'

He steps out of the kitchen and I hesitate before following him.

What is he talking about?

'Sure,' I murmur, 'I think everyone is . . . happy.'

The words trail out of my mouth and Duncan scans the sea of heads, all bent over their keyboards.

'Thanks, Bea,' he says, turning back to face me, 'you've been a big help.'

★

I glance down at my watch. It shines 17.27 back up at me. I cross one leg over the other and take a deep breath.

Ten more minutes and I'll be there.

Then an eight-minute walk to Sunfields. Give or take two minutes, depending on how quickly I can will my reluctant legs to move.

I uncross my legs and lean against the bus window.

I decided to wear jeans, my long-sleeved black top and a big woollen jumper. I figured old people tend to overheat, so I need to be prepared to be stuck in a room with potentially no heating on, even though it's almost December.

The bus comes to a sudden halt as we reach a line of traffic and I rock forwards, trying at all costs not to touch the woman next to me who keeps muttering into her sleeve.

After almost an hour of searching last night, I managed to find my trainers. Obviously, in an ideal world I'd be wearing my boots, but they felt a bit impractical.

Not that I'm expecting any of the residents to run away or suggest a game of tag rugby, but it will be nice to be prepared just in case.

Panic twangs through me as I start to recognise the dark roads the bus is twisting into.

I'm almost there.

My eyes flit back down to my watch.

17.32. I should have been there at 17.30, but we had a whole stream of school children troop off the bus like newly hatched ducklings, which added an extra five minutes.

Six, actually, once a parent had aggressively told off the boy who tried to push another child down the stairs.

I tuck my hands in my sleeves as my brain replays my schedule.

17.30: Arrive at Sunfields, meet Jakub.
17.35: Small talk with Jakub. Make friends. Bury hatchet.

17.40: Help old people. Find Nina, check she's fine.

18.00: Leave old people. Leave Sunfields, get bus.

18.30: Arrive home.

19.00: Microwave ready meal (macaroni cheese).

19.15: Put on pyjamas.

19.25: Watch *Hollyoaks* in bed.

I feel my breathing slowly return to normal as my evening slots into place in front of my eyes.

There is nothing to be nervous about. There is nothing scary about that schedule.

I'll be back at home within ninety minutes. In two hours, I'll even be in bed.

I reach forward and hear the light ding of the bell as the bus pulls towards my stop.

This will all be over in no time at all.

The bus tilts forward and lowers itself towards the kerb as it grinds to a halt by the bus stop.

I'm the only passenger to step off, standing lonely on the pavement like a small flag of surrender.

Maybe that's what I am. A small flag, ready to surrender to whatever terrible thing this Jakub maniac is going to make me do as punishment for saying his name wrong.

'Yakub,' I mumble to myself, practising the pronunciation as I walk down the dark street, 'Yakub, Yakub.'

Needless to say, mispronouncing Jakub's name only added to my growing list of anxieties about today. After me forgetting his name entirely, I ended up using Google to tell me how to say his name.

Which is *not* pronounced Jacob.

I also found out it's Polish, which I guess is where his accent is from.

I push my legs into the ground and power as fast as I can down Old Street towards Sunfields, which is sat in the corner like a forgotten doll's house. The wind whips past my ears and scratches at my naked ankles as I bury my head in my scarf.

My heart turns over as I spot Sunfields, tucked behind a large tree that is swaying in the wind as if it is beckoning me over.

I narrow my eyes as one of the spindly branches curls in my direction.

Christ, I really hope I'm not going to be murdered in this bloody old people's home. It really would be the perfect crime. For starters, nobody knows where I am, which is very out of character for me. Not that I obsessively tell people my whereabouts, I don't have to. I do the same thing every day. I go to work, I come home, I do my food shop at Tesco in Twickenham, and I go for a run every other day around Twickenham Green.

I push my neck further into my scarf.

Obviously, I couldn't tell Emma and Priya where I was actually going, not without telling them everything to do with Nathan. And how I wrote back to his letter by accident, and then wrote back to the next one on purpose.

I feel a small pang as my anxiety stirs under my skin.

It will be over soon. I will visit Sunfields, I will check Nina is okay. I will tell Nathan, and then I won't write again.

I walk past the final town house and feel my legs slow to a gradual halt as I come face to face with Sunfields, looming over me.

With great effort, I move my reluctant feet and walk forward. I mentally adjust my schedule.

17.45: Arrive at Sunfields.

Well, on the plus side, if I do get murdered in here then at least Joy can act as a witness. She's so nosey it wouldn't surprise me if she bugged that Bakewell tart I ate last year and now there's a permanent microchip lodged in my belly that Joy can track at her leisure, like I'm her prize greyhound.

I reach the plastic door and wedge it open. I try not to flinch as the thick scent of old drain cleaner swirls around me and sticks to the back of my throat like a dried cough sweet.

I glance back down at my watch as I reach the desk, empty yet again.

17.47: Greeted by Jakub.

I look around the reception area. It looks like a photo that has been left in the sun too long with all of the colours faded and drooping out of place.

It looks like it's all been forgotten about.

'Hello?'

Jakub has appeared behind the desk. I flash him a smile and wait for his face to respond as he recognises me.

He doesn't. He looks at me suspiciously, as if I'm going to try selling him some magic beans.

'Hi,' I say, 'Jakub, right?'

I try to hide a smile as I hear his name out loud, perfectly pronounced - like a real human.

Har har. That was said very well.

Jakub nods stiffly, his expression unchanged. The prickling optimism pinning my smile in place starts to bubble into sharp irritation and I try not to scowl.

Oh, come on. There is no way he doesn't recognise me. I was here yesterday! I was stood here literally twenty-four hours ago.

If he tells me to come back tomorrow, I'm starting a riot.

I could get the old people on my side. I bought Werther's.

I can almost feel his body tensing in front of me as he fights my smile, and for a second my eyes flick down to his arms.

How is someone who works in a care home so muscular?

Does he bench press the pensioners? I feel my eyebrows rise up my face.

Would I want him to bench press me? Would that be fun? Or would that actually be horrible?

'Right,' he says, looking over my shoulder as if someone more interesting might walk in, 'come on, then.'

His face stays solemn and I feel a frisson of annoyance.

Horrible. It would be horrible.

I glance back over my shoulder at the front door and then back at Jakub, who is waiting for me.

My feet jump forward as I follow him dubiously.

The door clicks open and Jakub turns back to face me. Automatically, I feel my face pull into a polite smile. His eyes stay fixed over my shoulder.

Who is he looking for?

'Okay,' he says, 'the residents are in there. How long are you here for?'

Without quite meaning to, my eyes flick back down to my watch.

17.55.

Hmm. Can I say ten minutes?

What's the minimum amount of time I could stay for? I'm already twenty minutes behind schedule.

Eight? Eight minutes?

I jump slightly as Jakub's eyes finally jerk down to mine.

Christ, he's intense.

'I'm not sure,' I mumble, my face burning under the pressure of his glare.

Jakub pulls a phone out of his pocket and turns it to check the time. His face changes to a bored expression as he holds the phone in his hand.

'Okay,' he says lazily, 'they eat at seven. You can help with dinner.'

Help with dinner?

'Now?' I say stupidly.

Oh no, what is he going to ask me to cook? Do I look like somebody who can cook?

'Not now,' Jakub snips, 'later.'

He starts to walk down the corridor. As I step warily after him, he turns around.

'Where are you going?'

I blink back up at him stupidly.

I don't know where I'm going. I've never been here before.

'The residents are in there,' he repeats in a very slow voice, raising his hand to the door behind me.

I turn on the spot and then look back at him.

Is he not coming in too?

'I've got work to do,' he says, catching my aghast expression.

I quickly force my face into a smile.

Right. Of course he does.

I nod. 'Sure,' I say, 'no worries. I'll be fine. Don't worry about me!'

The last word comes out almost as a song. Jakub raises his eyebrows in acknowledgement and turns back down the corridor.

Slowly, I feel my knees lock and my muscles clench as a fresh ooze of anxiety drips through my body like PVA glue.

I try to unclamp my legs, which are now welded to the floor like a set of signposts. I take a deep breath as Jakub disappears through another door.

Come on, Bea. You've already done the hardest part. You're in the home. You've made it in. You spoke to that scary Jakub guy and you made it here all by yourself. All you need to do now is speak to Nina.

All I need to do is speak to a stranger, alone.

I take a deep breath as I feel warm sweat gather under my arms.

She's not going to reject you. She's an old lady. Old ladies are nice. Everybody knows that.

My twitching eyes flick down to my watch.

18.03.

I can leave by six thirty. I can tell Jakub that I'm not feeling well. He can't argue with that. Then I will have kept my promise to Nathan and I'll never have to come here again.

I can do this.

I just have to get through this next little part.

I clench my clammy hands into moist fists and force myself to walk towards the wooden door. I reach out my hand and pull the door open, trying not to wince as the sickly smell swirls up my nose and I click the door shut behind me. My body burns under the weight of my thick jumper.

Good Lord, it is boiling in here.

I look around the room and I feel a twinge of confusion. It's practically empty.

Where is everyone? Why is there nobody here?

The walls are a dull pinkish colour, with dark shadows at the corners where the wallpaper has peeled away. There is a large photo of a field filled with flowers, hung proudly on the wall, and a small bay window letting in a sliver of light from the lamp post outside.

There are about eight chairs, all large and squishy, with high backs. Five of them are empty.

Maybe everybody else is in bed. Or they've gone out for the evening.

Can they go out?

I mean, this isn't a prison, so obviously they're allowed to.

I step forward nervously. Nobody has even noticed I've appeared. My heart burns in my chest.

Do they know I'm coming? Are they expecting me?

I don't want to just creep up on them. I might actually scare them to death.

That would be awful. Me trying to do a good deed by helping out at an old people's home, and one glance at my helpful face literally resulting in their hearts stopping due to fright.

My legs start to navigate my body towards the chair closest to me, which has a small woman propped on it. Her long fingers are holding a book open on her lap. Her head is craning over the book like it's providing her with oxygen.

Okay. I can talk to her. I like books. We can talk about books together.

My eyes squint as I try to read the title and I feel a zap of nerves as I spot she's reading *Wuthering Heights*.

Okay, this is a good start. I studied *Wuthering Heights* in A Level English. I mean, I hated it. But I still read it.

Although, is she going to want to talk about what the dark hills and rolling thunder represent?

Come to think of it, what do they represent? I can't even remember.

Is it something to do with someone's sexuality, or is that just me being a pervert?

I pull my nervous face into a smile as I reach the woman, and slowly sink into the small chair next to hers. She doesn't look up.

I take a deep breath, the new intake of stale air squashing the simmering anxiety down.

'Hi,' I manage in a small voice, 'I'm Bea.'

I feel my pained smile twitch as the woman drags her eyes up to meet mine. She has folds of creamy skin that sag slightly on her pointed face and thick, light grey hair is twisted on top of her head and fastened by a large comb. Her hooded green eyes fix on to mine.

'Hello,' she says, her thin lips barely moving, 'I'm Sylvia.'

I try to control my breathing. My chest threatens to cave in at the relief of her 1) responding, and 2) not dying.

She moves her eyes back down to her book and we drift back into the stale silence that hangs in the room.

I open and close my mouth, unsure of what to say next.

Is that it?

I shift my weight on the chair and look back around the room. There are two more residents sitting nearby, both propped in their large chairs. One, a man, is reading the newspaper, and the other woman is staring out of the window. Neither seem interested in my visit.

They're certainly not itching for me to come and chat to them.

I look back at Sylvia, whose attention is still firmly fixed on her book.

Does she want me to talk to her? Do people like being spoken to when they're reading?

Okay, I need to talk to her again. I can't just say hello to her and then leave. I just have to talk to her.

'I'm here for a visit,' I say, my smile still firmly fixed in place.

This time, Sylvia doesn't look up from the book and her slow drawl fills my ears almost instantly.

'Who are you visiting?' she asks.

I look back at her closed face.

Oh hell, I've been rumbled. I've been here for less than five minutes and the first woman I talk to cracks my entire plan.

Why didn't I think of a cover story?

'I'm here to visit everyone,' I hear myself say quietly. 'Like you,' I add half-heartedly.

Maybe she'll really want a visit! Perhaps Sylvia has been sat alone all day, fantasising about the idea of an unexpected visit from someone who can talk to her about *Wuthering Heights* and what a mysterious hunk Heathcliff is.

'I don't want a visit,' Sylvia says, as she turns another page in her book.

Oh.

I pause, trying to stop the smile from dropping off my face.

'Oh,' I say feebly, 'okay.'

Well, that's nice. What am I supposed to do now?

'Try Nina,' Sylvia says idly, holding a heavily beringed hand towards the window.

My heart jolts at the sound of her name and as I follow Sylvia's gaze my eyes lock on to the woman, folded into the chair by the large bay window.

My heart bangs in my chest as I look at her.

That's Nina.

'Right,' I say, my face burning, 'okay.'

Slowly, I pull myself to my feet.

As I walk through the room, the only man raises his eyes at me. I smile weakly in his direction, and his eyes instantly fall back into a glazed stare, away from mine, and I try to control the hard lump forming in the back of my throat.

Nobody here wants to see me.

Maybe I should just leave.

I reach Nina, fixing the familiar awkward smile onto my face.

Much like Sylvia, Nina doesn't break her gaze, and she continues to stare out of the window.

I shrink into my seat as I look at the face of a woman who I know has lost her child. Her skin is the colour of honey, and she has a dark plait that falls down her back. Her tadpole eyes are fixed out of the window and only the gradual movement of her chest makes it clear that she's alive. She is wearing a long skirt and a light blouse, and her small, papery hands are curled into each other.

I gaze at her for a second as my heart aches.

She looks like the saddest woman in the world.

'Hi, Nina,' I say quietly, feeling my voice drop as if someone could be listening in.

Nina's face doesn't move and I feel another spasm of nerves. She's acting as if she can't hear me.

Maybe she can't. Nathan didn't tell me why she was here. Maybe she's lost her hearing.

I glance around, hoping to spot Jakub, but he's nowhere to be seen.

'Hi, Nina,' I repeat, trying to make my voice slightly louder.

Once again, Nina's stare doesn't break and I feel my throat swell.

I just need her to tell me she's okay.

I lean closer to her.

'I just . . .' I continue, 'I just wanted to come here and check that you are okay. Well, not okay,' I say quickly, 'but I thought you might need someone to talk to. I wanted to talk to you.'

I stare at the side of Nina's face as she gazes out of the window. Her entire body is frozen as if she's an oil painting.

I pause, feeling my needy eyes lock on to her.

Come on, Nina. Please talk to me. Please tell me you're okay so that I can leave.

Nina's small chest inhales and I watch her desperately.

This is going terribly. One person doesn't want to talk to me, and the other is pretending I don't exist.

I look around hopelessly, as if someone might give me a trick to get her to hear me.

I sigh.

'I know Nathan,' I say, dropping my voice into a whisper, 'he's a friend of mine. Well, not friend. He writes me letters from . . . err . . . from prison. He asked me to come and see you, he told me about your daughter . . .'

My voice trails off. I feel an icy blade of emotion puncture the inside of my throat as I say the words out loud.

'He misses you,' I say quietly.

Nina's face doesn't move. For a moment, her glassy eyes shine in the reflection from the street light, until she blinks and the water vanishes.

I wait as she takes another small intake of breath, hoping she might speak. Within seconds, her chest sinks back down as the air skims out of her nostrils.

As I watch her, I feel my shoulders sink.

She's not going to talk to me. There is no point me being here. There is nothing I can do.

I look over my shoulder as Jakub pushes his way through the door.

I turn back to Nina, who hasn't moved.

'Well,' I say, 'it was really nice to meet you, Nina. My name is Bea. Maybe I'll see you again.'

I push my hands into my chair to propel myself back to my feet, when Nina's eyes click round to find me.

My stomach flips as Nina's dark eyes fix on to mine. I look back at her, as if she's magnetised me, and I feel a flash of emotion strike through my body.

Can she hear me?

Nina's eyes stay locked on to mine and I blink back at her, paralysed.

'You're Bea?'

Her voice is low and earthy, and she has the light twang of a faded London accent. Her voice causes a surge of fear to race through my body as I keep my eyes fixed on hers.

Does she know?

I give a small nod, unable to speak.

At this, she moves her body away from the window so that she is facing me.

'Nathan told me about you,' she says, 'he wrote to me and said you might visit. He told me about your letters.'

My heart stirs at the mention of the letters and flips over.

Nobody knows about the letters. I didn't think anybody would ever know.

I swallow and try to keep my smile in place as my brain fizzes. Nobody was supposed to know.

'Hello?'

I jump as Jakub's harsh voice hits my ears, and I suddenly realise that my body is shaking. I look round and see Jakub appear behind me. He looks from me to Nina, his face scrunched up like a used crisp packet.

'What's going on?' he asks.

I stare back at him as my heart rate speeds up and my body locks itself to the chair. I open my mouth to speak but every word inside of me vanishes.

'Bea is my Nathan's girlfriend,' Nina says proudly, 'my grandson. She's here to visit me.'

My face burns as I hear my lie pronounced in Nina's soft voice. Jakub frowns back at me.

'You know Nina?' he asks.

I look at Nina's smiling face and feel my head drop into a nod as guilt overwhelms me.

'Yes,' I say, my voice scratching out of my throat. 'Nathan asked me to come.'

Jakub looks at me for a second and then at Nina.

'Right,' he says.

'Do you want me to help with dinner?' I ask, desperate not to drop back into the unnerving silence.

Jakub's face breaks from confused back to his relaxed, bored expression.

'Sure,' he says, turning away from Nina and back towards the door, 'it's almost ready.'

I spring to my feet and follow him. As I walk away I make the mistake of looking back at Nina. Her small eyes are now round with hope as she gazes after me, and I feel guilt crawl up my body, grabbing hold of me by the throat.

What am I doing?

I never lie. I've never meant to lie. I didn't think she'd know. Nobody was supposed to know.

★

Jakub hands me a plate and raises his eyebrows at me.

'Can you carry two?' he asks.

I feel a stab of irritation.

Can I carry two? Of course I can carry two, I have two hands.

'Yes,' I say pointedly, sticking my free hand out.

Jakub hands me a second place and I grip the warm china and look down at the small pie and assortment of green vegetables. I glance up at the cupboard and notice stacks of bowls and plates.

Do they ever use that many?

Jakub pushes his way out of the kitchen and I follow him obediently, focusing on carrying the plates in the hope of it smothering the anxiety that has been gnawing at me for the last half an hour.

Ever since Nina recognised my name, I've felt a cold sense of numbness. I'm back on autopilot because I don't know what else to do.

I don't know how to fix this.

I follow Jakub down the corridor and through the door that leads back into the living room. Sylvia is now sitting up straight, her book neatly placed on the small table next to her and her green eyes watching us impatiently. Nina too is watching the door as we walk in, and to my horror I see her face light up as she spots me, as if she might have imagined the whole thing and seeing me again is confirmation that I am real.

Jakub walks straight over to Nina and pulls up a table to put her plate on. Awkwardly, I make my way over to Sylvia who eyes me as if I'm a teenage waiter serving her tea at the Ritz. I carefully put her plate down and turn to the sole male resident, the only person I haven't said hello to. As I meet his eyes, I feel a spike of sudden warmth.

The man has a square face and large ears. His skin is pale, and indented with wrinkles that line his cheeks as though several birds have landed in wet concrete. His eyes are baggy and the top of his head is shining, completely hairless. He's wearing a woollen, periwinkle-blue jumper that shrouds his padded body and is turned up around his wrists to free his small, plump hands.

I put the plate down in front of him, and almost jump as the man smiles at me.

'Thank you very much,' he says kindly, his mouth pulling apart to reveal several small teeth.

I look down at him, taken aback.

He's the first person here to speak to me first.

'That's okay,' I say, feeling a smile appear on my face.

He gestures to the seat next to him. I look back at Nina, and see that Jakub is still with her, and sink down into the mahogany chair.

The man leans forward, looking down at his meal, and then turns his grey eyes back to me. 'I'm Gus,' he says. 'What's your name?'

I look back at him, and to my alarm feel a sudden tug at the back of my throat at the kindness of his voice.

'Bea,' I say quietly. 'I'm Bea.'

Gus nods as he picks up his knife and fork.

'Oh yes,' he says. 'You're a friend of Nina's?'

The pie splits open under his fork and I try not to wince at his question.

'Yes,' I say, 'but I'm here to visit everyone.'

I glance back at Sylvia, but she's not even pretending to listen.

Gus smiles again. 'That's nice,' he says, 'although I think Nina is very glad you're here to visit her.'

I tuck my hands under my legs. 'Really?'

Gus spears a piece of pie with his fork and nods.

'Well,' he says, 'this is the first time she's spoken in about five months.'

My eyes skirt back over to Nina, who is smiling and talking quietly to Jakub. My heart turns over as I stare back at Gus.

'Is that when her daughter died?' I ask.

Gus nods and swallows his mouthful.

My eyes move back to Nina and I suddenly feel a powerful tug towards her, as if there's an invisible rope between us. She is smiling and talking to Jakub as she cuts up her dinner and I feel my entire body ache.

I can't leave her.

'But,' Gus says, pulling my attention back towards him, 'tell me about you. What do you do?'

I look back at him, my mouth dry.

'About me?' I repeat.

I feel a spasm of emotion shoot through me as Gus smiles.

Nobody ever wants to know about me.

Gus puts his fork down and smiles. 'Yes,' he says, 'tell me about your day.'

I look back into his wide eyes, my heart spinning.

He leans forward, waiting for my answer.

'Tell me how you are.'

★

I pull my jumper further over my hands and stick the damp sleeve in my mouth, my teeth grinding into the cuff of my jumper as if I'm a teething infant.

I turn a corner as I reach our road. The street light flickers yellow, like a fresh egg yolk, as I steer my cold legs down our street.

I didn't leave Sunfields until gone nine, way past my schedule. But when I was there, I didn't notice my schedule slip by. I didn't even notice the time. I spoke to Gus, and then I spoke to Nina. At one point, we were all sitting around and even Jakub was joining in. I don't even know what we were talking about. But I remember I went from feeling burning heat searing at my skin, to feeling warm.

And light.

I reach my front door and pull out my keys. As predicted, the entire house is coated in darkness and only the slight flicker of light from Priya's bedroom signals any life inside at all.

As I left Nina, the light inside me began to weaken as the cold, dark feeling of fear crept over me.

Nina knows about the letters.

She thinks I'm B.

The Accidental Love Letter

That was never supposed to happen. I never meant for it to go this far.

I spot Joy standing in her front garden, her craned head visible in a bright stream of light that pools out of her kitchen window.

She is squinting at me in concern.

My face quickly contorts itself back into a smile and I hold up my hand to wave.

How long has she been stood there? What is she doing?

I flash her another look, trying to satisfy her curiosity as I attempt to smother the sizzle of irritation that zaps through me as Joy stands there motionless.

I am so sick of her spying on me all the time. Hasn't she got anything better to do? What does she want?

I wriggle my door key free and jab it in the lock, when I hear Joy's front door click open. I fight the urge to roll my eyes as I consider pretending I haven't seen her and slipping inside.

'Bea? Is that you?'

I stand, frozen for a second, before turning to face her.

'Hi, Joy,' I say quietly, my voice echoing down the street.

I go to step inside my house when Joy's voice lures me back.

'I've got something for you.'

A hot strike of fear jolts through me and I turn to face her. She looks back at me, her eyes wide.

Another letter?

I turn on the spot and walk towards her house, trying to keep my smile in place.

How has he written back so quickly? He usually takes a week, five days tops. I sent my last letter two days ago.

I reach Joy's door and she smiles at me.

'You're back late,' Joy says, peering at me. 'Have you been anywhere nice?'

I look back at her, my eyes twitching as I try to suppress the rising sense of panic.

'No,' I say, 'just out. Do I have another letter?'

Joy pauses for a second, and then nods.

'Yes,' she says, 'it arrived this morning. I would have given it to Priya, but I didn't see her.'

'Don't!' I snap, the word firing out of my mouth before I can stop it. 'Please,' I add, 'please, only give these letters to me, Joy. If that's okay? They're private.'

I break off, my chest straining under the weight of my thick, suffocating jumper. I stare into Joy's eyes, trying to look normal as I feel the creature claw its way up my throat.

She can't give these letters to Emma or Priya. They can't know. They can't know what I've done.

They can't know what I'm still doing.

Joy steps back and picks up the letter, which is sitting on a small table, where her post always sits.

'Of course,' she says calmly, as she hands the letter to me, 'that's not a problem at all. I know how new romances like to be kept a secret.'

Her eyes sparkle at the word 'romances' and I try not to flinch.

'Great,' I mutter, 'thanks, Joy.'

Before I give Joy the chance to respond, I turn on my heel and run back towards my house, the letter held tightly to my chest. As I reach the front door, I look back at Joy who is still watching me and I feel a pang of guilt, which I quickly shake off.

I can't worry about Joy. She is not my problem.

I feel my shoulders sink in defeat as, alone in the darkness, the creature inside me reaches up and rakes its claws down my body.

I have enough problems of my own.

CHAPTER SIXTEEN

I knock on Joy's door lightly, glancing over my shoulder as Priya chugs down the street in Emma's Renault Clio. Within seconds, the door swings open. Today, Joy is wearing a pearly grey cardigan, buttoned all the way to the top, with a matching skirt.

Her expression moves from confused to delighted, and her familiar smile lights up her face.

'Good morning, Bea,' she says, looking over my shoulder, 'this is a nice surprise. I never normally see you in the mornings. You know, the post hasn't arrived yet.'

I smile back.

07.40: pop in to apologise to Joy.

'I know,' I say back, feeling a pang in the back of my chest, 'I wanted to apologise for the other day.' I try to look into her brown eyes but my eyes automatically dart away. 'I was really tired and a bit . . . err . . . stressed.'

I feel my hands jolt as they turn my letter between them, as heat burns up my neck.

I barely slept that night. Once I had managed to smother the roaring anxiety about Nina, a fresh wave of guilt poured over me about Joy.

I should never be rude to her. She is only trying to help.

'That's okay,' Joy says politely, 'I know how stressful it must be, being a working girl.' She smiles kindly and I feel myself relax.

'Thank you,' I say.

'Would you like to come in?' she asks, stepping back and gesturing inside her house. My fingers grip tightly on to the letter as my mind counts the time.

07.46-ish. I think I've been stood here for two minutes, maybe three. My bus leaves at 07.55. It takes five minutes to walk to the bus stop.

'I can't,' I say. 'Sorry. I've got to get to work. But I'll pop by this evening?'

Joy nods. 'Oh yes,' she says, 'it's Thursday, isn't it?'

I feel a wave of relief.

Although I've never told Joy my schedule, she knows it to a tee. I come round every Thursday after work, usually for dinner. It's been that way for the last two years, and she always sticks to it. We both do.

'Yeah,' I say, 'also, I wondered if you . . .' I hold the letter out, guilt squirming through my chest again as Joy's eyes flick down to my hands. She pauses for a second, her kind smile unwavering.

'Oh, of course,' Joy coos, taking the letter out of my clammy hands. 'I can post it for you today.' She glances down at the right-hand corner and smiles. 'Oh, another love letter, is it?'

She beams at me and I try to control my burning face as my heart races in my throat. I glance behind to check that Priya and Emma are out of sight, even though Emma didn't stay here last night and I just watched Priya leave.

'Yes,' I say in a small voice, 'but please don't—'

'I won't tell anyone,' Joy says, tucking the letter behind her, 'don't worry. It can be our little secret.'

I nod as I watch the letter disappear behind her back. I ripped Nathan's latest letter open as soon as I got inside, and wrote one back straight away. I told him all about Nina, and how she was, and all about how she made me feel.

I promised I would take care of her.

I promised myself too.

She needs me.

'Right,' I say, trying to sound normal, 'I'd better go to work then. Thank you,' I add, as I turn away, 'I'll buy you some stamps.'

Joy shakes her head as I walk down the drive. 'Don't be silly. I think I'll make us a casserole later.'

As I catch Joy's kind eyes, I feel the weight lodged in my throat loosen.

'Thank you,' I say earnestly, 'that sounds great.'

★

'Bea?'

I jerk forward out of my seat, ripping my thoughts away from Sunfields and the comforting image of Nina playing Scrabble.

Do old people like Scrabble? Or is that just a stereotype?

I don't want to offend her.

Maybe she'd prefer Boggle.

'Bea?'

I look up at Duncan, who has now managed to stride across the office to my sad, grey desk.

As we have this hot-desk policy, it means that my desk is always empty, aside from a mug of old tea and my sad-looking pencil case.

Faye did once buy me a plant as a 'gift' but it died the next day. She then asked whether or not I thought it was a symbol for something else that was withering.

Like my love life.

'Yeah?'

Duncan leans his soft elbows on the thin wall.

'How are you getting on with the beaver?' he says jovially, his mouth stretching to reveal his large, perfectly formed teeth. 'I think Angela would like to include it in next week's issue. Make it a hot topic, you know?'

I feel each vertebra bend as I cringe forward in my seat.

A hot beaver? Gross.

'Err,' I mumble, 'yeah, that's fine.'

I see a flash of joy spark over Duncan's round face.

'Excellent!' he booms. 'I realised this morning that I hadn't passed on the number for the couple. They're expecting your call.'

He pulls a crumpled piece of paper from his pocket and I stare at it dubiously.

How does he know these people? Are they two randomers he met at the pub?

I look down at the slightly yellow scrap and try to smile.

'Great,' I say, 'thank you.'

I look back up at Duncan, who is still towering over me, grinning.

Is that it? What does he want?

I pull my smile wider and raise my eyebrows at Duncan. His watery eyes flick down to the piece of paper and then back up at me and I feel a quiet tingle of panic.

He doesn't want me to call them now, does he?

'Now?' I say, my voice unusually high.

My question seems to break Duncan from his weird fantasy.

'Oh!' he says. 'Yeah, go on, then. Why not?'

I try not to roll my eyes.

Oh, great. So he didn't want me to call them right this second, he was just being weird. And now I've put the idea in his head, so he's going to stand there and loom over me while I talk to a woman I've never spoken to before about her erratic beaver.

Well done me. Great.

My limp hand reaches forward and I pick up my office phone, which has a light layer of dust skimmed across it like old icing sugar.

I hate talking on the phone. The only person I ever call is Mum, and she doesn't count.

My eyes move from the paper to the phone as I gently push the numbers. To my alarm, Duncan sinks into the empty seat next to me.

Okay, good. So he's clearly not going anywhere.

I dial the final digit and the phone clicks into quiet, unimposing rings that jolt through me like tiny electric shocks.

Please don't answer, please don't answer, please don't answer, please don't answe—

'Hello?'

I try not to jump as a woman's voice interrupts the rings and jangles in my nervous ear. I see Duncan nod next to me, apparently thrilled that the phone has worked.

'Hi,' I say, trying to keep my voice calm and professional, 'my name is Bea Smyth, I'm calling from the *Middlesex Herald* and I—'

'Who?' the woman barks down the phone and I stumble to a halt.

'Err,' I say stupidly. 'Bea Smyth?' I offer, as if she'd have any idea who I am. 'From the *Herald*.'

I pause as a stony silence rolls down the phone. I glance back to Duncan who is still grinning like an overexcited waxwork.

'The local newspaper?' I mumble, my face burning.

Why isn't this woman saying anything? How did Duncan get her number? Surely Duncan has already spoken to her. This isn't even her landline, it's her mobile! It's not like Duncan sat at home flicking through the Yellow Pages; she must have given him her phone number.

He said that she was expecting my call.

Expecting my call.

My teeth sink into my lip as my body burns.

This is ridiculous. Is she even still on the phone? Why isn't she saying anything? Even if she forgot that she gave her mobile number to Duncan, surely she knows what a newspaper is! Surely she has something to say about that. Surely—

'Duncan?'

I jerk out of my internal rant.

What?

Duncan?

Has she mistaken my voice for *Duncan's*?

Duncan is a man!

171

'No,' I say, 'Duncan passed on your phone number. My name is Bea Smyth, I work for the *Middlesex Herald*, the local paper. I'm writing a story about your beaver. Pet beaver!' I add quickly, suddenly realising how that sounds like I'm drafting a porno and want her to be the star.

Urgh! God, I would write the worst porno in the world.

'I wanted to talk to you,' I warble on, desperate to ask my stupid question before she hangs up, 'about your beaver and how you came to care for it.'

I can't believe I'm sitting at work asking a strange woman about her beaver.

This is how you get on the sex offenders' list.

'Do you mean fanny?'

My mouth falls open in horror.

What?

Oh holy hell. She does think I'm talking about her vagina! Oh my God.

What am I supposed to say? I don't want to enter into a conversation about somebody's vagina at four p.m. on a Thursday. That is unacceptable.

'Pardon?' I say, the word barely making it out of my mouth.

'Fanny,' the woman repeats matter-of-factly, 'our beaver.'

I open and close my mouth.

I can't deal with this. What am I supposed to say?

What is she talking about?

Is she talking about her vagina?

I can't have a conversation with a stranger about her vagina! I can't even talk about my own! For all intents and purposes, I often pretend I don't have one!

'We got Fanny a few years ago,' the woman continues, as if

she's talking about a lovely lemon drizzle, 'we just clicked instantly. She loved my husband, she always responded to him very well.'

My body jerks forward and I try to stop myself from throwing up all over the desk.

'She came around to me eventually too,' she says, 'and then, she just became part of the family.'

The woman stops talking and I relish the silence, my brain swelling under the pressure of a stranger telling me all about her vagina.

I almost fall out of my seat as Duncan cranes forward, trying to get my attention, and whispers something in my direction. 'Fanny is its name,' he says, his eyes wide.

What?

Why is he telling me that? I know what a fanny is, for crying out loud!

'The beaver,' Duncan continues, catching my wild look, 'the beaver's name is Fanny.'

I blink at him, fighting the urge to set myself on fire.

What?

No. Surely not. Surely this woman hasn't named her beaver Fanny.

I turn my head back to the receiver, trying to control my skittering voice.

I can't say the word 'fanny' to a complete stranger. I can't, I can't, I can't.

I *won't*.

'So,' I manage, 'when you lost, err . . . Fanny, is it?'

Arghhhhhhhhh.

'Yes,' the woman says, as if it's the most normal thing in the world, 'we're both big *Funny Girl* fans. I think Barbra would like her.'

I swallow.

What?

Who the hell is Barbra?

'Right,' I say, madly scribbling 'fanny' down on my notepad.

Duncan shoots me a thumbs up and stands back up.

I can't believe I've just written the word 'fanny' on my lovely pink notepad. Right next to my shopping list. You won't find one of them loitering next to the eggs.

Thank God.

'Great job, Bea,' he whispers. 'Keep up the good work.'

I stare desperately after him as he toddles back to his office. Numbly, I move my attention back to the phone.

'So,' I say weakly, 'how did you realise your Fanny was missing? Fanny!' I almost shout in desperation. 'How did you realise Fanny was missing?'

Oh my Lord.

This is ridiculous. Why am I - an aspiring, serious journalist - asking a woman about her fanny going missing?

I should be reporting on local drama and politics!

'Oh,' the woman says, 'I just knew. You do, don't you? I just woke up and said to my husband, something's up with Fanny.'

Is she doing this on purpose? Does she think that's an acceptable answer to give in an interview with the local paper?

She's not flirting with me, is she?

If she asks about my fanny, I'm hanging up.

'Right,' I say weakly. 'And, sorry, just for the story, what's your husband's name?'

If she says Richard, I'll die.

'William.'

Oh, thank God.

I feel my chest cave in relief. Okay, that's not that bad. Maybe I'll be able to write some sort of story that doesn't sound like it's written by a sex-crazed maniac. If I just manage to—

'Willy for short.'

I open and close my mouth, unable to speak.

Great.

CHAPTER SEVENTEEN

My damp fingers clasp on my phone, leaving small swirls of moisture on my screen as I walk through the street and the week replays itself in my mind. Somehow, I made it to Friday without combusting under the pressure of lying to everyone I know.

I wince as the cold wind strikes my bare skin and I look at a small town house, draped in Christmas lights and flashing invitingly. If I concentrate, I can almost hear the house singing to me. Every house down this street is decked in lights, with fat little figures propped outside, their mechanical arms juddering back and forth in an odd waving motion. The house at the end of the street has a plump Santa who shouts hello every time somebody walks past.

Needless to say, I almost wet myself the first time it shouted at me.

I spot Sunfields, the only house on the street not shimmering under the sparkle of Christmas lights. As I look at it, I feel my chest expand.

I'm going back. For the first time, I am willingly going back on my own accord. Not under the pretence of doing a good deed, or helping Nina. Or even helping Nathan. I don't need to go back. I've done what I said I'd do. I could just disappear and write the entire thing off as a weird memory.

But I haven't. I'm going back. I push my hands further into my coat pockets.

I'm going back because I want to see them. I want to see Nina and Gus. In a weird way, I almost want to see Sylvia.

When I last arrived at Sunfields, my body was in knots. It was as if I was made of rubber, and a child had pulled at my limbs, stretched my organs and moulded me into a contorted shape. I jerked and twitched under the pressure of holding my body still, but it felt unnatural. I wasn't supposed to be that way.

But then I started talking to them. And as I did, my body unfolded itself. Slowly, the knots unravelled. I spoke to Gus for hours. I don't even know what we spoke about, but I didn't want to leave.

I left feeling warm.

I haven't felt warm in years.

I need to feel warm again. I need that feeling back.

My legs power forward as I reach Sunfields. I feel my phone vibrate in the tight grip of my hand and I turn the flashing screen towards me.

Florrie Nannoo posted for the first time.

My legs slow to a halt as I glare at the phone. Irritation spikes inside me.

Oh, for God's sake. Why? What is she posting? Why is Priya back on that stupid account? I thought she'd deleted it.

I press the intercom and then push my body against the faded front door. I feel my ears recoil at the harsh scraping sound the door always makes as it wheezes through the frame. The heavy smell swirls into my open mouth and I feel an immediate rush of heat as the insanely high temperature of the home washes over me.

'Hi.'

I look up from my phone and see Jakub, who has appeared behind the reception desk.

Oh good, I'm not going to have to ring that stupid bell.

'Hi,' I say back, a smile springing on to my face. As always, Jakub's face stays straight.

I fight the urge to roll my eyes at him.

Why does he never feel the need to smile back at me? Does he have no manners?

It's not even manners, it's social pressure. How can he look at me blank-faced while I, a human being, stand opposite him smiling?

I mean, even dogs smile back.

Sort of.

There is a pause as Jakub and I look at each other, not speaking.

I wait for him to start a conversation.

He doesn't.

'How are you?' I ask, my smile still in place.

Is he going to show me where to go? Or show me what he wants me to do? Or am I going to stay out here for the next two hours?

Why does he always treat me like I'm a total stranger?

'You're back,' he says simply, his eyes not moving from mine. He says the words with no expression. He isn't surprised to see me, or even annoyed.

He's just stating a fact.

I open my mouth and close it again.

That's a weird thing to say.

'Yup,' I say, 'I'm back.'

Did he not want me to come back? Was it a one-time invite?
I keep looking at him, but his face doesn't move.

Argh! Why is he always so bloody awkward? What does he
want?

'So,' I say, 'shall I just—'

'They've been waiting for you,' Jakub says. 'Nina said you
were coming at six.'

His eyes finally move away from my face and look up at the
white plastic wall clock. The hands tick to 6.15.

I feel a stab of annoyance.

Okay, fine. Yes, I'm fifteen minutes late. I'm well aware. I'll
now be fifteen minutes late for my entire evening.

Five minutes can be discounted for this ridiculous conversation Jakub is forcing me to have with no purpose or direction.
And the bus was late. I can hardly control that.

'The bus was late,' I say simply, feeling my eyes narrow as I
look back at him.

I'm not apologising for being late for something I'm volunteering for.

'Okay,' Jakub says, his voice dropping back to his standard
bored tone, 'they're all waiting for you.'

He gestures to the door behind him and I try to squash the
sudden burst of anxiety at the thought of seeing Nina again.

I barely spoke to Nina before. After I'd introduced myself,
she sat back next to the window and craned her body towards
the window until eventually I could only see her long plait
hanging over her arched back.

But I did catch her looking at me. Once.

I didn't think she heard what time I was coming today. I only really spoke to Gus.

I glance up at the wall clock and feel my mind slot together my schedule.

18.15: Arrive at home (now 18.15 thanks to unreliable bus driver).

18.20: See Jakub, make small talk.

18.25: Chat to Nina, Gus and Sylvia.

19.00: Help Jakub bring out dinner.

19.15: Leave as they all eat, catch bus home.

20.00: Back home. Straight into PJs and heat up leftover pasta bake.

20.03: Potentially send passive-aggressive text to Priya and Emma when I discover that one of them has eaten it (very possible).

20.30: In bed, watch *Hollyoaks*.

21.00: Watch *RuPaul's Drag Race*.

22.00: Go to sleep.

I take a deep breath.

Easy.

I walk past Jakub, my chin high in the air as he watches me leave.

He really is the worst host in the world. He hasn't offered me a cup of tea.

He hasn't even shown me where the fire exits are!

I turn in the corridor when my phone vibrates again in my hand. I slow to a stop and look down at the screen. It's from Priya.

Where are you?

The little fizz of anxiety brewing under my skin sparks. I slip my phone into my back pocket and push my way through the door.

I can't tell her where I am.

I can't tell anyone.

She never used to care where I was. Although that could be because I spent every day in the same place. So there wasn't much—

'You're late.'

I look around at Sylvia, who is propped up in her high-backed bottle-green chair. Her hair is pinned up, identical to how it was the last time I saw her. It's almost as if she's been frozen in time since Friday.

'The bus was late,' I mumble, looking around for a spare chair. 'Sorry.'

Why is everybody so obsessed with my time-keeping? I give myself enough grief to stay on schedule, I don't need it from them too.

At the sound of my voice, Nina looks up from her chair by the window and smiles as I sit down in a squishy blue armchair. Gus folds up his newspaper and I notice Nina turn her head to face me, but she doesn't leave the window.

I feel my cheeks pinch as Sylvia, Nina and Gus all look at me, their eyes wide, as if I'm about to divulge the latest scoop.

'Hello,' I say stupidly, 'everyone.'

'It's nice to have you back.' Gus's crinkled face relaxes into a smile. 'Did you have a nice weekend?'

At Gus's question, Nina moves her head back towards the window, but her body is slightly leaning towards me.

Sylvia opens *Wuthering Heights* and raises her eyebrows.

Well, she pretended to care about me for longer than last time.

'Yes,' I say automatically, giving the exact same answer I give Faye every morning, 'it was very nice, thank you.'

I fold my hands neatly as we drop into silence.

This is usually the part where I turn back to my computer and Faye starts wittering on about her weekend.

I feel quite naked without a computer to hide behind.

'Oh good,' Gus says, 'and what did you do?'

My eyes flit over to Nina, who has rested her hands on her lap. Her sunken eyes are wide and expectant.

I look back at her hopelessly.

What did I do?

I did the same as I do every weekend.

I did my washing, my ironing, my food shop and my cleaning.

Emma was with Margot, and Priya stayed at her parents'.

In short: I did nothing.

'Not a lot, really,' I say, my chipper voice wavering, 'just this and that.'

We fall instantly back into silence and I look round at their kind, open faces.

'Just life stuff,' I say, 'like . . . washing and that . . .' I trail off, feeling my face flare.

I wish I had something to say. Why do I never have anything to say?

I look up at Nina, a sharp pain striking across my chest as I catch her eye.

She must think I'm the most pathetic girl in the world.

'You should have come here.'

My eyes look round to Gus, whose kind smile hasn't moved.

'She doesn't want to come here, Gus,' Sylvia says dryly, not looking up from her book. 'What's she going to do? Sit and play bridge with you?'

I try to stop myself from glaring at Sylvia. I look back at Gus to see if he's hurt but, if anything, his smile has grown.

'That seems to be enough for you, Sylvie,' he says, a gravelly laugh pumping from his chest.

Sylvia keeps her lips pursed, but I can see a spark of laughter playing with the corners of her eyes.

'I'm sure she's got better things to do than sit around with a bunch of old people playing bingo,' Nina says.

'No,' I say quickly, 'I mean, I'd love to. I love bingo.'

My heart bangs against my chest as I look from Nina to Gus.

'We don't play bingo any more,' Sylvia says flatly. 'Not since Diane left.'

'Oh.'

We drop back into silence and I twist my damp hands together.

'So,' I say, 'are you looking forward to Christmas?'

The word Christmas sends a spark through Gus, and Nina sinks further into her chair.

'Oh,' Nina says, moving her eyes away from me, 'it's soon, is it?'

I feel a flash of alarm as I look at Gus and Nina, who both look like slowly deflating balloons. As if my question has punctured them.

I thought everybody liked Christmas.

'Aren't you spending it with your families?' I offer.

Sylvia makes a scoffing sound as she flicks another page. I look to Gus, desperate for him to say something light.

'To be honest, dear,' he says quietly, 'I think we'd forgotten all about it.'

★

'Why isn't the home decorated?'

Jakub looks up at me as I charge into the kitchen. He's stirring a large pot, which is wafting swirls of peppery steam.

My thumping, enraged heart returns to normal as I look at his unimpressed face.

'What?' he says, his accent reducing every sound to the same level.

I take a deep breath and puff my chest out.

'The home,' I say, gesturing behind me, 'this home. It's not decorated for Christmas. Why?'

The words tumble out of my mouth and Jakub looks up from the pot and observes my stern expression, which is twitching under the pressure of keeping it straight.

'Pass me some bowls.' Jakub raises his eyebrows at me.

What?

'They're behind you,' he says. 'I need three.'

I flounder, feeling my legs move at the compulsion to always be helpful. I open the cupboard door and pull three bowls from the tower of crockery.

'Did you hear me?' I say.

Jakub takes them off me and gives the pot a stir. 'Yes.'

I stare at him, waiting for him to answer.

He doesn't. Again.

Why is he so impossible to have a conversation with? He acts as if he's living on a limited daily word count.

'Well?' I say incredulously. 'Gus said that they'd forgotten all about it. That's really bad, that they feel so unfestive here that they could have forgotten—'

'They haven't forgotten,' Jakub says simply, lining up the bowls.

'What?' I say, my face burning. 'Yes, they have. Gus just said so.'

For the first time ever, I see Jakub smile. I feel a weird squirm of emotion.

He looks much less like a serial killer when he smiles.

'That man reads the paper every day,' he says, picking up a ladle, 'you think he doesn't know what the date is?'

I flounder, feeling my face prickle.

'But then why—'

'They don't want it this year.'

His words cut across me and I close my mouth stupidly.

'This year?' I echo. 'Did they celebrate last year?'

'Yup.'

'So why don't they want to this year?'

Jakub cocks his head as he spoons the soup into the last bowl. I loiter in the silence hopelessly.

I don't understand.

'Has something happened?' I say, lowering my voice. 'Did somebody here die? Was it that Diane lady? They said she'd left.'

I see Jakub's face change.

'She did.'

Oh my God.

Somebody died here?

'So, she died?' I say, my heart pounding.

Jakub shakes his head, running the pot under a jet of water. 'No. She left. Everyone left.'

I look at him, my tense body softening.

What? Left?

'What do you mean?' I say. 'Why?'

Jakub switches the tap off and looks back at me. His permanent scowl has vanished.

'They're closing the home,' he says. 'They have until the first week of January to find somewhere else to live.'

My heart sinks.

'Or what?' I say.

Jakub picks up two of the bowls and turns to face me.

'I don't know.'

Jakub gestures to the third bowl, steaming on the counter, as he walks past me. I stand still, floored.

They're closing the home? How can they close it? How are they allowed to? People live here.

It's their home.

I grab the bowl and chase after Jakub, cursing as the hot soup splatters on my wrist.

'Wait,' I say roughly, as my legs power after him, 'what do you mean they're closing the home? Why? How can they?'

Jakub keeps walking. 'It's been sold,' he says plainly.

Sold?

I reach him as he finally stops to turn into the living room. He goes to push the door open and I feel my heart leap into my mouth.

'Wait!'

My free hand shoots out in front of Jakub's chest like a barrier. He raises his eyebrows at me expectantly and I look back at him, my heart heavy in my chest. As he moves his blue eyes to meet mine, for a moment I see a flicker of something as we stand in silence. The hot bowl burns against my cramping fingers and I open my mouth hopelessly.

Jakub stares back at me, waiting for me to speak.

I don't know what to say.

'They can't,' I say eventually, the sad protest falling out of my mouth.

I see Jakub's shoulders drop slightly, breaking his rigid posture. He looks back at me again before pushing through the door and into the living room. I hear Gus cheer at the sight of him and I push my back against the wall as an overpowering thought pulses through my mind.

If they close the home, then I can't come here any more.

If I can't come here any more, then I go back to being cold.

This thought cues the creature resting in my gut to flex its claws and I try to ignore the hot tears welling in my eyes.

I can't go back to being cold. I can't.

Chapter Eighteen

My eyes flit down to my notepad as I rap my pen against my desk.

15.15: Afternoon visit from Faye.
16.00: Final tea break of the day.
16.15: Finish press release and send to Angela.
16.50: Shut down computer ready to leave.
17.00: Run for 17.08 bus to Sunfields.

I look back at the clock and see its red plastic hand tick to 3.30 p.m.

Faye is late, annoyingly. She must be talking to someone she actually cares about.

Or perhaps she's found a mirror.

'Working hard, eh, Bea?'

I look up as Duncan strides past my desk, a wide grin pulling at his puffy cheeks. Today he's wearing a thick woollen jumper over his shirt and tie, and I feel a pang of familiarity.

I wonder if his wife made that for him.

I shoot him a half-smile and look back down at my monitor.

I don't know what he expects me to say back to that. Yes? No? Kind of, but I'm also watching a tutorial on how to make my own short-crust pastry?

'Keep an eye on your emails,' Duncan calls, forming his fingers into small guns and shooting them in my direction. 'I've got some exciting stuff coming your way.'

My smile quivers.

Oh great.

We finally published the beaver story this morning and, as predicted, no one cares. Not even Angela, who used it against me when I said I hadn't had time to file the invoices.

It didn't get a single like on Facebook, and our post about Teddington's record-breaking sausage got two hundred.

I guess people care more about sausages than beavers.

I rest my cheek on the palm of my hand as I refresh my emails. As promised, an email from Duncan is waiting at the top of my inbox like an unexploded firework.

It's a round robin.

I peer around the office, trying to spot if anybody else has noticed Duncan's latest spout of madness. Nobody stirs. I snap my finger on my mouse and feel my insides shrivel as Duncan's email pings onto my screen.

Hiya guys!! Thought it was time for another DO! This time I want to get cReAtIvE so have come up with three options on what we can do. Whichever gets the most votes WINS!!!!!

  Peace and love

  Big D.

I blink at the email, feeling hot sparks of panic flitting through me as I will myself to scroll down to read the options.

I really hope Duncan has no idea what 'big d' means.

My body burns with embarrassment at the thought.

Right. Come on. Let's see what he has to say. I'm probably worrying about nothing. I mean, it's a work do! Obviously it will be a meal at Pizza Express or some kind of drinks at a quirky bar. Maybe he wants to do something like make our own cocktails. That would be fine. That I can deal with.

My finger creaks over the mouse as I scroll down the page.

Or maybe he wants to push the boat out and go for a curry instead of the normal Chinese. That would be fine. I mean, I'd have to look up the menu beforehand but everything is pretty much online now, isn't it? I could choose what I want before, and just ensure that—

My eyes judder to a halt as I spot the three options glistening on my screen.

Oh no.

So guys! Here are our three options . . .
   1) *Staff karaoke ?!*
   2) *Staff fashion show ???!!!?*
   3) *Staff calendar shoot ?!!!????* SHOTGUN DECEMBER

I blink at the screen in horror.

What the hell is this? Why would anyone want to do any of these things?

I mean, a staff fashion show? Christ! What are we going to model? Our work outfits from the Next sale?

I bet Faye came up with these horrible ideas. What's wrong

with a curry? Why can't we just go for a nice korma? Everyone knows where they stand with a naan.

I snap the email shut and get to my feet.

Right, well, I will just have to make sure that I am ill for this ridiculous staff event. If I pretend I have a urine infection then nobody will question it and everybody will be too embarrassed to ask any questions.

I grab my mug and make my way into the kitchen.

Although they'd better not go with the staff calendar idea, because they might wait for me to be better so I can shoot my month.

Urgh.

If that's the case then I'll have to up my illness so that I'm off work for a considerable amount of time. Maybe I'll get glandular fever.

But will I need a doctor's note? I can't fake one.

God, maybe I'll have to actually break my leg.

'Oh!'

I bound straight into the kitchen and spot Faye. She is leaning over the kitchen counter with her back to the door, her long hair hiding her face like two curtains. Her head jerks up at the sight of me and I spot small black pools gathered in the corner of her eyes. She quickly whips her head away from me.

Is she crying?

'Sorry,' I say stupidly, leaning towards the kettle, 'I was just . . . do you want a . . .?' I trail off as Faye spins back round to me. The small splodges of black from under her eyes have vanished and her mouth is split in a wide, toothy smile.

'I'll have a coffee if you're making one,' she says in her usual chipper tone.

I look back at her. 'Are you okay?'

I've never seen Faye upset before.

'Black, please,' Faye adds, as she swans past me, 'I'm on a dairy ban. Thanks.'

★

'Hi, Joy,' I ramble, 'is my letter here? Do I have one?'

Joy pulls her door open, a smile appearing on her face at the sight of me. As soon as she clocks it's me, she turns on her heels and walks back into her house, the door swinging behind her.

'Come on in, Bea!' she calls over her shoulder. 'Sorry, I'm making a cake.'

I hover at the door frame, peering after her as her copper head disappears into the kitchen.

I frown.

It's a Wednesday. She knows I don't come in on a Wednesday. I do my ironing on a Wednesday.

Dubiously, I step inside, pulling my feet out of my grubby trainers. As soon as I push her door shut, a light scent of vanilla wraps itself around me and I feel my taut muscles relax.

Joy's house always feels so clean and warm.

'Thank you,' I say, following Joy into the kitchen, 'I can't stay long, I just want to see if . . . wow!'

My mouth drops open as I spot Joy, craning over a staggering cake in her kitchen. Her buttercup-yellow jumper is rolled up to her elbows and she has splats of flour over her pink apron. The cake has been crafted into a castle, made of small squares of sponge stacked together like bricks with layers of buttercream.

I gawp at Joy as she presses another piece of sponge into the smallest wall.

'Joy!' I cry. 'That's amazing!'

Joy flashes me a smile as she slowly lifts her hands up from the piece of sponge, then picks up another one.

'Oh this?' she says. 'It's not as impressive as it looks.'

Gosh. What I wouldn't give to live in a castle made of cake.

'Do you need any help?' I ask.

Please say no, please say no.

Joy looks up at me, her eyes bright.

'Go on, then.'

Damn it.

'If you could just hold this part in place,' she says carefully, gesturing to the wall she's building, 'while I cut up some more sponge.'

She catches my stricken expression and laughs. 'You'll be fine,' she says.

I hold my anxious hands up to the cake.

What happens if I sneeze and jerk this whole thing over? Or if a wasp comes in and tries to sit in my ear? Or I get an involuntary cramp and end up clapping my hands together and crushing the cake to smithereens?

Joy cranes over a large, square piece of sponge as she holds her ruler up to it.

'This is so cool, Joy,' I say, clenching my quivering muscles as I hold the cake.

Christ, this is worse than holding a newborn baby.

What's going to happen if my hands start sweating?

Joy smiles and picks up a small knife.

'Do you like it?' she says. 'I used to make it for Jenny all the time, for her birthdays.'

I smile, as the image of Joy as a young mum unfolds in front of my eyes.

I bet she was a great mum.

'Who's this one for, then?' I ask. 'Are you posting it to Jenny in Australia?'

I try to shoot Joy a grin but she doesn't look up as she runs the knife over the sponge.

'No,' she says, 'this one is for the school fête tomorrow, up the road. They're always looking for cakes, and I don't mind.'

I feel my eyebrows creep up my face.

She's made all this effort for a school fête? She doesn't even have a child at the school.

'Right,' Joy says, picking up the ruler and measuring the lines of sponge again, 'now I just need to cut these.' She squints at the sponge and picks up the knife. Her eyes flick up to me and she almost does a double-take, as though she'd forgotten I was there.

'Sorry, dear,' she says, her smile pinging back on to her face, 'I've just dragged you in here to help with my cake. Did you want something?'

I feel a pang in my chest.

'Oh,' I say, 'I just wanted to see whether you had any letters for me.'

It's been a week and Nathan hasn't written back. He usually writes back within three days. But this was the first letter that was really from me. Well, I still signed it like I always do. But I said things that I really meant.

I told him about Sunfields. Then I told him about Nina.

Her kind eyes look at me and I feel my insides twist.

'No,' she says, 'sorry. I haven't received anything.' She turns back to the sponge. 'Is it another love letter you're waiting for?'

The back of my neck pricks with guilt.

'Yeah,' I say in a small voice.

Joy swipes the knife across the sponge and beams down at the perfectly cut squares. She gestures to my hands, still cupped over the tower of sponge.

'You can let go now, dear,' she says kindly, 'it's set.'

I slowly take my hands away, my heart racing as I stare at the wall of sponge, which stands proudly before me.

'Phew!' I laugh. 'It didn't break.'

Joy smiles at me, and admires the wall.

'No,' she says softly, 'it's stronger than you think.'

CHAPTER NINETEEN

I eyeball Jakub as I shove my shoulder into the front door, my arms burning under the weight of two large carrier bags.

He looks back at me from behind the reception desk, blankly.

I glare at him.

Why isn't he helping me?

He watches me shove my shoulder against the door again, which creaks open slightly, before wedging itself into the carpet. I stick my head through the gap and stare at Jakub furiously.

'Can you help me, please?' I yelp, sounding like a furious mother of five.

Jakub walks towards me, his mouth fixed as a straight line across his face. He pulls the door open with ease and I try not to stagger through the door as the bags swing off my shoulder.

Jakub raises his eyebrows at me. 'What are those?'

I look up at him as I bumble past.

'It's a game,' I say, hoisting one of the bags up on to my hip.

I shoot him a look, daring him to break his permanent look of indifference.

Honestly, I think I could tell him there was a swarm of locusts in these bags and he'd still look at me like I'd asked where the toilets are.

To my surprise, he reaches forward and hooks the bags out from my clenched fingers and holds them like they're filled with feathers.

Good Lord, he's strong. How is he so strong when he works in a care home?

'A game?' he repeats, following me as I walk towards the living room.

I know where they all will be now. I don't need Jakub to show me. Not that he would, or ever really has.

'Yup,' I say, pushing my body weight against the door, 'you can play if you like.'

Jakub leans forward and holds the door open for me.

'I don't play games,' he says.

I try not to roll my eyes. Of course he doesn't.

I stumble through the door and flash a smile at Sylvia, who is sitting in her usual chair and peering at me from *Wuthering Heights*. Gus is grinning at me from the moment I walk in and Nina is sitting, as she always is, by the window. She glances over at me as I walk in, but moves her head away within seconds.

I try to squash the flutter of anxiety as Jakub puts the bags down gently on the table.

'Fine,' I say, meeting his cool stare, 'we'll play without you.'

'Play what?' Gus asks, his square head resting low on his shoulders.

I open my mouth to reply, when I hear the click of the door. I turn and see that Jakub has left.

Good. I'd rather him not be in here anyway.

I smile back at Gus. 'Bingo!'

'We don't play bingo,' Sylvia says dismissively. 'We haven't since Diane left. She had the kit.'

'I know,' I say, 'but that's why I've got this.'

I wriggle the big box out of the plastic bag and drop it on the table proudly. Gus laughs.

'You play bingo?' Sylvia asks, lowering her book on to her lap.

'No,' I reply, 'but I thought we could play today. I bought this,' and I tap the box, feeling a zap of warmth strike through me.

Why am I so excited to play bingo? Is this the new me?

I catch Gus winking at Sylvia, and she turns the page of her book.

'Look at that, Nina!' Gus calls towards the window. 'Look what Bea has bought us.'

My eyes follow his gaze. Nina hasn't moved.

A cold feeling spreads through me.

I thought she wanted me here.

'Would you like a game, Sylvie?' Gus leans forward and rests his hands on his knees, his head turned towards Sylvia.

'No, thank you,' Sylvia says pointedly, dropping her chin towards the book.

Gus slaps his leg. 'Oh, come on,' he says, 'you used to be the champion.'

Sylvia turns a page. 'I know I did,' she says.

'Scared you'll lose, then?' Gus says, leaning towards her. 'Scared Nina will beat you?'

Sylvia lifts the book closer to her face. 'Of course not,' she says matter-of-factly. 'Nina won't play.'

My eyes stray towards Nina again, who still hasn't moved. As always, she is sunk in the high-backed chair with both of her hands stretched out and resting on the arms. Her gaze is fixed out of the window, her eyes only flickering slightly when a strip of light skims through the glass.

I slowly move towards her, my heart picking up its pace as I get closer.

I know she doesn't want to talk to me. I know she doesn't want to talk to anyone.

But I can't let her just sit there, alone. She's always sat there on her own.

Nobody wants to be alone.

'What are you looking for?'

I hear the words before they pass through my mind and I almost flinch at the bluntness of my question. Nina's eyes twitch, but they don't stray.

'A robin,' she says quietly.

I follow her gaze out of the window and look out at the jagged tree, its angry, naked branches jerking out at odd angles.

I sink into the chair next to her, peering out of the window.

I can't see any birds. There isn't any wildlife at all.

'Why?' I ask. 'Have you seen one before?'

I glance over at Nina as I wait for her answer, and I see her large eyes glass over.

'Once,' she says, her light London accent playing with the word, 'a long time ago. One came right up to me and Melanie to say hello. I've never forgotten it.'

I feel my heart swell inside my chest as the creature inside me wraps its claws around my throat. A hot, familiar feeling swirls up inside my throat and I swallow.

'Is Melanie your daughter?' I ask, already knowing the answer.

Nina nods, the movement of her head causing a few tears to run down her cheeks and seep into her blouse. Her eyes stay firmly fixed on the view out of the window and her lips are clamped together defiantly.

I reach my hand forward and place it on top of Nina's and at the touch of her hand, the anxiety inside me is silenced.

Chapter Twenty

'Hello?' I shout, pushing my way through the front door, my heavy shopping bags thwacking the backs of my legs.

18.15: home after my weekly food shop.

'Hiya!' I hear girls' voices yell in unison.

I stagger into the living room with my bags and see Priya, Emma and Margot, all curled up on our sofa and clasping large mugs. Margot is leaning forward on her knees and watching Priya as she runs her fingers through her hair. Emma gets to her feet and grabs one of the bags from my hand. I smile at her gratefully as she takes it with me into the kitchen. She drops the bag on to the kitchen counter.

'You're just in time,' she says, picking up the kettle and filling it with water. 'I'm just about to make a tea. Would you like one?'

I start unpacking my shopping.

Peppers, onions, broccoli and spinach. Bottom left-hand corner of fridge.

'Yes, please,' I say.

Milk, butter, Babybels. Second shelf of fridge.

Emergency Dairy Milk, hidden behind celery in fridge.

'How are you?' I ask, as Emma pulls mugs out from the cupboard.

'Yeah,' Emma sighs, 'okay. Haven't had the best week at work. Just a lot of people shouting at me.'

She shoots me a smile over her shoulder, but I know she's not joking. Emma works in sales, which comes with a large pay packet and lots of fancy perks. But they don't tell you about the targets when you start. It's all about the targets, as Emma always repeats. She pours the boiling water in the mugs and I lean my weight against the fridge.

'That's horrible,' I say. 'I hate that people are so mean to you at work.'

Emma shrugs, reaching behind me to grab the milk. 'It's fine,' she says. 'Work all right for you?'

She picks up two of the mugs and nods her head towards the other two. I pick them up and feel a light squirming sensation.

I never feel like I can complain about my job in front of Emma or Priya. My job is stressful, but nothing compared to either of theirs.

I place Priya's tea by her feet and sink to the floor, cradling my hot mug between my fingers.

'So you don't miss him, then?' Margot asks, her calm voice interrupting Priya's erratic hair flicking.

'The thing is,' Priya says, her voice light and carefree, 'there's nothing to miss any more. We didn't actually have anything that special. I've come to realise that now.'

I hold the mug up to my lips.

'And now that I've realised this,' Priya continues, 'it's helped me make space in my mind for what I really want to do with my life.'

I frown.

'What do you mean?' I ask. 'You love your job.'

Priya shrugs as I shuffle closer to her. 'Well,' she says, 'yeah, I do. But I feel like I could be doing more.'

'So,' Margot says, glancing over towards me, 'what is it you want to do now?'

My eyes jerk away quickly.

Priya tilts her head. 'I don't know,' she says airily, 'I'm still trying to work that out.'

I open my mouth to speak when the doorbell rings.

I scrunch up my brow.

Who is that?

Emma arches her back towards the window and pulls at the net curtain.

'Oh,' she says, 'it's Joy. She's brought our post round.'

Emma goes to stand up when I lurch forward with such force that tea splats down my front.

Emma scoffs at me. 'Bloody hell, Bea,' she laughs, 'you desperate for an electric bill or something?'

My face pinches as Margot and Priya look round at me.

'Yeah,' I mumble, darting towards the door.

She must have my letter. Nathan must have written back. What else could it be? She never calls round at the weekend.

Carefully, I push the door to the living room shut and pull open the front door. Joy jumps slightly as the sight of me and I try not to wince at the icy air that whips through the hallway.

Joy's perfect hair is tucked under a neat little hat, and she's wearing a padded coat that wraps around her body like small purple pillows. She smiles as I meet her eye, and leans forward.

'Hello, Bea,' she says brightly. 'How are you?'

Instinctively, my eyes dart towards the letters in her hand. Straight away they land on the letter clasped between Joy's fingers. I notice Nathan's scrawly handwriting immediately. My heart leaps into my mouth as I raise my eyes and look back at Joy.

'Fine, thank you,' I gabble, my hands gripping the door frame. 'You?'

'Yes, yes,' Joy says, shifting her weight between her feet. 'I'm all fine, thank you. Are you excited for Christmas?'

'I—'

'Hi, Joy.'

A jolt of fear strikes through me as I hear Emma behind me. I whip my head around and see Emma pulling on her shoes. She shoots me an odd look as I feel my face flame, and I quickly look back to Joy. And then the letter.

She can't see it. I need to get the letter before she sees it.

'Hello, Emma,' Joy says pleasantly. 'How are you? How did the latest batch of banana bread turn out?'

Emma grins. 'Yeah, all right!' she says, as she shoves her foot into her shoe. 'Not a patch on yours, though.'

My eyes burn into the letter. Can I grab it? Can I reach forward and snatch it? Would they notice?

'Have you got our post again?' Emma asks, walking towards the door.

Before I can register my actions, my arm snaps forward and grabs the two letters out of Joy's hand. Emma blinks at me.

'Yeah,' I say, trying to control my heart racing, 'stupid post.'

I try to laugh, but only a weird squawk emerges from my mouth.

'Right,' Emma looks at me and then back at Joy. 'Well,' she says, 'thanks, Joy. We really need to speak to our postman, though.

It's madness you bringing our post round all the time.' She laughs and picks up her keys. 'I'm just running to the shops.' She looks back at me, 'Do you need anything?'

My eyes jerk over to her as I feel a hot wave of relief.

She's leaving. Thank God. She's not going to try to look at the letter. She didn't notice.

'No,' I say. Actually, 'Milk!' I practically shout as Emma slips out of the door. 'Milk. We've just used the last of it.'

I watch Emma's car roll out of the driveway before I look back at Joy. Her large eyes are blinking at me.

I look over my shoulder to check Priya and Margot are still in the living room, and then shut the front door slightly behind me.

'Thanks,' I say, 'for collecting our post and that. But please don't bring it round.' My eyes dart around her anxiously as I try to keep my voice steady. 'I'll come and get it, okay?'

The last bit fires out of my mouth with more anger than I meant, and I see Joy's wide eyes shrink.

'Right,' she says, her voice light and chipper as always. 'I'm sorry, Bea. I know that you normally come and get it on a Tuesday, but I just thought you'd be anxious to know that he's written back.'

'Thank you,' I say, 'but I'll always come and get it, okay?'

Joy slips her hands into her coat pockets and nods. 'Righty-o, Bea,' she says.

I push the door back open and step inside. 'I'd better go, Joy,' I say, trying to pull my taut face back into a smile. 'Have a nice evening.'

'Yes, love,' Joy says, already turning back towards her house as I tuck the letter into my pocket, 'you too.'

I push the door shut and feel my cheeks pinch.

Why has he taken so long to write back?

'Has Emma gone?'

I poke my head into the living room, my hand still firmly gripping the letter. Margot is smiling at me.

'Yeah,' I say, 'she's literally just gone.'

'Ah,' Margot says, 'I want some chocolate.' She pulls out her phone. 'I'll text her.'

I turn to walk into my bedroom when Priya leans towards me.

'Margot,' she says, batting her eyes towards Margot and me, 'have you heard Bea's hot news?'

I freeze, a small frisson of electricity shooting through me.

'What are you talking about?' I say, walking into the living room.

Priya grins. 'You think you're so smart and elusive, Bea, but I know you.'

I look back at her, agog.

'What is it, Bea?' Margot beams at me.

'Nothing,' I say, feeling my face prick.

Does she know?

Priya purses her lips at me and then flits her eyes towards Margot. 'Bea's got a boyfriend,' she sings.

At her words, my fingers coil around the letter.

'What?' I splutter. 'No, I don't!'

'Do you?' Margot says excitedly. 'Who? You can tell me!'

'No one,' I say indignantly. 'I don't have a boyfriend.'

'Yes, you do!' Priya fires back, jabbing her finger towards me. 'Where else have you been? She's out almost every night, Margot.' She looks at Margot as if she's telling on me. 'And she doesn't get back until late.'

I stare at her, feeling hot spikes of panic sprout inside me.

Shit. She's noticed. I didn't think anyone would notice.

I can't tell her where I've been. She won't understand. I'm not even sure I understand it myself.

'Well?' Priya laughs, raising her eyebrows. 'If it's not a boy then what is it?'

I've been going to a care home to hang out with old people that I don't know.

I open and close my mouth as all possible excuses scuttle out of my mind.

My eyes flit to the clock: 5.50 p.m.

'Fine,' I say in defeat 'fine, you got me. I'm seeing someone.'

Priya squeals and claps her hands together.

Margot gasps. 'Does Emma know?' she asks.

'Nobody knows!' Priya cries. 'This is your dirty little secret. What's his name?'

My mind pulls up my internal schedule. I've got to leave in ten minutes.

I need to read this letter before I leave.

'I'm not telling you,' I say quickly, walking out of the living room to grab a cereal bar from the kitchen.

Priya shouts after me, 'Why not?'

'It's a secret,' I say, walking out of the kitchen. 'It's early days. I don't want to jinx it.'

Priya shoots Margot a hurt look, but Margot's calm face stifles her arguments.

'We understand,' she says in her cool, mellow voice, 'we're just excited for you. Being at the beginning of the relationship is the best. Everyone deserves to feel that excitement.'

I look back at Margot, my fingers gripping the letter inside my pocket.

'Yeah,' I say, feeling a small spark shoot through me, 'I think so too.'

★

'How long has she been sat there for?'

Jakub looks up from his stack of paperwork and follows my arm, which is stretched towards Nina, sitting in the same spot where she always sits, staring out of the window.

Jakub slumps his shoulders in a shrugging motion, staring at the papers on his lap.

I feel a spark of irritation.

'I'm worried about her,' I say, eyeballing Jakub. 'She's not okay.'

Jakub snaps his pen and scribbles something on the paper. 'I know.'

This is the third day this week I've come to Sunfields. I've had my chat with Gus, and I even managed to squeeze out small talk from Sylvia.

But Nina didn't move. She barely even looked at me.

'I'm worried about her,' I say again, looking at Nina's curved back.

I've found out that Nathan knew Sunfields was closing. He wrote that Nina has been rehomed to a new care home, but he doesn't know where it is.

I don't really know how much he cares.

Jakub sighs and props his face in his hand. 'What do you want from me?' he says in a bored voice.

'I want you to help her!'

'She doesn't want my help,' Jakub says, moving his hand over to a new sheet of paper, 'I've tried.'

'Well, try harder.'

The words leave my mouth before I can stop them, and Jakub finally fixes his icy-blue eyes on me. I feel a bolt of electricity shoot through me as I stare back at him.

'I don't have time,' he says evenly, keeping his stony eyes fixed on mine. Slowly, he pulls his eyes back down to the stack of paper and I stare back at him, my heart thumping. I turn back towards Nina, feeling my body ache as if she's holding my heart in her small hands.

'Fine,' I say stubbornly, 'if you won't help her then I will.'

I shoot Jakub a defiant look over my shoulder, but he doesn't even acknowledge me.

How on earth did he ever get a job here? He doesn't seem to care about anything.

I turn on my heel and walk towards Gus, who is bent over a newspaper.

I don't think I've seen Jakub smile once. Not even when I brought in a surprise Starbucks for him (a small attempt of bribery that went down like a lead balloon. Honestly, he acted as if I'd brought him a steaming cup of poison.)

'Gus,' I say, pulling up the spare chair next to him.

Gus lifts his eyes from the newspaper, and peers at me through his glasses, which are resting on the bridge of his nose.

I try not to stare as my eyes flit over to his ears.

Christ, Gus's ears are enormous. They're like two hammocks hooked on the side of his face.

I smile at him. 'Hi.'

I bloody hope my ears never get that big. I mean, I know your nose and ears never stop growing (hideous) and there isn't much I can do about it.

But his are just ridiculous.

Why would you ever need ears that big? Like, what is he listening for?

Don't even get me started on my nose. Mine is already big enough to stop traffic. If it keeps growing until I'm ninety, then I'll be snapped by David Attenborough as a rare breed of toucan.

'I wanted to ask you . . .' I say. 'You know Nina?'

I see Gus's smile twitch as he nods.

My heart buzzes in my chest as the idea swirls into my mind. I glance over to check Jakub is still buried in paperwork as I lean closer.

'How well can she walk?'

Chapter Twenty-One

'Bea?'

I almost fall off my seat as Duncan jumps into the spare seat opposite me and swings it round in a circle like a spinning top.

I quickly minimise my screen and blink at him, dumbfounded.

What on earth is he doing?

'I wanted to chat to you about the beaver,' he says, swinging his legs back and forth like a toddler.

I try not to glower at him.

Of course. Of course he does. What else would my boss want to talk to me about at 11.30 on a Wednesday?

'Right,' I say, trying to control my cheeks from burning.

'Well?' Duncan grins, skidding to a halt from his relentless spinning. 'How did you get on? What did you think?'

'Bea, did you make a coffee? Oh,' Faye stops by my desk and smiles sweetly, 'hi, Duncan.'

I glance up at her.

Why is she asking me that? We never make each other coffee.

'Err . . .' I look between Faye and Duncan stupidly, 'yeah, all right.'

'Did you enjoy it?' Duncan says hopefully.

No. No, I did not. I hated every second.

'Yeah,' I say, wincing as my voice pings up at the end like an elastic band.

Duncan slaps his hands together, a fresh smile splitting his round face. 'Great!' he cries. 'Well, Bea, that was a bit of a test run for you, but I think you did really well! I'd like you to think of your own stories now, find something you want to write about.' He leans on the desk and looks at me earnestly. I notice Faye leering over.

What does she want?

'Oh,' I say, 'wow. Thank you.'

Something I really want to write about? Does he mean my pitch?

'Have a think, Albus,' Duncan says, standing up and smacking his hands together. 'Best to do something you can really get your teeth stuck into. Something you really care about.'

I smile weakly as I watch Duncan walk away. I feel a warm glow spread across my chest and a small spindle of an idea begins to spin in my mind.

CHAPTER TWENTY-TWO

I edge towards Sunfields.

Am I about to break the law?

I glance at my watch. 12.07. I'm three minutes early. A cold bluster of wind wraps around my neck and I shrink into my scarf.

I'm not really breaking the law. I mean, I wouldn't go to prison for this.

It's not like I'm wearing a balaclava.

I sneak towards the faded plastic door, wait to be admitted and then push it open with my shoulder. Jakub looks up at me and, for once, I see the shadow of an expression sweep across his face.

Is he pleased to see me?

'What are you doing here?'

Ah. Of course not.

I smile, ignoring the anxiety leapfrogging about my body like a small cluster of toads.

'I thought I'd come in today,' I say lightly, walking straight past Jakub and through the heavy door behind the reception desk. As always, Jakub ignores me.

I poke my head round the door leading to the living room and wave to Gus, who gives me a thumbs up. I follow his gaze and spot an old wheelchair propped up against a table. I feel my heart skip.

I must buy Gus a thank-you present.

Glancing over my shoulder to check Jakub is out of sight, I slip into the living room and march straight up to Nina, who is sitting in the chair facing the window. Sylvia doesn't look up from *Wuthering Heights*, but Gus winks at me as I walk past.

'Hi, Nina,' I say, dropping down to her level.

Her eyes flit over to me.

'Hello,' she replies.

'I've got a surprise for you,' I say quietly. Before I give Nina the chance to answer, I reach forward and grab the wheelchair. I shake it open and catch Nina's bewildered stare.

'What are you doing?' she asks, her voice hoarse as if it hasn't been used in days.

'We're going out!' I say brightly.

I steer the wheelchair next to her and hold out my arm for her to hold. Nina looks down at my arm and then back at me. For a moment, she just stares at me and I feel my face twitch in the silence.

'No, thank you.'

I blink at her, trying to catch my smile as it slips off my face. No?

I falter. I wasn't expecting her to say no.

She can't say no.

'Come on!' I say. 'It'll be fun!'

I look over my shoulder, my heart racing in my chest.

Come on, Nina. Come on. You have to come with me before Jakub comes in.

Nina moves her head to look back out of the window and locks her gaze on the bare tree, shivering under the ice.

She needs to come with me now. If I leave it much longer, Jakub will notice. Then this will all be for nothing.

I can't leave it. I need to take her.

I drop down to my knees and rest my hands on her armrest.

'Nina,' I say, the brightness of my voice fading away, 'you'll like it. I promise.'

I stare at the side of her face.

She needs to come with me.

'Please.'

Nina's eyes slowly move towards me, and she locks her eyes on mine. I stare back at her, my body aching as she looks at me.

I reach forward and touch her hand. 'You can trust me.'

★

'I can walk, you know,' Nina says. 'I don't need this chair.'

I wince as a pert rucksack thwacks the side of my face and I mumble an awkward apology as I squash into the woman next to me.

I look down at Nina. 'Gus said you'd be more comfortable in the chair,' I say carefully, as the bus swings around another corner.

Christ, who the hell is driving this thing?

I glance down at my watch and feel a jolt of nerves. 12.48.

'Are you hungry?' I say, leaning closer to Nina. 'We'll have lunch soon.'

Nina moves her head towards the window as my question is swallowed by the screeching of a passing horn.

I don't even know what she eats. Does she have any allergies? Oh God, what if she's a vegan?

I curl my hand around the yellow pole and feel my arm tense as the bus tips forward again.

One more stop.

I did leave Jakub a note, telling him exactly where we are going and when we'll be back. Obviously, he'll be angry, Jakub seems angry about everything, but at least he won't be worried. It's not like I've kidnapped Nina. She did get in the wheelchair voluntarily.

Sort of.

I look up as a crowd of teenagers troop down the stairs, all laughing and jostling together. I feel a small jolt of fear as I glance towards Nina, sat in her chair and staring out of the window. Without quite meaning to, I step in front of her like a guard dog. The bus rocks forward past another set of traffic lights and my thumb dings the buzzer. I notice Nina look in my direction in curiosity. She hasn't asked where we are going. I'm not sure she really cares.

I feel like she doesn't care about anything.

I grip the handles of Nina's chair as the bus groans to a stop and push Nina out of the door. The chair jolts at the uneven pavement and I hear Nina grunt as she knocks against the back of the chair.

Shit. Is there a knack to this chair that I don't understand?

The wet December air swirls around us and I wince as a car streaks past us, spraying us in a shower of blackened icy water.

'Right!' I say brightly, trying to make my voice carry over the shriek of traffic. 'It's just down here.' I wheel Nina around and lean my body against the chair to push it down the pavement.

Nina places her hands on the armrests of her chair as we move down the pavement. Small specks of rain fall from the sky and she remains silent.

I glance up at the signs, trying to ignore the creature stirring in the pit of my stomach.

I really thought she'd be more excited about this. I know she doesn't know where we're going. But I thought she'd want to go with me, I thought we'd created a bond together.

I thought she liked me.

My fingers grip the handles tightly as I power through the streams of angry-looking people, storming through the pavement against the rain.

Maybe this was a bad idea. Maybe I shouldn't have taken her out of Sunfields at all. Maybe I should have just left her by the window.

This thought cues a sharp pinch of fear in my heart.

What am I doing? I barely know this woman. I've only met her a handful of times, and I've barely managed a conversation with her. I'm just assuming that she'd like this when I know nothing about her. I didn't even ask if she'd want to come.

I push the chair down a small side street, my eyes searching for the sign. Although I don't need to look at the signs, I know where I'm going. I used to come here all the time.

We don't have to stay long. If she hates it, then we can go

home. We could turn straight around. We could be back home by two thirty. Jakub might not even notice that we've gone anywhere.

An icy burst of wind whips the back of my neck and I glance down at Nina. Although she is wrapped up in a big puffa coat (that I forced her into), I can see her bare hands are twitching.

'We're almost here,' I say, my voice dipping as I catch my breath, 'I'm sure it's just here . . .' My voice fades away as I turn another corner and spot the large building. Its old, shining lettering is proudly engraved on the front, exactly how I remember it. As I look up, warmth washes over me.

RICHMOND GARDEN AND BIRD SANCTUARY.

My eyes flick down to Nina and for the first time since I met her, I see her face curve into a smile.

I take a deep breath.

'I thought we might have better luck seeing a robin here.'

*

I push Nina through the clean, glass door, which slides open invitingly. As soon as we step into the sanctuary, the crisp smell of freshly cut grass nips my nostrils and I feel my heart lift. I notice Nina's tense grip on her armrest has loosened.

'So,' I say, as we make our way through the reception, 'I thought this might be a nice place to spend the day. I used to come here a lot when I was a child. There are so many birds here and—'

'I'd like to walk, please.'

I stop in my tracks at the sound of Nina's ropey voice.

'I can,' she says firmly. 'I'll be fine.'

I hesitate. She does walk around Sunfields, I've seen her.

'Okay,' I say, stepping in front of the wheelchair and holding out my arm.

Nina reaches forward, curling her small hand around my bare arm. Her hand is icy cold, and I flinch when she leans her weight on me as she pulls herself upright. Her grip stays firm on my arm as she reaches her full height, and her chocolate button eyes lock on to mine. For a second, we stare at each other, until Nina slowly peels her hand off my arm and stands unsupported.

I step backwards and park the wheelchair by the door, glancing back to Nina, who is watching me.

Please don't fall over. Please don't fall over.

'Okay,' I start again, 'I think it's through here.' I walk back to Nina and offer her my arm, which she ignores. 'That's where they all used to be,' I add, hearing my voice fade away.

Nina nods, and as we reach the next set of double doors my breath is snatched from my chest.

We've entered a giant greenhouse, which arches over thirty feet into the sky. Rays of white sunlight streak through the glass and swirl around us. The greenhouse is filled with proud trees, curling around each other and flexing their branches to show their fat green leaves. As the thick smell swallows me, I feel a hot spark of joy.

I haven't been here since I was a child. I used to love coming here.

Nina steps forward and I follow her, and we slowly make our way along the light grey path, occasionally masked by the dark shadows of the larger trees. I hear a light tinkling sound coming from a pearly blue pond, dropping specks of water out of a dinky water feature. I look over to Nina, who is looking at an array of fat lily pads, floating on a dark pond.

'Have you been here before?' I ask, stepping towards her.

Nina shakes her head. 'Never,' she replies.

I glance down at my watch. I've worked out that we can stay here for one hour. Ninety minutes at the very most. Any more than that and Jakub would have full licence to kill me.

I glance ahead.

'Hello!'

I jump slightly as a bright-eyed girl pops up in front of me. Her mocha ponytail swings at the top of her head and she grins at us both.

'Hello,' I say politely.

'Welcome to Richmond Garden and Bird Sanctuary,' she chirps. 'What are you hoping to see today?'

I look back at Nina, who is still watching the lily pads.

She's not going to jump in, is she?

'The birds,' I reply. 'They're just through the next room, right?'

Nina looks up at my question and steps towards us.

The girl nods. 'Sure,' she says, gesturing us to follow her, 'I'll show you.'

I start to walk after the girl, checking Nina is by my side, and to my alarm I feel a lump form in my throat.

I really hope she likes it. I really, really hope she likes it.

Please let her like it.

'So!' the girl says as we reach a set of large double doors. 'It's just through here.'

She punches a square button on the wall and the doors swing

open in front of us. As we step forward, the lump swelling in the back of my throat drops.

There is nothing here.

I look around madly at the empty room. There are several trees, towering over us, but not a single bird.

Where are all the birds?

My eyes flit over to Nina's face, and I see her smile has faded too.

She hates it. Why aren't there any birds here?

'Is this the bird sanctuary?' I say in a small voice.

'Yes!' the girl says. She shoots me a large grin and then catches my eye. 'Look up,' she adds, nodding her head to the ceiling.

Slowly, my head tips towards the ceiling and I gasp. Hundreds of birds sweep across the ceiling, dipping and weaving in and out of the trees. There are small, zippy green ones, shooting through the air like rockets, and fat grey ones, pocketed together on branches like little balls of cotton wool. I watch in amazement as they dip and dive and all sing together, chirping away to each other like a large, mismatched family.

I twitch as I feel something on my arm, and as I look down, I realise that Nina has curled her arm around mine. Her head is craned backwards as she watches the birds, and I feel my heart grow.

★

'Here you are.' The young boy smiles at me as he places a fat teapot on a tray. 'One pot of Earl Grey tea.'

'Great,' I say, sliding my hands out of my sleeves and curling my fingers around the tray, 'thanks.'

'That's five pounds, please,' he says.

I try to control my face from shooting him a look of outrage.

Five pounds? Five pounds for two cups of tea? Is it made from an actual Earl?

I scrabble around in my pockets and manage to fish out my flimsy debit card.

I don't even know if I like Earl Grey. I only bought it because that's what Nina wanted, and I wanted to seem cultured.

I tap my card on the machine and feel my chest coil in anticipation.

Please don't get declined. Please don't get declined.

It's the eighth of December. I get paid on the first. I've literally just been paid. The rent and all of the bills come out on the second. I definitely still have five pounds in my account. Surely. I must do.

The card machine beeps approvingly and the boy glances up at me.

Oh, thank God.

I pick up the tray and turn on the spot, thick fumes of perfumed tea swirling from the spout of the teapot.

Urgh, that smells disgusting.

Why does it smell like some kind of horrible witches' potion?

I make my way towards Nina, who is seated in a violet chair and smiling in my direction. Her hands are folded neatly and resting on the circular table and for the first time since I've met her, her shoulders are no longer sunk into her frame.

She looks happy.

I feel my face ping into a grin as I reach her.

'A pot of Earl Grey . . .' I say, sliding the tray on to the table.

Nina moves her hands, her mouth curving into a smile.

We spent forever in the bird house. It was as if the beating wings showered us with glue, welding our bodies to the ground. The only part of us that moved was our eyes, which skimmed across the room at each bird that dipped and dived. Apart from the light chatter between them, there was no sound at all.

I could have stayed in there all day.

That is, apart from the incessant anxiety nipping at my brain at the idea of Jakub finding my note and Nina being away from the home a second longer than the three hours that I promised.

I pull a small china teacup towards me.

'Would you like some?' I ask Nina, reaching my hand towards the teapot.

'No,' Nina says at once, freezing my hand instantly, 'not yet. You have to let it brew.'

I blink at her.

What?

Nina catches my expression.

'You have to let the tea brew,' she says, lifting a finger towards the teapot. 'It won't be ready yet.'

'Oh.'

I drop my hand on to the table.

Gosh. I'd hate for her to see how I make tea at home in my Sports Direct mug.

Can you add sugar to Earl Grey? I think I'm going to need about six.

'Thank you for bringing me today.' Nina looks up at me.

I smile. 'That's okay!' I say instantly, in my usual stretched expression of glee.

It's the same voice I use for everything. When Angela asks

223

me to reload the paper in the photocopier, or when Emma apologises for never taking out the bins ever, ever, ever.

It's like I'm on autopilot. I don't even mean it. I just hear myself say it.

'I'm sorry there weren't any robins here,' I add, shifting in my seat.

Nina looks up at me and smiles.

I was desperate for us to see a robin. I didn't even think to look before. I mean, it's a bird sanctuary, I thought it would be a given.

'Did you tell Nathan?'

I jump as Nina's soft voice breaks my thoughts.

What?

My eyes blink up to Nina, who is looking back at me innocently.

Tell Nathan what? Why is she asking about him? We never talk about Nathan.

'About today,' Nina continues, 'that you had planned this.'

Oh.

Sometimes I forget Nina knows anything about Nathan.

I wish she didn't.

I'm starting to wish I didn't.

'No,' I say, my face burning. 'But I will,' I add.

We drop back into silence and I twist my hands together, my eyes throbbing.

I glance up at a couple who shift past us, squeezing themselves through the tiny gap as they shuffle towards their table. They dip their heads at us approvingly.

'Do you come here very often?'

I look back at Nina. 'No,' I reply honestly, 'I haven't been here since I was a child.'

'Why not?'

Nina's dark eyes watch me and I feel my heart twitch as the answer swims around my mind. Instinctively, I feel my hands grip my phone.

I catch Nina's eye and shoot her a half-smile.

'Don't know,' I mumble, trying to ignore my face, which is burning with embarrassment.

But Nina doesn't break my gaze. She watches me, her hands fanned out on the table. Eventually, she lowers her eyes to the teapot.

'Go on,' she says softly, 'I think it's ready now.'

★

I shove Nina's wheelchair forward, trying to ignore my watch ticking accusingly on my wrist.

I don't want to know what the time is. All I know is I'm late. I'm really late.

I didn't mean to be, I'm never late. I hate being late. But once me and Nina started talking, I stopped thinking about the time.

I spot Sunfields at the end of the street. Nina's hands grip the wheelchair and I glance down at her as my legs pump into a light jog.

I really hope she doesn't fall out of the chair. What if I trip over my own feet and push Nina down on to the pavement? Christ, I'd be in prison alongside Nathan.

At least I'd save money on stamps.

Or, Joy would.

'Sorry,' I grunt, as I suck in an icy breath of air.

At least there's no chance of Nina dropping off. Unless she has a heart attack, which is very possible considering I feel like I'll have a heart attack if I don't get there soon.

I slow to a halt, trying to stop myself from buckling over the wheelchair in relief as I push Nina into Sunfields.

Nina looks up at me. 'Why are we running?'

The heavy door swings shut behind us and I almost fall over as my eyes land on Jakub, who is stood behind the reception. His huge arms are folded and his eyebrows are knitted together in a fierce glare.

Oh shit.

'Hello, Jakub,' Nina says, as if everything is completely normal, 'how are you? We've just been on a day out.'

I stare back at Jakub, unable to pull my eyes away. Nina unfolds herself from the chair and walks forward.

'I think I might go and tell Gus about our day, Bea,' Nina says lightly. 'See you in a bit.'

Keeping his eyes fixed on mine, Jakub pushes his hand against the door and holds it open for Nina. He looks like a steaming kettle, ready to boil over at any second.

A seething, venomous kettle.

I break eye contact with Jakub and manically uncoil my scarf. As soon as I look away, my eyes skirt around the room.

'Sorry we're late,' I babble, 'the bus took a while. Is everyone in the living room?'

'Where have you been?'

Jakub's voice strikes across me and I feel my chest tighten.

'I took Nina out,' I say, my voice pinching under the pressure. 'We went to a bird sanctuary.'

I go to walk forward but Jakub steps in front of me.

'You took her,' he says coldly. 'You can't just take them like that.'

My heart twitches and I try to keep my smile in place.

'I left you a note,' I say.

'You have no right,' Jakub says, 'it's not your place.'

My eyes fly back up to Jakub's, and suddenly the anxiety brewing in my chest is replaced by a stronger feeling.

'Well, then, whose place is it?' I snap, the words firing out of me. 'She's sad, she's grieving—' I break off, my eyes stinging in shock. As I look back at Jakub, his face moves and for a moment, we just stare at each other.

'She needs someone to look after her,' I say eventually.

I lift my chin to stalk past Jakub, but as I reach him he takes my arm.

'I care about her,' he says. 'You're not the only one who cares about them. You have no idea.'

I throw his hand off me. 'Well, then, why aren't you doing anything?' I say. 'These people are about to lose their home and you don't even seem to care.'

He glowers at me, his icy eyes boring into mine.

'You have no idea,' he says again.

I feel a cold strike of pain slice through me. I lean closer to him, feeling my jaw lock.

'Neither do you.'

CHAPTER TWENTY-THREE

I drill my fingers on the desk, ideas zapping through my mind like small volts of electricity.

I glance down at my latest letter to Nathan and feel a flash of embarrassment at my scribbled handwriting. I usually take real pride in my letters, I spend ages curling each word on to the paper, but this one fired out of me.

I need to find someone who cares about this. I can't sit by and watch them tear Sunfields down. It's not fair.

It's not right.

'What's up with you?'

I jolt in my seat as Faye appears next to me. My scrunched-up brow loosens for a moment and I raise my head from my hands. Faye is frowning at me.

'Hi,' I say, feeling my heart race as if I've been broken from a trance, 'you okay?'

Today Faye is wearing a high-neck black dress, her impressive blonde hair is swirling down her back and her light pink lips are pursed.

'What are you doing?' she asks, her voice dripping with suspicion as she peers over my desk. To my horror, I notice her eyes flit towards my letter and I reach forward and grab it.

'Nothing,' I say quickly, 'working. You?'

Faye raises her eyebrows at me, a smile playing at the corners of her mouth. 'Are you writing someone a letter?' she asks gleefully,

I shove the letter in my bag.

Great.

'No,' I say roughly, turning back to my computer.

Faye pauses, her wide eyes blinking at me as I silently will her to leave me alone.

'So,' she says, 'great news about Duncan . . .'

'What?'

'Letting you write something?' she finishes, pulling some of her hair through her fingers.

Urgh.

Why does she say 'letting' as if Duncan is doing me a favour? I'm a reporter, it's my job.

'Thanks,' I say shortly.

Go away.

'Do you know what you're going to write about?'

'Yup,' I say automatically, and then immediately want to kick myself.

Why did I say that? Now she'll never leave.

'Really?' she says, like clockwork. 'What?'

She leans her body closer to my desk, as if the answer is hiding under my coffee cup.

'I can't talk about it yet,' I say, randomly opening an email and tapping at my keyboard. 'It's not confirmed.'

I feel Faye's body tense and I click on another email.

Her smile drops. 'Okay,' she says tartly, 'fine. See you later, then.'

I glance up at her and feel myself breathe out in relief as she stomps through the office, probably on the lookout for someone else to annoy.

Honestly, does she ever do any work?

I pick up my mug and make my way into the kitchen.

How does she get away with it? I don't think I've ever seen her sit at her desk for more than ten minutes at a time. If I did that then Angela would end up—

'Oh.'

I stop in my tracks at the sight of Duncan, who is leaning over the kettle. I feel my mouth curve into an automatic smile.

'Hi, Duncan,' I say politely.

As soon as Duncan spots me, his face rearranges itself into his regular animated expression.

'Hello, Bea!' he booms, in his best Butlin's Redcoat voice. 'How are you?'

'Fine, thank you,' I say, flicking the kettle on. 'What were you looking at?'

I hear the words leave my mouth before I think it through, and I feel myself flush.

Why did I ask him that? That's so personal, he could be looking at anything!

For a second, Duncan's smile falters.

'Oh,' he says, 'just this.' He leans forward and opens his wallet.

I look over as he pulls out a photo of two fat babies, propped up against a sofa and laughing. Their squidgy hands are shoved in their mouths, and one of them is trying to crawl. I smile down at the photo.

'Aw,' I say, 'are those your children?'

I notice Duncan's shoulders sink slightly.

'Yeah,' Duncan says, 'twins. Annabelle and Amelia.'

'They're lovely,' I say, glancing sideways at him.

For a second, Duncan stares down at the photo. His hands cradle the photo carefully, as if it might break if he held it too tightly.

'Yes, they are,' he says.

Duncan never talks about his children. It's like he's a cartoon character, drawn specifically for work, who would be out of place anywhere else. He snaps his wallet shut and his bright eyes focus on me.

'Right!' he says. 'Back to work then, Albus!' He claps me on the shoulder. 'Make mine a strong coffee, will you?'

I watch him bumble out of the office, feeling the warmth inside me leave with him.

'Sure.'

★

I push my way through the red door and storm straight up to the reception desk. Jakub is seated behind it, staring at papers. Like he always is.

'Who decided to close the home?'

Jakub looks up. I see his expression wither at the sight of me.

'Why?' he asks, looking straight back down at the papers.

'I want to write to them,' I say, clicking my pen and flicking open my notepad. 'I want to stop it.'

'You won't,' he says in a bored voice, 'they know exactly what they're doing. They've been doing it for a year.'

'But people should—'

'We've tried.' Jakub's voice cuts across me and he gets to his feet. 'There is nothing we can do. It's closing in three weeks now. It's done.'

Jakub walks through to the living room and I follow him, irritation popping in my chest.

If people knew about this then they would help. If people knew what was going to happen to Nina, Gus and Sylvia then they would try to stop it. It's not right, they're tearing down their home.

They're real people.

'But,' I start again as we walk through to the living room, 'if we just—'

'Bea?'

I look round at the sound of Nina's voice and feel myself do a double-take. She's standing by the table, looking down at a newspaper.

My heart beats faster.

She's not sitting in her chair.

I smile as Nina walks back towards her chair, gesturing me to follow. I try not to look daggers at Jakub as he sits down next to Sylvia, who drops her copy of *Wuthering Heights* as he pulls up his chair.

Nina lowers herself into a high-backed, bottle-green chair and I drop into the small chair next to it. I try to pull my face into a smile as I sit down, but Nina frowns at me.

'What is it?' she asks.

'What?' I say, my voice strained. 'Nothing! I'm fine! How are you?'

'Why are you fighting with Jakub?'

I falter.

I'm not fighting with Jakub. We're fighting.

'We're not!' I chirp back, my smile still firmly fixed in place.

'You are.'

Nina narrows her eyes at me and I feel her gaze chip away at my fake smile.

'Oh,' I say lightly, 'we're just talking about Sunfields. I just don't want it to close.'

The last words tumble out of my mouth before I can stop them, and I feel my chest tighten.

Nina's face doesn't move.

'Why?'

I look back at Nina as I feel a hot flash of emotion strike through me.

Why?

I shrug, my face pulling into an awkward smile as I ignore her gaze.

'I like coming here,' I say in a small voice.

'Bea?'

I flinch as Jakub's harsh voice echoes across the room. I look round to see him standing at the other end of the room, and I feel a flutter of panic.

Is he about to throw me out?

I was quite rude to him.

'Yeah?' I say, trying to keep my expression neutral.

If he does try to throw me out, I won't go without a fight. Not that I'd physically fight him, obviously. He could squash me under his thumb like a flying ant. But I'd pretend I couldn't hear him. Or that I'd lost my scarf and that I couldn't possibly leave without it. Yes, that's a good plan.

First, though, I will have to hide my scarf.

Where did I even leave it?

Right, so to start with I must—

'Would you like some dinner?'

I blink at him.

What?

'Sorry?' I say stupidly.

Nina leans forward.

'What is it we're having, Jakub?' she asks. 'Is it goulash?'

Jakub nods, keeping his eyes away from mine as if he's been forced to ask me.

I feel a rush of heat swamp me.

'No, thank you,' I say pompously, lifting my chin and looking away from him.

Christ. The first man to ask me to dinner in about three years and it's someone who hates me.

Great.

Nina frowns at me again. 'Why not? Are you leaving?'

'No.'

'What will you have for dinner at home?'

I blink at her.

I can't tell her that all I have in my cupboard is a barbecue chicken Pot Noodle.

'Right,' Nina says decisively. 'Yes, please, Jakub. Bea will be staying.'

Jakub nods and sweeps out of the room. I stare after him.

'You'll like this goulash,' Nina says, her eyes twinkling. 'I'm sure we had it last week. It's very nice.'

I smile at her weakly and get to my feet.

Why is he asking me? He can't actually want me to stay. I

don't want him feeling like he has to ask. Maybe I've outstayed my welcome.

I walk out of the living room and into the small kitchen. Jakub is leaning over a pot and looks up at me as I walk in. For the first time, I feel myself really look at the kitchen and flinch at the state of the cupboards, bursting with mugs and plates. Far more than are needed for a home with three people in it.

'It's fine,' I say quickly, 'really. I'm fine for dinner, but thank you.'

Jakub pauses.

'You don't have to,' I add. 'I'll eat when I get home.'

'Do you not like goulash?'

I blink at him.

'I'm not sure,' I admit, my face prickling.

Jakub turns back to the pot and starts ladling it out.

'It's nice,' he says, 'but you don't have to eat it if you don't like it.'

I watch him scoop the meat and vegetables into bowls.

Why does he want me to eat it?

I hope he hasn't poisoned it.

Jakub hands me two bowls and for a second I almost see his poker face break into a smile. I feel a flash of emotion spark in the pit of my stomach and my cheeks tingle.

'Okay,' I say, as I turn and walk out of the kitchen, 'thanks.'

★

I stick my fork into a fat piece of meat and spear it into my mouth as Gus laughs.

'It was never the same,' he says, slapping his hands together. 'She didn't even accept my poems.'

I chew on the meat, rich flavour oozing into my mouth.

If this is poisonous, at least it's delicious.

I smile at Gus as I swallow my mouthful. He's been telling stories for the last ten minutes about his younger life as a cockney Casanova. I had no idea he was such a stud.

Although I'm not sure why I would have known that before.

'You wrote her a poem?' I ask, sipping my water.

'That's why she didn't want anything to do with you,' Sylvia says, angling her head towards Gus. 'They obviously weren't very good.'

Gus chuckles into his meal and I see small circles of pink form on Sylvia's cheeks.

'I can't believe you wrote her a poem,' I say.

I don't think anybody has ever written me a poem.

'Rubbish!' Gus chimes. 'Are you telling me this boyfriend of yours has never written you a poem?'

I stare at him, baffled.

Boyfriend?

What boy—

'I don't think Nathan would write poems,' Nina says, dipping her spoon into her bowl.

My heart twitches at his name.

Oh, that boyfriend.

'No,' I say, fixing my eyes on my meal.

'Get rid of him, then,' Gus says matter-of-factly. 'That's what Jean did to me.'

'No,' Sylvia says, a small smile playing on her lips, 'Jean found someone who was better at poetry.'

I laugh as I swallow my mouthful, then glance over at Jakub whose spoon is resting in his empty bowl.

'Have you got a girlfriend, Jakub?'

I almost drop my spoon in shock as I hear the question being asked in my own voice.

Why on earth did I ask him that? I hate it when people ask me that question!

Jakub shakes his head and we fall into silence. I fight the urge to stab myself with my fork.

Urgh. Now look what you've done. Everybody was having a perfectly nice time until you asked an awkward question and made everyone feel uncomfortable.

You arse.

'So, Bea,' Sylvia says, 'what do you do for Christmas?'

I look at Sylvia, her green eyes fixed on me.

Sylvia never speaks to me.

'Oh,' I say, 'I usually spend it with friends, but I'm not sure this year.'

'What about your family?' Jakub asks, his stern expression cracking slightly.

I look away, as I suddenly feel a wave of anxiety sweep up my body.

I force a fake smile on to my face.

'No,' I say, 'not with family.'

My hand twitches towards my phone and my eyes flick up to Nina. As she looks back at me, I feel as if a silent message has moved between us. I dip my spoon back into my meal and try to fight the heat creeping up my back.

'This is really nice, Jakub,' I say, lifting my spoon.

Jakub nods in appreciation.

'Can you cook, Bea?' Sylvia asks.

'I didn't cook this,' Jakub adds quickly, before I can respond to Sylvia's question.

I don't really have anyone to cook for any more.

I swallow another mouthful. 'Yeah,' I say, 'some things. I can make a good roast.'

'You'll have to make one for us one day!' Gus says, grinning at me as he places his spoon into his empty bowl.

I look back at him, feeling my chest swell.

'Yeah,' I say, 'I'd like that.'

★

'Goodnight, then.'

I watch as Gus, the last one awake, leaves the living room. I hold up a hand and smile at him as I stack away the bingo kit and slot it under the table. It's almost ten o'clock now, I'm usually gone by nine at the latest, but I didn't want to leave. I still don't.

We all ate dinner together and then sat and played a game of bingo. Even Jakub finally abandoned his prized stack of paperwork to join in, and Sylvia cracked a smile when she won, just like she said she would.

I look up as Jakub reappears from the kitchen. He walks towards the table and starts spraying it down.

'Right,' I say, clapping my hands together as I stand back up, 'I think that's me done, then. I'll try and come over tomorrow, but if not I'll definitely come next week.'

Jakub raises his eyebrows in acknowledgement as he wipes the table down. 'Okay,' he says.

I pick up my coat from the chair and slot my arms into the sleeves.

'What time do you finish?' I ask, wrapping the coat around my body.

'Whenever.'

I frown.

Well, I guess he is the manager.

'Does it take you a long time to get home?' I ask.

Jakub wipes the last corner of the table and tucks the cloth into his back pocket.

'I live here,' he says.

I look back at him.

'Oh.'

He lives here? With the residents?

I always assumed he lived with family, or friends.

A cold wave of guilt seeps through me as reality dawns.

'So,' I say slowly, 'when the home closes, where will you go?'

The words hang in the air and I feel myself wince silently as I hear them. Jakub doesn't answer and my body burns with embarrassment.

Why did I ask him that? What's wrong with me? What a horrible thing to ask. I stare at him as he continues to wipe the table down, and I feel a sudden urge to give him a hug.

'Sorry,' I mumble, my face hot, 'I'd better go. I'll see you later.'

I pick up my bag and duck my head as I walk out of the living room. As I walk past Jakub, he turns.

'Wait,' he says.

I stop to look at him, guilt rippling through me.

'Do you want a drink?'

★

I watch in alarm as Jakub tips the clear liquid into a glass and doesn't stop until it's half full. He catches my expression and stops pouring.

'Too strong?' he asks, lifting the bottle away from the glass.

Christ, is he trying to kill me?

I nod weakly, looking at the icy vodka in my glass.

'It will put hairs on your chest,' Jakub says, pouring his own glass.

I try not to frown.

I don't *want* hairs on my chest.

I pick up the glass and hold it on my lap.

'This is how we drink in Poland,' Jakub says, holding his glass up to me in a 'cheers' motion. I lift my glass and clink it against his. I tip the glass towards my mouth, and try not to gag as the sharp taste fills my mouth.

I haven't drunk vodka since university.

I cough slightly. Jakub laughs, tipping the drink down his throat as if it's water. I feel a tingle as I laugh back at him. It's the first time I've seen him smile.

'So,' I say, rubbing my mouth with the back of my hand, 'how long did you live in Poland for?'

Jakub puts his glass on the table, rests his elbows and leans forward. 'Twenty-five years,' he says, meeting my eyes. 'I moved to England three years ago.'

'Why?'

Jakub looks up at me. A shadow moves across his face for a moment, and then he looks away.

There is a silence and I feel my cheeks redden.

Should I not have asked him that?

He shrugs as we drop back into silence, turning the glass between my hands.

'Why are you here?'

I look up as Jakub's question breaks my thoughts, and I feel a sharp wince of pain in my chest at his question.

Why am I here?

'I wanted to see Nina,' I say quietly.

'You like coming here,' Jakub says matter-of-factly.

I feel a jab of irritation.

'Yeah, so?' I say sharply. 'Why is that a bad thing?'

Jakub shrugs, taking another sip of his drink.

'It's not,' he says. 'I like being here too.'

I shuffle in my seat, my coat squirming underneath me.

Why did I stay? I should have just gone home like I said I would. Why did I think I'd enjoy spending time with him?

My eyes wander around the room and I spot a framed photo in the corner. A woman is smiling up at me, her arm hooked around a young child with piercing blue eyes and a big, gappy smile.

'It was better before,' Jakub says. 'The house was full.'

I look back at him. 'Full?'

Jakub nods. 'We had twenty-two residents, all in their own rooms. We had more staff, we had activities. It was a real home and then, one by one, everyone left.'

He tips the last of his drink into his mouth and I feel a pang in my chest.

'Where did they go?' I ask.

Jakub shrugs. 'Some went to family, some got sent to new

homes. The staff were let go. I said I could manage the last few weeks alone. They send the meals here and everything we need.'

'Oh,' I say, 'right.'

I look around the dark living room, trying to imagine what life was like here before. All of the colourful, fat chairs filled with residents, chatting and laughing. Perhaps they had visitors all the time, and several nurses bustling in and out.

'I know you want to change it,' Jakub says quietly, 'but you can't. It's done.'

His words get under my skin and I feel my eyes sting. I quickly blink the tears away and flinch as I notice Jakub looking at me. I shoot him a half-smile and to my alarm, he reaches forward and touches my hand. I feel my body burn.

'They'll be okay,' he says. 'They'll be sent to nice places. They won't be homeless,' he adds, giving my hand a squeeze.

I take my hand away and wipe my eyes, my big grin springing back on to my face. My eyes flick away from Jakub and land back on the framed photo.

'Do you miss your family?' I ask. 'Being in England?'

Jakub follows my gaze and looks at the photo.

'Yes,' he says quietly, 'but it's different there now. My family aren't all together in Poland. And these guys,' he gestures around the empty room, 'they're my family now too.'

He moves his eyes back to mine and I feel my heart contract.

'Yeah,' I say, this time holding his gaze, 'I know the feeling.'

Chapter Twenty-Four

I knock on Joy's front door, my hand curled around my letter as if it could blow away in the wind. I pause as the loud knocks are drowned by the sound of the heavy rain and I watch Joy's fat Christmas wreath shake in the wind as I try to peer through the window.

Joy never takes long to answer the door. She usually answers before I've even finished knocking.

I raise my hand to knock again, when Joy pulls the door open. As soon as she sees me, her face breaks into a warm smile and I smile back at her.

Maybe she was on the loo.

'Oh,' she says, 'hello, Bea. Do you want to come in?' She looks behind me. 'This weather is horrible, isn't it?'

I tug my hood further over my head, and step inside. 'Thank you,' I say. 'I can't stay long, I've got to get to work.'

My eyes flick up to her clock, on the hall stand: 7.38.

I need to leave in two minutes.

Joy's eyes flit down to my hand. 'Another love letter?' she asks.

My heart lurches.

It's more than a love letter this time, it's about the home.

'Joy,' I ask, the thought dropping into my brain, 'have you ever been to Sunfields before?'

Joy frowns at me. 'The care home?'

'Yeah,' I say. 'Did you know that they're closing it down? So all of these people won't have anywhere to live?'

Joy looks at me, perplexed.

'No, dear,' she says, 'I didn't know that.'

'Well,' I say, handing the letter to Joy, 'it's terrible. Anyway,' I add as I step back out of her house, 'thank you so much for this. I'm going to buy some stamps today so I can stop bothering you.'

'No!'

Joy's voice breaks from her in a shrill, pinched tone.

'It's fine,' Joy adds, her voice returning to her usual, calm manner. 'I'm happy to do it, dear. You have enough going on. It's really no bother.'

I pause.

Is she okay?

'Okay,' I say, pulling my hood tightly around my head. 'Well, I'd better get to work. Have a nice day.'

I turn on my heel and duck into the darkness. I spot Joy waving after me, one slippered foot stepping into a puddle.

'You too, dear.'

★

I thwack my shoulder against the door, wincing as it creaks open, and I feel the bag stuffed under my arm shake.

'You okay?'

I look up at Jakub who hurries forward, grabbing the tumbling bag from under my arm. I look up at him, all puffed up under my thick coat and knitted woollen hat, my cheeks flaring at the sudden heat. As our eyes meet, I feel a bolt of electricity shoot through me.

'Thanks,' I pant, kicking the door shut behind me as the icy wind whirls into the home.

Jakub props the door open for me. 'What's all this?'

'It's a surprise,' I say, shooting Jakub a grin as a limp piece of gold tinsel swishes out of my bag like a horse's tail.

I make my way into the living room, a wide grin plastered across my face as I stagger towards the large table. Gus looks up from his newspaper.

'What's all this, Bea?' he asks. 'Are you moving in?'

I hear a small laugh from Sylvia as she turns another page of *Wuthering Heights*, and I turn to Gus.

'Not yet,' I laugh.

Nina is seated in the chair next to Gus, a fan of playing cards spread across her small hands. She looks up at me and smiles.

'Are you two playing cards?' I ask, shaking my coat off as the burning heat of the room sinks into my skin.

'Gus is trying to teach me bridge,' Nina says, pulling a face at me.

'She's getting quite good!' Gus says, his eyes flitting over to Sylvia, who has finally put her book down.

'What's in all of your bags?' Sylvia asks, her small silver-framed glasses pushed to the bridge of her nose.

'Ah!' I spring back round to the table and shake some tinsel out of my large shopping bags. 'I thought it was about time we decorated this place.'

As I hold pieces of tinsel in my hands, Gus's smile softens.

'I don't think we're doing Christmas this year, love,' he says. 'I don't think we can.'

'Of course we can,' I say at once, almost shocking myself at my brisk tone, 'I've got everything here, see?'

I stick my hand into the largest plastic bag and wrestle out a large box with a photo of a Christmas tree on the front.

Sylvia puts her book down and rests her hands on her lap as Jakub walks into the living room. His eyes sweep the table, which is covered in glistening tinsel and packets of bright baubles.

'I can't return it,' I add, 'I didn't keep the receipt.'

As I look round at Gus, Nina and Sylvia, I feel a flash of worry spark inside me.

Nina looks back at me, and Gus's smile stays fixed on his face.

Oh God. I've just made things worse. Why didn't I listen to them? What was I thinking?

'It's okay,' I say quickly, stuffing the tinsel into a ball, 'we don't have to, I'll just—'

'Right!' Sylvia claps her hands together and I jump. 'I'll start on the tree. And Gus,' she says pointedly, as she pulls herself out of her chair, 'Nina will beat you at bridge later.'

Sylvia walks towards me, her arms outstretched, and I feel a wave of relief. I look at Jakub who is standing at the door. He winks at me.

'Great,' I say, my heart lifting. 'Who knows how to put a tree up?'

★

I steady the round stool and look down at it dubiously.

Can this carry my weight? I'd be mortified if I broke it.

Carefully, I place one foot on the stool and hoist myself up, my entire body tensing.

Please don't break, please don't break, please don't break.

'Okay,' I say slowly, trying to steady myself, 'pass me the tinsel then, Gus.'

Gus rifles through the carrier bag. 'Any particular colour?'

'Not the gold,' Nina calls, as she loops strings of tinsel across the pink walls. 'That needs to go on the reception desk.'

Gus nods and fishes out a string of red tinsel, little cherry-coloured shards of glitter scattering across the table. I hold my arm out as Gus passes it to me.

'Have we got a fairy?' he asks, peering into the bag. 'For the top of the tree?'

I weave the tinsel as best as I can through the plastic branches.

'No,' I answer, feeling the stool rock dangerously as I lean forward, 'I've got us a star instead.'

Gus pulls the dainty plastic star from the bag and looks at it. He holds it in front of his crinkled eyes and smiles.

'My grandsons used to love putting the fairy on the tree,' he says. 'They'd fight every year about whose turn it was. We could never remember.'

I hook the last string of red tinsel around the tree and glance down at Gus.

'I didn't know you had grandchildren, Gus.'

I reach out my hand as Sylvia passes me some silver tinsel.

'Oh yes,' Gus chuckles, 'one son, but three grandchildren. All boys.'

I feel a flutter in my chest as I drape the tinsel over the tree.

I never thought Gus would be a grandfather. He's never mentioned grandchildren before.

'Oh, that's lovely,' I say, hopping off the stool. 'Do they live nearby?'

Gus drops the star back on to the table. 'Yes,' he says, 'about an hour away. But they're ever so busy. They've all got a lot to be getting on with.'

I look at Gus as he twirls the star between his hands. I turn to Sylvia, who has pulled open a box of glistening reindeer.

'What about you, Sylvia?' I ask, taking a reindeer from the packet and hooking it on a branch, 'Are you a grandma?'

Sylvia shoots me a look from behind her glasses as if I've asked her if she's a Nazi.

'Do I look like a grandma?'

I bite my lip.

Yes. Of course you look like a grandma. You're literally about eighty.

'No,' she says crisply, 'you have to be a mother first.'

I prop another decoration on a branch.

'I was always quite happy on my own,' she adds lightly, placing her reindeer in the middle of the tree.

I smile at her, trying to ignore the question bubbling around my head.

If neither of them have any family, then where will they go when this place closes?

'Where do you want this tree?'

I look up as Jakub walks into the room and puts down a tray of steaming mugs. He flashes me a smile and I beam at him.

'I'd say in the middle of the room,' Sylvia says, 'by the coffee table. But we're not finished yet,' she adds, as Jakub steps towards the tree.

I look over at Gus, who is still turning the plastic star between his hands.

'Gus,' I say, 'do you want to put the star on the top of the tree?'

Gus looks up at me and laughs.

'I'm too old for that,' he says, shaking his head.

Sylvia shoots Gus a look.

'Nonsense,' she says sternly, 'you should do it if you want to. What's the point in living life only thinking about what you'd like to do?'

Gus looks up at Sylvia. Jakub steps forward and claps Gus on the shoulder gently.

'Come on,' he says, 'we'll help you.'

I glance over at the rickety stool nervously.

Oh no. Why did I suggest this? If Gus falls off that stool, he might crack a rib.

Gus looks around the room, fixing his eyes on Sylvia, who still has her eyebrows raised at him. Eventually, his face breaks into a smile and he gets to his feet.

'Go on, then,' he says, laughing to himself, 'why not?'

Jakub moves the stool and holds out his arm. Gus grips Jakub's forearm and I find myself holding my breath. Sylvia hands Gus the star, and he reaches forward and props it on the top of the tree. Nina sighs.

'Oh,' she says, 'that looks lovely, Gus.'

Gus carefully steps down from the stool and admires the tree. He turns to me and smiles.

'Thank you.'

I beam at him.

'How about we all have Christmas together, this year?' I say, hearing the words out loud before I've registered them. 'We could invite your grandchildren, Gus. And I could cook. I make a good roast, so I reckon I could manage a Christmas dinner.'

I look around the room at the four smiling faces.

Nina walks over to me and places her arm in mine.

'That sounds like a great idea, Bea.'

Chapter Twenty-Five

I shake my mouse and stare at my screen, the blank Word document blinking back at me. Bubbles of excitement pop under my skin as I prop my dusty phone between my cheek and shoulder.

'Thank you for calling, your call is important to us. Please note that our opening hours are Monday to Friday, nine a.m. to six p.m. Somebody will answer your call as soon as possible. We are currently receiving a high volume of calls.'

I roll my eyes as the timer clicks to eight minutes.

Eight minutes I've been on hold to the council. As soon as I pressed 'call' I seemed to go straight on hold, which is a continuous loop of the same droning voice.

'Thank you for calling, your call is important . . .'

I hold the phone away from my ear, desperate not to hear the speech again.

I finally managed to pluck up the courage to speak to Angela this morning about my story. I told her I wanted to write about Sunfields, and how it is closing down. People should know about it. People would care.

Maybe someone would be able to do something about it.

So, like a good reporter, I'm starting this investigation by collecting quotes. My first stop being the council.

'Thank you for calling, your call is important . . .'

That is, if they ever pick up the damn phone.

'Hi.'

I flick my eyes up at Faye, who is leaning over my desk.

'Who are you on the phone to?'

I move the receiver away from my mouth.

'The council,' I say.

Faye frowns.

'Why?' she asks. 'You're not allowed to make personal calls in the office, you know.'

I try not to scoff at her.

That's rich, coming from the girl who spends half of the working day taking selfies.

'Thank you for calling, your call is important . . .'

'It's not a personal call,' I say, 'it's for my story.'

Faye's eyes flick down to my notepad, and her face twitches.

'Oh,' she says, 'right. The story Duncan gave you.'

I feel a stab of annoyance.

'He didn't give it to me,' I say tightly, 'I had to go find it myself so—'

'Hello?'

I jump as a loud voice trumpets down the line. I almost drop my phone in fright.

Argh! Why is it so loud?

'Oh!' I say. 'Hello, could I please speak to somebody about homes?'

I notice Faye furrow her brow next to me and I try to ignore her.

Go away.

'Council tax?' says the voice.

I pause.

What?

'Err,' I say, 'no. Residential homes, please. Or care homes. That department.'

'Is this regarding council tax or an update of address?'

I open and close my mouth.

What? What on earth is she talking about?

'No,' I start again, 'I need to talk to somebody about residential homes.'

There is a long pause and I watch the seconds tick away.

Ten minutes. I've been on this phone for ten minutes now, and I still haven't—

'Please hold.'

I jolt as the phone switches into an odd country song.

Great.

What song is this?

'Are you writing a story about a home?' Faye asks.

'Sort of,' I say, my face flushing.

'Has Angela approved this?'

I shoot her a look.

'Yes,' I say tightly, 'actually, she said—'

'Hello?'

'Oh!' I jolt again, my heart flipping over. 'Hello.'

'Hello,' a man's voice resonates through the phone, 'you're through to the council tax department. How can I help?'

What? Why? I specifically said not council tax!

'Oh,' I say, trying to sound calm, 'sorry. I don't know why she put me through to you. I need to talk to someone about residential homes.'

'Right,' the man says in a bored voice, 'well, we deal with council tax in this department.'

I take a deep breath.

'I know that,' I say slowly, 'but I need to please speak to someone about residential homes.'

'Would you like me to transfer you?' he asks.

Without quite meaning to, I shove my fist into my mouth.

'Yes, please,' I manage.

And just like that, the phone clicks again and the monotone voice spills back down the line.

'Thank you for calling, your call is important . . .'

'Why are you writing a story about care homes?'

I glance across at Faye, who is still sitting in the chair next to me.

Why does she care? Why can't she just leave me alone?

I force my twitching face into a smile.

'Because,' I say in a strained voice, 'I want to write about—'

'Hello operator . . .'

Argh! The operator? Why am I back with the damn operator?

'Hello!' I chirp, my voice flying up seven octaves higher than usual. 'I need to talk to somebody about council tax, please. NO!' I shout, as my brain catches up with my words. 'Not council tax! I need to talk to someone about residential homes.'

I hear the operator tapping her keyboard, and I try to control the urge to hurl the phone across the room.

'Sorry,' the girl says, 'did you say council tax?'

If she puts me through to council tax again, I will storm down to the council's offices and break their headsets.

'No,' I say through gritted teeth, 'I need to talk to somebody about residential homes. I'm a reporter from the *Middlesex Herald* and I'm writing about Sunfields Care Home being shut down by the council. I'd like a quote, please.'

The last part spills out of me in a high-pitched warble and, to my horror, the phone goes dead.

Did she hang up on me?

Did she hang up on me?

'You're writing about a home shutting down?' Faye asks.

I jump and slam the receiver down. I'd almost forgotten she was there.

'Yes,' I say, heat flaring up my body. 'Yes, I am.'

★

I stick a stamp in the corner of the envelope and tuck it in my bag as I make my way down the stairs.

16.58:   Leave work.
17.05:   Post letter.
17.15:   Catch bus to Sunfields.
17.45:   Arrive at Sunfields.

I jump down the final stair when I hear footsteps scurry behind me.

'Wait!'

I turn to see Faye a few steps behind me. I hold the door open for her and we walk through reception together.

'Thanks,' she pants, 'are you getting the bus?'

I feel my insides shrivel.

I once made the mistake of telling Faye which bus I get, which led to her saying how she could get the same one as me and resulted in an hour of non-stop talking about her weekend and how many boys she's dating.

'No,' I say, 'not today.'

Faye frowns at me. 'Are you not going home?'

'Nope,' I say, as we push the front door open, 'I'm going out.'

Har har. I'm going out. I have plans on a weeknight. Look at me go.

'Bea?'

I spin round as I spot Priya, leaning against the building. Her phone is clasped in her hand and her body is wrapped in a large puffa coat. I stare at her.

What is she doing here?

'Priya,' I say, walking towards her, 'hi.'

'You took ages,' she says grumpily. 'I need your help. Please don't say you're seeing your boyfriend tonight.'

I feel a zap of heat whip through my body.

'Boyfriend?' Faye repeats. 'I didn't know you had a boyfriend, Bea!'

Oh, great.

'I'm Faye,' Faye says, toddling up beside me. 'I'm Bea's friend from work.'

Friend? Are we friends?

'Oh,' says Priya, sounding distracted, 'hey. I'm Priya.'

'Right,' I say quickly, desperate to stop any further conversation about my imaginary boyfriend. 'So I'll see you tomorrow, Faye.'

Faye looks at me and her smile quivers for a second.

'Yup,' she says, turning on her heel, 'bye, then.'

She saunters down the street and I turn to Priya, who has pulled her phone back out and is holding it in front of her.

'You all right?' I ask nervously.

Priya has never met me outside work. I didn't even realise she knew where my building was.

'Yeah,' she says. 'Actually, no.'

I try to steer her down the street as the icy December wind grips my face, but Priya roots herself to the ground.

'Look at this.'

She turns her phone to face me and I feel my shoulders sag. It's a message from Josh.

Miss you.

'Oh,' I say, 'right.'

'He sent it this morning. What do you think it means?'

Priya bats her large tadpole eyes at me and I stare back at her hopelessly.

I really am terrible at this.

'That he misses you?' I offer.

What else am I supposed to say?

'Come on,' I say, hooking my arm in hers and steering her down the street, 'let's go home and talk about it there. It's freezing out here.'

Priya refuses to budge and I jolt backwards.

'No,' Priya says, 'I've been thinking about this all day and I need to go and see him.'

I blink at her, my mind scrabbling to work out what the time is.

I need to be on my bus in three minutes.

'Bea,' she grips me tightly, 'I can't go on my own, will you come with me? Please?'

★

I shove my hands deeper into my pockets as Priya paces up and down the pavement like an incontinent Labrador.

'Priya,' I say wearily, burying my head into my scarf, 'can you just knock on the door? Or, like, not knock on the door and then we can go home? I can't stand here much longer, I'm freezing.'

We've been loitering on the pavement for the best past of half an hour. A shimmering sheet of ice has crackled across the street and my breath has started to fog in front of me like hair-spray.

Suddenly, Priya stops pacing and stares at me.

'Is it the right thing to do? To see him?' she asks, blinking her large eyes at me. 'I mean, he said he missed me. Why would he say that if he didn't mean it? I have to see him. Right? That's what he wants me to do? Maybe he wants to get back together.'

I stare at her as her questions bounce off my head.

'Sure,' I say eventually, 'just go see him.'

'Right,' Priya says, finally breaking her restless pacing and stepping towards Josh's flat, 'right.'

'But,' I say quickly, reaching forward and grabbing Priya's arm, 'do you want to get back together, Pri? I mean, he was pretty horrible to you and you've been, well,' my grip loosens on her arm as I stare into her watery eyes, 'you were heartbroken.'

I keep my hand on Priya's arm as she blinks the tears away.

'I just have to know,' she says in a small voice. 'I've been imagining this conversation for weeks. I can't leave it.'

I nod, letting go of her arm as my skin cracks in the frozen wind. She steps towards his house and I follow her.

'Okay,' she says, 'I'm going in.'

'Okay.'

'You don't have to wait for me.'

I nod again.

'Okay.'

'Thank you for coming with me,' she says, her voice wobbling, 'and just for, you know,' she shrugs, 'being there.'

I reach forward and pull Priya into a hug.

'Always,' I say, giving her a squeeze.

Priya lets me go and nods, turning on the spot to face the front door. She lifts her hand to knock and gasps, before ducking down hurriedly. I run forward.

Oh my God, is she hurt?

'What?' I cry. 'What is it?'

'Get down!' Priya hisses, tugging me to the floor.

'What?' I manage, as I hunker down next to her. 'Why?'

I try to look through the window but Priya forces me back to the ground. I turn to her and see that her dark eyes are swimming with tears.

'He's in there with another girl.'

CHAPTER TWENTY-SIX

I smile up at Sunfields as I walk towards the house. I see the lights of the Christmas tree twinkling through the living-room window and the proud wreath is stuck firmly on the door, like a real home.

I reach the door and wait to be admitted. I barely even look at reception as I walk straight into the living room, my heavy bag weighing me down.

I managed to slip away from work a few minutes earlier today to get the bus, I don't think anyone even noticed. Duncan shut himself in his office all day, he didn't send any of his ridiculous mid-afternoon quotes, and Faye was too absorbed by her phone to notice me leave.

'Hi, everyone,' I say, as I walk into the living room.

Sylvia lowers her book and Gus raises his eyes to look at me as his hands shuffle a pack of cards.

'Hello, Bea,' Sylvia says. 'I think Jakub is just making a cup of tea.'

I drop my bag on to the table, suddenly noticing that Nina isn't in her usual spot.

'Okay,' I say, unzipping my bag, 'so, I was thinking, how about we do our Christmas Day meal on Christmas Eve? That way your family will be able to come, Gus – and any other family members anyone wants to invite,' I add, my insides squirming.

I don't think anybody else has any other family.

'Lovely,' Sylvia says, going back to her book. 'That sounds good, doesn't it, Gus?'

I look over at Gus, who has dipped his head towards his cards. For the first time since I've met him, he's not smiling at me.

'What's that?' Gus asks.

Sylvia skims her index finger down a page, her face taut.

'Having a Christmas meal on Christmas Eve?'

'So you can invite your family,' I add, desperate to make Gus smile.

What's going on?

Finally, Gus lifts his eyes to meet mine. Although the smile is back on his face, the usual spark behind his eyes isn't there.

'Oh,' he says, 'yes. Although, I don't think Sam and the boys will be able to make it.'

He keeps his eyes locked on to mine for a second, and then looks back down at the cards. For a moment, I almost see a flush of colour skim across his lined face.

A hot flash of emotion sparks through me.

Why not?

'Oh,' I say, keeping my voice light, 'okay, well, that's okay. It will just be the five of us, then.'

I smile broadly down at Gus, who keeps his head lowered towards the cards. Anger nips at my skin.

Why aren't his family coming? What could they be doing?

261

I've been coming here for weeks now and they haven't come to visit once. I don't think I've even heard them make a phone call.

I look over at Sylvia. Her face is still taut as she keeps her eyes fixed on the pages of her book.

My hand reaches into my pocket and grips my phone.

What could be more important than your family?

'Bea?'

I look round to see Jakub hovering in the doorway.

'Can you come here for a second?' he asks. 'Nina wants you.'

I glance down at Sylvia and Gus. They both have their heads buried in their activities and haven't even noticed Jakub.

What's going on?

'Sure,' I say, following Jakub out of the living room. 'Is she okay?'

'Yeah, she's fine,' Jakub replies, as we walk down the corridor towards the fire exit, 'she just wants to speak to you.'

I frown as Jakub pushes against the fire exit. An icy wind storms through the open door and I instinctively fling my arms around my body.

'Out here?' I cry, my body shaking. 'Why is Nina outside? It's freezing!'

I step out into the small garden and into the blanket of inky darkness that swallows me up as soon as I shut the door. Only the faint flicker of the orange street light in the distance allows me to spot Nina, who is sitting on a wooden bench. Her body is wrapped up in her large coat and her small hands are curled around some paper. Next to her, swaying in the wind slightly, are two red balloons.

'Hey, Nina,' I say, walking over to her, 'are you okay? It's freezing.'

Nina looks up at me. In the darkness, I can barely see her features, but I notice her swollen face, squeezing her eyes into two small pouches of skin. I feel a flash of pain as I sink down next to her, and suddenly I can't feel the sharp wind scratching at my skin. I reach forward and place my hand on hers.

Has she been crying?

'Hello, Bea,' Nina says quietly, 'I was hoping you'd be here today.'

'Of course,' I say quickly, shocks of icy air filling my lungs. 'Nina, it's freezing out here. Let's go outside, it's the middle of winter.'

Nina looks away and I stare at the side of her face as she looks forward, into the darkness. I look down at the paper on her lap and I notice neat handwriting curling across the page. Under the faint shadow of the orange street light, my eyes pick out two words. My heart jumps.

To Melanie

Nina's eyes follow mine and she smiles.

'She loved Christmas,' she says, 'she always did.'

I tighten my grip on Nina's hand.

'Have you written her a letter?' I ask, the words forcing their way out of my mouth.

I've never done that.

Nina gives me a small nod.

'She wasn't meant to die,' she says, her voice barely audible. 'She was too young. She was never meant to die.'

Hot emotion burns at the back of my throat.

'I know,' I say.

Nina looks down at the letter, her thumb moving across her words.

'There is so much I never said to her,' she says.

'You always think you have more time,' I hear myself say.

Nina moves her eyes to look at me. Suddenly, I feel my face is wet. She reaches over and picks up a blank piece of paper. For a second, we just look at each other, a thousand words floating between us.

'Do you want to write one?'

I stare back at her, my throat squeezing in pain.

'I don't think I can,' I manage, giving a small laugh.

Nina squeezes my hand, her kind eyes locked on to mine. She turns away and folds her letter into an envelope. There is a small hole in her envelope, and she threads the string of the balloon through it.

I watch her, unable to speak, as she passes me a balloon.

'You don't have to write anything,' she says, taking my hand back in hers, 'you just need to feel it.'

I grip my balloon, which waves at me in the sharp December wind. Thousands of thoughts rip through my brain, hot flashes of emotion pierce my skin like daggers and fear wraps itself around my throat. But, as always, the loudest thought thumps through my brain.

She wasn't supposed to die.

Nina gives my hand a tight squeeze and nods. Like a silent signal between us, both of our hands open, sending the balloons into the night. The red circles dance with each other as they are swept up in the wind and, slowly, they are swallowed up by the inky black sky. Nina curls her arm around mine, and as I move my eyes away from the sky, I notice a robin has landed at our feet, and for a second, I almost feel like she heard me.

I miss you, Mum.

★

I clutch a letter in one hand and raise the other up to Joy's front door, which clicks open instantly. A thick smell of sugar wafts into the frosty morning air and she dusts her hands on her apron.

'Oh,' I say, 'something smells nice! What are you making?'

Joy smiles at me. 'Oh, just some muffins,' she says. 'Would you like some?'

My stomach aches.

I'd love some, but if I say yes then I'll have to go inside and I don't have time. I need to get to Sunfields before midday.

'No, that's okay,' I smile. 'But thank you. They smell lovely.'

Joy tucks her hands into each other. 'Are Priya and Emma in today? I could bring some round for them.'

I glance over my shoulder at our dark house.

'No, they're both out.'

Emma is looking around flats with Margot, and Priya has gone to stay with her parents for a few days. Which is the best place for her. I'm still waiting for her to react properly to seeing Josh with another girl. She has barely said a word about it since the other day. If I didn't have a yellow bruise on my knee from Priya yanking me to the pavement I'd think I made the whole thing up.

'What are you up to today, then?' Joy asks.

I drop the letter to my side as I feel the familiar warm glow filling my chest.

'I've taken the day off work. I'm just going off to Sunfields, I visit them quite a lot.'

I see a brief frown flit across Joy's face.

'The residential home?' she says.

I nod. 'Yeah. I've been volunteering there. I'm actually spending Christmas with them. They weren't going to have a Christmas dinner otherwise; none of their families could be with them.'

Joy looks at me, and for a second her smile slips.

'Oh,' she says, 'how sad.'

'Yeah,' I say, my eyes flitting down to my watch.

9.07. My bus leaves in eight minutes.

'Anyway,' I say, 'I wanted to say that I bought some stamps,' I wave the letter about proudly, 'so I wanted to offer to post some of your letters today, if you have any. There's a postbox on the high street, right?'

A shadow passes over Joy's face. She reaches forward and takes the letter from my hand.

'That's okay,' she says, 'I can post it for you. I need to send a last-minute Christmas parcel to Jenny anyway. I shouldn't have left it so late, I can't believe it is only a week away.'

Joy places the letter on her mantelpiece and then turns back to smile at me.

'What would you like for tea later?' she says. 'I could make us a pie.'

I feel a cold thud in my chest as I look back at her.

It's Thursday. I'd forgotten.

How could I have forgotten it's Thursday?

'Oh,' I say, 'Joy, I'm so sorry but I can't do tonight. I promised I'd go to Sunfields.'

Joy places the letter on the mantelpiece behind her and looks back at me. 'Oh,' she says, 'not to worry. We can always do next Thursday.'

I nod, glancing down at my watch.

'Definitely,' I say. 'Well, I'd better go, my bus arrives soon.'

Joy leans out of the doorway as I walk down the path.

'Okay,' she says. 'Have a nice day, Bea.'

'You too.'

★

'You want to write a story?'

Jakub drops two tea bags into the large china teapot and looks back at me.

'Yes,' I say, 'a news story. I'm a reporter, that's what I do for a job.'

I feel a frisson of pride as I hear myself say these words out loud with such force. I usually mumble my job title if anybody asks me. I'm not embarrassed by it, obviously, I've just never felt like a real reporter.

Jakub looks over his shoulder and smiles at me.

'I just feel,' I say, taking two teacups from the shelf, 'that if people knew what was going on here, they would do something about it. They would help. Like, this is their home.'

I place the teacups on the tray. Jakub shrugs.

'Maybe,' he says, 'but the home closes in about two weeks now. I don't think the council will change their mind.'

He gestures towards the door and I prop it open. He nods his head in thanks.

'But they might,' I say, following him out. 'We won't know if we don't try.'

I push open the living-room door and angle my body to prop it open as Jakub gets closer to me. I hold the tray of mince pies awkwardly.

Argh, what am I doing? There is no way we'll both fit through this tiny gap.

I look up at Jakub to acknowledge my stupidity, but to my alarm he starts to shimmy his way through the gap. As he shifts past me, I feel his chest graze against mine and I try to stop myself from blushing furiously.

My God! If he doesn't hurry up and get past me my head is going to explode! Does he really need to be this close to me? Couldn't he have waited until I'd moved? I mean, we're practically having sex!

'Oh, is that a cuppa?'

Gus's chipper voice breaks through my thoughts and, suddenly, Jakub is through the door. I try to control my legs, which feel like they're about to crumple to the floor, as I step away from the door. It swings back behind me as though nothing has happened.

Gus rustles his newspaper and Jakub smiles, carefully putting the tray down on the table.

'It sure is,' he says, 'and Bea has bought us some mince pies.'

'Oh, I say,' Gus remarks.

Jakub goes to pour the tea and I find myself sticking my hand out to stop him.

'Wait,' I say, 'you have to let the tea brew.'

Jakub raises his eyebrows at me and I can't help but laugh as I hear Nina murmur her approval from her chair.

'Is there anything good in the paper, Gus?' I ask, taking the fat mince pies out of the packet and placing them on one of the patterned plates.

Gus smooths out the paper again. 'Oh yes,' he says, 'there is a story in here all about a man who tried to rob the NatWest in Teddington. He ran in with a pair of tights over his head, but they had a ladder in them! The idiot.'

I sit down in the chair next to Gus and look at the story he is showing me.

'Did you write any of these stories?' he asks. 'I can't see your name anywhere.'

I scan down, noticing Angela's name printed at the bottom.

'No,' I say, 'not any of those ones.' I look up at Jakub, who is engrossed in conversation with Nina. 'But I do want to. I want to write a story about this place, and how it's closing.'

Gus raises his hooded eyes to look at me.

'I wanted to ask if I could interview you, and Nina and Sylvia,' I say.

Gus chuckles. 'Me?' he says. 'In the paper?'

I nod.

'Oh,' Gus says, 'I don't know about that.'

'Your son could read it,' I say, 'and your grandchildren.'

Gus looks back down at his paper.

'Yes,' he says, 'I suppose so. Excuse me.' He pulls himself to his feet and I watch as Gus slowly walks out of the living room.

I move my body round to face Sylvia, who is reading her book.

'It's such a shame that his family can't come for Christmas,' I say. 'He's such a great man.'

'He's a coward.'

I blink at Sylvia in shock.

What?

'Gus?' I say. 'What do you mean?'

Sylvia looks up at me from her book. 'He never asked them,' she says. 'He lost his nerve.'

I frown at Sylvia.

'But why—'

'Bea?' Nina says, looking up from her conversation with Jakub. 'You can pour the tea now.'

CHAPTER TWENTY-SEVEN

I watch my computer screen impatiently as Facebook blinks back at me optimistically.

Come on, reply! Why aren't you replying? What else are you doing? Everybody has Facebook on their phones these days. Surely he's read the message.

'Bea?'

I look up at Angela and feel a zap of emotion as she walks towards my desk. Her back is arched over and she rubs her eyes with the back of her hand as she leans on the side of my desk. My finger snaps on my mouse and my story fills my screen, I feel a swell of excitement.

I've been waiting for Angela to come and speak to me all day. I never like to bother her, she always has her head buried in her work, and the odd time I've tried to strike up a conversation she's acted as if I've pulled her out of a trance.

'Good morning, Angela,' I say brightly, 'how are you?'

Angela looks at me, a confused expression flitting across her face.

'Oh,' she says, 'yes, I'm fine, thank you, Bea. I wanted to tell you that I've got a few press releases that I'll be emailing over to you this afternoon that need to be typed up.'

'Sure,' I say. 'Angela!'

Angela turns to leave my desk and stops.

'I wanted to show you something. I've finished writing my story, I wanted to see what you think.'

Angela pauses and I look up at her hopefully.

She needs to read it. It's a really good story, it's the best one I've ever written. I managed to talk to Gus, Sylvia and Nina about Sunfields. I even managed to get a quote from Jakub. Nobody will be able to read it without wanting to help.

'Oh, right,' Angela says. 'Has Duncan seen it?'

My eyes flit over to Duncan's office. The grey blinds are pulled down over his windows and his office door is firmly shut. He hasn't left the office all day.

'Err . . . no,' I say, 'but he did say I should work on something.'

Angela nods.

'Great,' she says, 'let's show Duncan now. If we're both happy with it then you're in time to make this week's edition.'

My heart turns over as I grab my printed story and follow Angela.

In this week's edition?

'Are you going to speak to Duncan?' Faye's blonde head clocks round as me and Angela walk past.

'Yes,' I say, 'to have a meeting about—'

'Great,' Faye springs to her feet, 'I need to speak to him too.'

I feel my eyes roll as Faye totters after us.

Why does she have to be involved in everything?

We reach Duncan's office door and Angela raps on it with

her knuckles, pushing the door open before Duncan has the chance to answer. As the door swings open, I feel my eyes widen.

Duncan's office is usually filled with coffee mugs and sweets, his desk empty of any real work, and all his windows are always flung open, letting in rays of natural light. My eyes squint at Duncan as if they are out of focus.

He jerks up, pulling his head from his hands and freeing his eyes from a sea of papers, all fanned across his desk and surrounded by an avalanche of biros. There is a large Starbucks cup at one end of his desk, and at the other end a paper bag is languishing, with tiny welts of grease swelling in patches. His tie is askew around his neck, and his face forces itself into a smile as soon as he sees us. The excitement brewing in my mind is replaced by a cold wash of emotion, and I suddenly want to leave.

'Sorry, Duncan,' Angela says absent-mindedly. 'Is now a bad time?'

Duncan slaps his hands together, and then quickly tries to organise his desk.

'No!' he cries. 'Never a bad time! My door is always open, remember? How can I help you ladies?'

I glance back at Faye, whose eyes are wide at the sight of Duncan.

'Bea has finished writing her story,' Angela says, striding towards Duncan and handing him the piece of paper. 'I think we should read it, in the hope of including it in this week's edition.'

Duncan fumbles the paper in his hands, his eyes widening and scrunching up again, as if he's using them for the first time today.

'Oh, right,' he says, 'of course. Well done, Bea. How exciting.'

He pushes his thumb and forefinger against his forehead as he squints down.

'Remind me,' he says, looking up at me. 'What was this about?'

I look around, my mouth suddenly dry.

I'm back. I'm back in the same position I was in all those weeks ago. Duncan, Angela and Faye all here, ready to hear my pitch.

My hand curls into small fists and I take a deep breath.

'It's a story about a local care home, Sunfields, that is being shut down by the council. I want to raise awareness of what is happening in our community. They are kicking these people out of their home—'

I break off, my heart thumping loudly in my ears. Duncan is looking at me, his watery eyes sad.

'That's awful,' he says softly, and then he quickly looks back down to the paper. 'Terrible!' he adds, his voice returning to his normal, cheerful manner.

'Why do you want to raise awareness?' Faye asks, scanning her eyes over the story.

Why is she so interested?

I look back at her defiantly.

'Because I want to get them to change their mind.'

★

I race through the door, my heart thumping from charging down the street. I push my way into the living room and drop my shopping bag on the table with a large thud.

Gus gasps. 'Bloody hell, Bea!' He laughs. 'Have you got a body in there?'

I grin as I hear Sylvia chuckle softly behind her book.

'No,' I say, 'I've got us a turkey. I managed to get the last one in Tesco.'

And what an ordeal it was. Christ, I never thought it would be so hard to get a turkey. Christmas is two days away! I thought I had loads of time!

'Oh, lovely,' Nina says, walking across from the window. 'That looks like a nice one.'

Sylvia pulls a face. 'I hate raw meat.'

Jakub appears from the hallway. He spots the turkey and looks impressed.

'Whoa,' he says, 'that's huge.'

I shrug. 'Well, we can have turkey sandwiches for the next few days.'

Jakub drops the turkey back into the shopping bag and carries it out towards the kitchen. Nina pulls up a chair next to me and smiles.

'How did the story go down at work?' she asks.

I smile.

'Good!' I say. 'They really liked it! I just want to reread it myself a few times and make sure it's definitely good to go.' I smile at Gus and Sylvia who are watching me. 'I think we might publish it next week!'

Sylvia dips her head at me. 'How exciting,' she says.

I open my mouth to reply when I feel my phone vibrate in my hand. Priya's name pops up on the screen.

Where are you? Are you in tonight or are you staying at your boyfriend's house?

I look down when she texts me again.

Whatever his name is.

I feel my face pinch as I push the phone into my bag.

'So,' I say, a grin spreading across my face, 'is everyone excited for tomorrow?'

I turn to Sylvia as she starts talking, when my phone lights up again. I look down into my bag and my heart jolts.

Sam Thomas has messaged you.

Chapter Twenty-Eight

I glance over my shoulder as I hear the front door click open. I press my back against my bedroom door and scan the letter one more time.

Dear B,

I can't believe all that you are doing for Nina. I never knew you had it in you. I guess I never should have questioned it. It's amazing that you've managed to get a local reporter to write about it. I didn't know you read the paper, do you read it every day? They post so much, sometimes stories just disappear. I'm doing okay. It feels weird being in here at Christmas. I have made friends, but you're the only one I'd want to spend Christmas with. It makes me miss Mum a lot. Hope you're doing okay and you're with your family for Christmas. Tell your parents I say hi, if they don't hate me.

Love you always.

Nathan x

'Bea?' The door shakes behind my back. 'Bea? Are you in there?'

My heart jolts as I quickly shove the letter under my bed and jump up. I pull the door open and look at Priya. Her eyes are wild and she's blinking madly. Too much. Why is she blinking so much?

'Hey,' I say, 'are you okay?'

'Yeah!' she says, her voice bouncing around the walls. 'I'm good! I'm great, actually.' Her eyes flit over my body, resting on my coat. 'Are you going out?'

'Yeah,' I say, reaching for my bag.

It's the morning of Christmas Eve. I've got to be at Sunfields in an hour to get everything ready.

Priya's face drops.

'But it's Christmas Eve!' she whines. 'We always spend Christmas Eve together.'

I look at her.

We haven't spent Christmas Eve together in about four years.

'No, we don't,' I say, 'you always spend it with Josh.'

I flinch as I hear the words leave my mouth.

'Sorry,' I add quickly, 'sorry, I didn't mean that. I just meant, I didn't realise we had plans together this year.'

I squeeze my way past Priya. She turns around and follows me.

'Are you going to your boyfriend's house?' she snaps.

A wave of heat scurries up my neck, but Priya doesn't stop.

'You are, aren't you?' she says. 'You spend so much time with him, Bea. Why haven't we met him? Why doesn't he ever come here? I don't even know his name.'

I walk into the kitchen and I start filling up my water bottle, desperate to avoid Priya's glare.

'You will,' I murmur, my face burning as the lie comes out of my mouth.

I turn back to Priya who has slumped down on the sofa. I feel a pang of guilt.

I wish I could tell her. She'd love everyone at Sunfields, they'd love her too.

But I can't. Not without telling her everything else. She wouldn't understand.

'I'm sorry,' I say. I walk forward and pull her into a hug. 'We'll spend some more time together soon, I promise.'

Priya hangs in my arms, her phone gripped tightly in her fingers.

'I just miss you,' she says in a small voice. I let go of her and she turns her face away. 'I don't like being here on my own.'

I look down at her, and for a moment I feel my heart sink.

I know that feeling.

'I'm sorry,' I say, 'I—'

Priya waves her hand in front of me. 'Don't apologise,' she says, shooting me a smile, 'just because you have a life and I don't. Anyway, I go home tonight for Christmas,' she says. 'I'm not back until the twenty-seventh. I think Emma has already gone. I somehow managed to get a few days off,' she shrugs at me, 'probably because I worked all of Christmas last year.'

'Well, we'll hang out then,' I say. 'Why don't you text Emma too? We can all do something together.'

Priya nods, keeping her eyes away from me. I pick up my bag and swing it over my shoulder, trying to squash down the guilt simmering inside me.

'Bye, then,' I shout, as I step into the frosty air and pull the front door to a close. 'Have a nice Christmas.'

★

I kneel down, squinting through the small window in the oven door at the glistening turkey.

'How's it looking?' Jakub asks, swirling a glass of red wine in his hand.

I look up at him. He's leaning against the kitchen counter. For the first time since we've met, he's not wearing his blue overalls. Instead, he's wearing a copper-red woollen jumper, stretched over his broad chest, and faded jeans.

It feels a bit weird seeing him in ordinary clothes, almost like seeing a teacher outside the classroom.

'Almost there,' I say, straightening up. 'Another half an hour or so. Right on schedule,' I add, before I can stop myself.

Jakub smiles as I hear Nina laugh loudly from the living room.

'So what was Christmas here like last year?' I ask, picking up my own drink. 'Did you have a big meal?'

Jakub nods. 'Oh yeah,' he says, 'we had all the residents here, and some of the nurses. There were about thirty of us, all in all.'

'Wow!' I say. 'Thirty? I wouldn't want to cook a roast dinner for thirty.'

Christ, imagine peeling all of those potatoes!

Jakub laughs lightly. 'We had help.'

'So,' I say, 'you had thirty people here last year? How many of them were residents?'

Jakub's smile drops slightly. 'Twenty-two.'

I look back at him, my heart twanging.

Nineteen people. In the last year, nineteen people have left.

The microwave dings and I look round as Jakub pulls the door open. A sweet scent of mince pies drifts into the space between us and he hands them to me proudly.

'Right,' I say, 'time for more mince pies, then?'

Jakub nods and we walk back into the living room. Gus insisted on pulling the crackers before we did anything else, and now has an emerald-green paper hat at a lopsided angle on his square head. Nina is sitting next to him, laughing as he reads a joke off a small, crumpled piece of paper, and Sylvia has her head in her book, again.

'Anyone for a mince pie?' Jakub asks.

'Oh, go on then!' Nina says, a smile stretching across her doughy face.

I shake my head as Jakub holds the plate towards me, and then I look towards Sylvia. My heart fizzes as I reach into my bag.

'Oh,' I say, 'Sylvia, here is your Christmas present.'

I pick up the large box and place it on the table next to her with a light thud. Sylvia looks up in surprise.

'A Christmas present?' she repeats. 'Who is it from?'

I sit down in the seat next to her. 'Me,' I say, heat rising up my body.

Sylvia looks around the room, her milky face pinched.

'But you—'

'Just open it,' I say, pushing the present closer to her. 'It's only something small.'

Sylvia hesitates for moment, and then reaches her hands over to the box. Slowly, she tears the bright wrapping paper, her green eyes squinting behind her glasses, until the paper falls away. I hear a small gasp escape from her mouth as she reads the words printed on the box. As I watch her, a smile spreads across my face.

'The complete works of the Brontë sisters,' she says softly.

'It's all the books!' I say happily, my heart swelling with pride. 'I thought you might like to read some more.'

Sylvia looks up at me, her eyes still wide.

'Maybe we could read one together,' I add.

Sylvia looks back down at the books and runs her hand across all the neat spines. I watch her, my heart beating rapidly in my chest.

'Thank you,' she says, her voice soft, 'I will cherish this.'

'Sylvie?'

I look round at Gus, who is holding a piece of paper away from his face and squinting.

'Here's one for you. Who delivers presents to dogs? Santa Paws!'

Nina laughs and I smile at Gus, who winks at Sylvia. A small smile lights up Sylvia's face.

'Why is that one for you?' I ask. 'Did you have a dog?'

I look round stupidly, as if there's a Staffordshire bull terrier who has been living here all along.

Sylvia is still smiling. 'Yes,' she says, 'his name was Bruno. Great big thing. He loved the sea.'

I frown. 'The sea?'

I'd always assumed Sylvia had lived all her life in London.

Sylvia tucks her hands back neatly into her lap. 'Cornwall,' she says, 'I used to go down there for my holidays. Bruno loved it. Silly old thing.'

'Cornwall is the best place to go,' Gus says, dropping his cracker on the floor, 'it soothes the soul. Was it Falmouth, Sylvie?'

Sylvia nods.

I open my mouth to reply when I hear the front door swing open. My heart leaps as my eyes fly towards Gus.

They're here.

'Be right back,' I mutter, getting to my feet and scurrying through to reception. Excitement bubbles in the pit of my stomach as I turn the corner and see a man wrestling with a small child. He's standing next to a woman with cropped, dark hair and a toddler on her hip. She's holding another small boy by the hand. Although I've never met either of them before, I recognise Sam's square jaw instantly.

'Hi.' I step forward, holding out my hand. 'Sam and Elaine?'

Elaine looks up and smiles, shaking my hand. 'Yeah, are you Bea?'

I nod. 'Thank you for coming. He'll be so—'

'Grandpa Gus!' one of the boys shouts, fighting against his dad's restraint. 'Where is Grandpa Gus?'

I blink down at the child. He has pale skin and large, wonky teeth that stick out of his pink gums. His blue eyes shine up at me and I can't help but grin.

'He's just through here,' I say, 'I'll show you.'

As I step back, I suddenly feel a flutter of nerves.

Should I have warned Gus about this?

Before I can speak, the young boy escapes from his dad's clutches and races past me. I chase after him, but before I can stop him he's leapt through the living room and on to Gus's lap.

My hands fly up to my mouth.

Oh Christ! He could give Gus a heart attack doing that!

'Grandpa Gus!' the boy squeals. 'Grandpa Gus! It's me, Tommy!'

Gus's smile is wiped off his face as he stares at Tommy in

amazement. Slowly, he looks round to Sam and Elaine and the two other children.

'Hi, Dad,' Sam says, stepping forward. 'Merry Christmas.'

'What . . .' Gus manages, his voice barely audible, 'what are you doing here?'

Tommy clings with his arms around Gus's neck like a monkey, and I quickly move a chair for Elaine to sit on.

'We were told you were having a Christmas meal today,' Sam says, 'and we wanted to come.'

Gus flicks his eyes up to me and I feel my heart do a somersault.

'Would anyone like a drink?'

I look up and see Jakub, who has reappeared, a Santa hat perched jauntily on his head. He hooks his arm over my shoulder jovially and I feel myself laugh.

Elaine and Sam murmur their responses and I notice Sylvia has placed her hand on Gus's arm.

'So,' Elaine looks up at me, bouncing a small child on her knee. 'Do you work here,' she asks, 'or are you family?'

My smile wavers. I open my mouth to speak when I feel Nina wrap her hand around my arm.

'She's family.'

And in that moment, it is as though the creature inside me doesn't exist. In that moment, I finally feel like I belong.

I have a family again.

Chapter Twenty-Nine

I hop off the bus, the damp air clinging to me as I step on to the pavement. I've barely been outside for the past three days. Except for popping out to get some milk, I haven't left Sunfields at all. Jakub let me stay in one of the spare rooms, and we didn't have any reason to leave. We spent the days talking, cooking meals and Gus even taught us all how to play bridge. Sylvia won, just like she said she would.

I turn into my street and notice Joy's house is in darkness next to ours. I frown.

That's weird. Joy never has the lights off in the day.

Maybe she ended up going away for Christmas, after all.

I walk towards my house, spotting the living room lights on and Emma and Priya's shadows.

I push the door open, my keys still in my hand.

'Hello?' I shout, kicking the door shut behind me.

I cannot wait to have a shower. The shower in the room at Sunfields was barely more than a dribble and their heating is always so abnormally high, I feel as if I've lost half my body weight in sweat.

'Hi, Bea,' Emma says. 'Can you come in here, please?'

I drop my bag in the hallway, the stillness in the house making me feel nervous.

Why?

I walk into the living room, trying to keep myself upbeat.

'Hey,' I say, as I see Priya and Emma sitting next to each other on the sofa, 'how was your Christ—'

The words die in my throat as my eyes fall down to Emma's lap and I spot my letters. The letters from Nathan.

My letters.

Panic splits through me and I feel my legs lock.

What are they doing with my letters?

'Where . . .' I manage, my voice hoarse, 'where did you get . . . ?'

Emma looks at Priya, and then back at me.

'Bea,' she says slowly, 'did you write back to that man?'

I stare at her, my heart thundering in my chest as everything crashes down around my ears.

They know. They've found out.

'Come here,' Priya says, reaching forward and pulling me on to the sofa. 'It's okay, Bea.'

She puts her hand on my leg but I feel nothing. Fear is whipping up my body as I stare at the letters, paralysed, desperate to snatch them out of Emma's hands and run away with them.

They've found out. They know my terrible lie. It's all over.

'Bea,' Emma says again, 'did you write back to that man in prison?'

Priya's grip on my leg tightens. 'It's okay,' she says quietly, 'we're not mad. You can tell us.'

Very slowly, I nod. I move my head and I feel my body crumple as the creature inside me flexes its claws.

'How many times?' Emma asks, fanning the letters in front of her. 'I mean, shit, Bea. There are so many letters here. There are about ten. Did you write back every time?'

My body starts to twitch as my eyes fill with burning tears. I nod again.

'But why?' Priya says quietly. 'We don't understand.'

Of course they don't. Nobody would understand.

Priya and Emma stare at me, waiting for me to answer. I look down at my hands, twisting them together as my face stings.

They would never understand.

'Like,' Emma pulls out a letter, 'he's writing as if he knows you, he's talking about things you used to do together and that he loves you and stuff.' She holds a letter up incredulously. 'Do you know him?'

'Have you been to see him?' Priya asks.

I shake my head. 'No,' I say quietly, my face burning with humiliation as I wait for them to piece it all together.

Emma looks down at the letters, and then slowly looks back at me. Her voice is low, and hearing her words out loud makes me feel as though I could die.

'Have you been pretending to be her?' she says slowly. 'This girl. This "B" person?'

'Is that where you've been?' Priya says suddenly, turning to face me. 'All this time, when you said you've been with your boyfriend? Have you been with him?'

'No,' I say quickly, holding on to this sliver of truth. 'No, I haven't.'

'Well,' Priya says, exasperated, 'where have you been? We don't understand, Bea.'

I open my mouth, my throat tightening as anxiety grips my body. I can't lie to them any more. I have to tell them the truth.

'I've been at Sunfields Care Home,' I say quietly. 'Nathan's nan lives there. He asked me to check that she was okay.'

Emma stares at me.

'How long ago was that?' she breathes.

'I don't know. About a month ago.'

'But,' Priya says, 'you've been away loads. Is that where you've been going all the time?'

I stare down at my hands, trying to fight the tears that are threatening to spill over. I nod.

'But,' Priya says again, struggling to hide her bewilderment, 'why?'

'They're my friends.'

The words leave my mouth before they pass through my brain. I blink away the tears that are welling at the corners of my eyes.

Emma blinks at me.

'Bea,' she says softly, 'I don't understand. Why have you been hanging out with old people and writing to a criminal? I don't get it. Where has this come from? Why would you do this?'

Because they listen to me. Because they like to see me. Because they make me feel wanted.

I bite my lip, my head hanging low.

Priya squeezes my leg. 'Are you still writing to him?'

I suddenly feel a sharp pain in my chest and I push the back of my hand against my wet eyes.

Emma leans forward, her elbows resting on her knees. 'Bea,' she says firmly, 'you can't write back to this man any more. You can't keep pretending to be someone you're not. You're messing with people's lives here.'

Her words cue the creature to rip through my body, tearing at the back of my eyes and squeezing my heart.

I never meant to hurt anyone.

'You need to stop this,' she continues. 'I'm sorry if you don't feel like we've been there for you. But you can't keep this up. It's not normal. It's not right.'

Priya looks between me and Emma desperately.

'Look,' she says, 'why don't I make us a tea? We can sit in and watch the *Strictly Christmas Special* like we said. I don't want this to ruin our evening.' She turns back to me. 'We're sorry, Bea. We don't want to upset you. We just want you to be happy.'

Priya squeezes my leg and nods at Emma, who walks into the kitchen and sticks the open kettle under a jet of water.

I shoot Priya a half-smile as I feel my body fold in on itself, and every spark of happiness inside me dies.

It's over, then. It's really over.

CHAPTER THIRTY

I hang my heavy head in my hands. My temples are throbbing with the thoughts that are spinning around my mind as I hear the office kettle whir in the background. My eyes squint around at the bright lights, stinging as I try to keep them open.

The entire street was in darkness this morning – not even Joy's house was lit up – and Priya and Emma don't go back to work yet.

My phone vibrates in my hand. I turn it over and read a text from Emma.

Hi girls, how about this as a fun getaway? If we book this month then it's a third off?

My heart sinks as I lock my phone.

Priya and Emma went back to acting as if everything was completely normal, and ended up suggesting that we all book a weekend away to spend some quality time together. It took all of my energy not to sit and cry.

I'm going to go back to Sunfields one final time to say goodbye. I can't leave Nina without that.

I shake my mouse in an attempt to refresh my emails as Faye swans past my desk. I try to keep my anxiety at bay. It has been simmering under my skin since I woke up, like a kettle on the brink of boiling. I must have fallen asleep eventually last night, but it didn't feel like I did. My eyes were wide open through the night, anxiety pinning my lids back with bolts and wrenching me out of sleep with thoughts that sliced through my mind.

What have you done?

What were you playing at?

None of it was real, you made the whole thing up. They don't even know who you really are.

Faye shoots me a look as she walks past and I feel a flutter of confusion as her usual smirk is replaced with an odd half-smile.

'Bea?'

I force my tired eyes to focus on Angela, walking towards my desk and looking like she does every day. The murky yellow bags are still hung under her eyes like hammocks and her thin lips have a lighter shade of pink slicked across them.

Maybe she got a new lipstick for Christmas.

'How are you?' she asks briskly. 'Did you have a nice Christmas?'

I nod, a dagger of panic shooting through me.

Angela nods back.

'Good,' she says, 'right, I'm about to send you a press release. I've already typed it up, so it's ready to go, I just need you to check for spelling mistakes, okay?'

I try to pull my features into a smile as my body twitches.

Angela smiles and turns on her heel, heading back towards her desk. I look at my inbox numbly, waiting for her email to appear.

I shouldn't be at work. I should have stayed at home. I can

barely speak without breaking. But I couldn't face being stuck at home with Emma and Priya all day. I didn't even want to look at them.

Angela's email pops on to my screen and I click it open. As my aching eyes try to focus on the words, my brain finally wakes up.

LOCAL MAN LOSES HIS APPEAL

Nathan Piletto, latterly of Lion Road, Twickenham, has lost his appeal against both conviction and sentence.

Piletto, 30, was convicted last June for fraud and sentenced to three years' imprisonment. Dismissing the appeal, Mr Justice Latham said that the jury had not been misdirected by the trial judge and that the sentence imposed was proportionate to the seriousness of the crime.

As I scan the last sentence, hot waves of fear engulf me as I look down at Nathan's pixelated face. My eyes flit across the room as my heartbeat thumps in my ears.

Who else has Angela sent this to? Who else knows about Nathan? I look at Faye, who is chatting to Jemima and laughing.

What are they laughing about? Has Faye worked it out? Does she know I know Nathan? What if she asks me about him? What would I say?

Heat rolls up my body and I try to swallow the sour nausea that climbs up my throat.

Is that why he wrote to B? Because he knew his sentence might change?

My eyes fly back to the top of the press release and I read through it again.

Did Nathan try to tell me about this? I've been so swept up

in organising Christmas at Sunfields and writing the story that I'd almost forgotten about his letters. I spent three days at Sunfields over Christmas, so maybe Joy has had a letter waiting for me for days.

I should have known about this before. I should have—

'Bea?'

I jump as Angela reappears. She's holding an empty coffee cup and looking down at me.

'Have you read it?' she asks. 'Is it good to go?'

I look up at her, my mouth dry.

'Yeah,' I say weakly, 'it's fine.'

★

I race down the road, my skin pinched as the wind whips my collar away from my face.

I need to get to Joy, I need to see if she has any letters for me from Nathan. And then I need to go and see Nina. Priya and Emma don't need to know anything.

I turn into my street and look at the houses. Joy's house is still in darkness. My heart twinges.

Is she still away? Where has she gone?

I need her to be at home. I need to talk to her.

My feet slow to a halt and I feel my body sag in defeat, until I notice her small car, parked on her drive. I frown.

That's weird. Joy doesn't go anywhere without her car. She never gets public transport.

I look back at the house, sat in a pool of darkness. Like it has been for days.

My heart rate picks up as I walk towards her house.

When was the last time I saw Joy?

I lift up my hand and knock firmly on the front door. The sound echoes through the cold air as if it's the only sound the house has made in days.

Joy always answers.

I squint through the window, trying to see something in the darkness.

Something's not right.

'Joy?' I call, rapping my knuckles harder. 'Joy? It's Bea, are you in there?'

My skin pricks in fear as a cold wave ripples through my body. I drop my hand and press my face against the window.

'Joy?' I shout again. 'Joy?'

Before I can register my thoughts, I race round the back. The blinds are pulled halfway down over her kitchen window and I pummel my fists on the back door.

'Joy,' I shout again, cupping my hands to the kitchen window and trying to peer underneath the blinds. 'Joy?'

I screw up my eyes, desperate to see through the thick blanket of darkness that covers Joy's house. As a car swings out of a neighbour's garage, a light is cast over Joy's kitchen and I spot her, sitting in her chair in the hallway. Her eyes are open.

My heart leaps into my mouth in relief.

She's okay.

'Joy!' I shout, louder this time. 'Joy, it's me! Let me in!'

I see her head move as the lights of the car vanish.

She's ignoring me. My frozen hands drop from the window.

'I'm not leaving until you let me in,' I say, my voice harsh.

Slowly, Joy moves her eyes towards me, but she doesn't speak. I raise my eyebrows at her challengingly.

'Let me in,' I say firmly.

Joy looks back at me, her mouth a straight line across her pale face. I can just make out her features in the dark shadows, as though she's a ghost.

Eventually, a small sound escapes from her mouth, but it's swallowed by the darkness.

'What?' I shout. 'I can't hear you! Just let me in!'

This time, her voice sounds louder and pierces the silence in the house like a knife.

'I can't.'

★

I lean back in my chair, turning the hot polystyrene cup between my hands and trying to stop it from scorching my frozen skin. Joy sits in the chair next to me, her hands placed in her lap and her lips pursed. She's barely spoken to me since I broke into her house. I smashed her kitchen window before I even had the chance to question what I was doing. Her key was in the lock, thank God. I don't know how I would have managed to get in otherwise.

I glance over at Joy and feel a spasm of worry as my eyes linger on the purple bruise on the top of her head.

Joy always smiles. She can't look at me without smiling, no matter what I say to her. This is the first time I've ever seen her look anything but happy. She looks broken.

I take a sip of my coffee. The harsh, burnt-tasting liquid swirls around my mouth, making me wince.

I had to carry Joy to the taxi. She could barely stand.

'Okay . . .'

I look up as a woman in purple overalls walks towards us.

'Joy Turner?'

Joy looks up and I instinctively touch her hand.

'So you're all fine. We've checked you out thoroughly after your fall, and you're all okay. I've got here that you weren't taking your medication?'

Joy's face doesn't move.

I look at her nervously. Come on, Joy. Please smile. I just want her to smile again. She doesn't look like her usual self.

'I forgot,' Joy says in a small voice, 'and then I couldn't.'

Joy's stiff hand twitches slightly under mine. Her hands have puffed up, like a fresh pair of armbands, and her knees are swollen, stretching the fabric of her trousers, like two fat melons.

I feel my grip tighten. I'm not letting go.

'Right,' the nurse says, 'well, you must remember to take your medication to avoid these flare-ups, okay? But I've also given you some new bottles,' she holds out a paper bag and I take it from her, 'which are much easier to open. I think you'll need some help over the next few days while the tablets kick in. Do you have anyone who can help?'

The nurse moves her eyes to me and I feel my body jerk.

'Yes,' I say quickly, 'me. I'll help her.'

The nurse looks back down at her clipboard. 'Are you her daughter?' she asks.

I feel my face prick.

'No,' I say, 'I'm her neighbour.'

The nurse writes something down on her notepad and then smiles at us both.

'Right,' she says, 'well, then, we're happy for you to go, Mrs Turner.'

'Thank you,' I say, finally prising my hand from Joy's as I put the plastic cup under my chair.

The nurse nods and turns towards another patient.

I look back at Joy. Her eyes are fixed forward and her hands are placed neatly in her lap. Only her chest is moving, which is slowly rising and falling with her shallow breath. I feel guilt tug at my chest. I've never seen Joy like this.

'Has this happened before?' I say.

My body squirms in the silence. She never ignores me.

'With the arthritis,' I add.

Very slowly, Joy shakes her head, her eyes still fixed forward.

'You can go now,' she says, her voice soft. 'You don't have to stay with me.'

A shock of heat hits me.

'I want to!' I say earnestly. 'I want to make sure you're okay!'

'Why?'

I blink.

Why? How can she ask me that?

'Because . . .' I say, 'because I care about you.'

We sit there in silence and I twist my hands together until the question that's been playing on my mind finally announces itself.

'How long had you been sat there for?' I say, my eyes glued to my hands.

My question hangs in the air, and I feel my cheeks burn.

I shouldn't ask her that. I know I shouldn't. But I need to know.

Joy sighs.

'I don't know,' she says. 'Jenny was going to call on Christmas Day, she said she wanted to have a video call, but I couldn't get my laptop working. I got so distracted that I forgot to take my pills. When I tried to go to bed I tripped, and everything went a bit . . .'

She trails off and I stare at her.

'Fuzzy,' she says. 'The next thing I knew, I was sat there in darkness until you appeared.'

She moves her eyes to meet mine and I feel a pang in my heart.

Christmas was three days ago.

Why didn't I go and see her sooner?

We fall back into silence and I take a sip of my coffee.

'Why were you at the house?'

I swallow another mouthful of coffee as guilt shoots through me.

I was at the house to see if there were any letters for me. I wanted to see if Joy had my post.

I wasn't there to see Joy.

I never am.

How long would Joy have been sitting there in the dark, if I hadn't found her?

How did I never notice that Joy was alone? I always knew she was alone, but I never really saw it.

I lean back in my seat, and place my hand back on Joy's.

I never thought anyone else could feel lonely.

CHAPTER THIRTY-ONE

I click open Joy's door and slip her key into my back pocket. The front door opens to reveal Joy's immaculate house, the white glow of the street light streaming through the window and showing everything perfectly in its place as though nothing has happened.

I hold the door open to Joy and step inside. I can't remember the last time I was inside Joy's house.

'Hello? Bea?'

Emma appears from the kitchen, her hair pinned back in a large clip and her sleeves rolled up.

'You just missed the handyman,' she says. 'He's fixed your window, Joy.'

Joy smiles as I lead her to an armchair. 'Thank you, dear.'

'And I've brought you round some Christmas cake,' Emma says, walking back into the kitchen. 'We had loads left over at home, and what's a cup of tea without some cake, eh?'

Joy sits down and I drop her bag on the floor.

'Are you okay?' I ask. 'Do you want a cup of tea? I think Emma is making one.'

Joy reaches forward and takes a magazine from the coffee table.

'Yes please, love,' she says. 'I'll go to bed soon.'

I nod and join Emma in the kitchen.

'Where's Priya?' I ask. 'Is she not here?'

'She was,' Emma says, reaching down three mugs from the cupboard. 'She left about five minutes ago. She had another Josh drama last night.' Emma reads my face. 'I know,' she says. 'I'm not sure where she went.'

I sigh and lean against the worktop. As my eyes scan the kitchen, I notice a small stack of post by the sink. Emma follows my gaze and I feel myself jump.

'Hey,' Emma says, 'I've got some exciting news.'

'Oh?'

Emma grins. 'I think I'm going to move in with Margot, rather than us finding a place just for the two of us. Her house-mate is never there anyway.'

I look up at Emma, my heart pounding. I'd almost forgotten about that.

'Oh, wow,' I say, 'that's great.'

'We're quite keen to do it as soon as we can,' she continues, 'and as you're the landlord, well, do you mind when I move out?'

I shrug. Mum left the house to me, but I never think of myself as a landlord.

'Whenever,' I say.

Emma nods and I try my best to give her a smile.

'Oh,' Emma says, turning back to the tea, 'I'm sorry about your story. It's a shame it didn't work out.'

I look back at Emma.

What?

'I read it this morning,' Emma continues, dropping the tea bags into the bin. 'I didn't realise they'd made the decision already and the home was due to close so soon. I guess you'll want to go back and say goodbye to them, before it happens.'

I stare at Emma, my heartbeat thudding in my ears.

What is she talking about?

Emma catches my expression. 'Have you not seen the paper?'

Emma sticks her hand in her back pocket and pulls out her phone. I watch her, my mouth dry, until she turns the screen to face me.

THREE RESIDENTS HOMELESS AS SUNFIELDS RESIDENTIAL HOME CLOSES

After much discussion, Sunfields Residential Home is closing on 2nd January, leaving the three remaining residents forced to find new homes. The decision was taken by the council, who claim that the residential home is no longer sustainable for the number of residents. A spokesperson said they have helped all the residents find suitable alternative accommodation.

But where does this leave the three remaining, vulnerable residents with nowhere to turn? Sunfields Residential Home, which was originally home to twenty-two residents, now has only three left as they struggle to find a new home before the January deadline.

A statement from the council claims that the 'health and well-being' of the residents has been 'paramount' throughout this process and they will do whatever they can to assist the final three residents with their move into their new homes.

But with only a few days left, do they have any homes to go to?

My mind trips over the words, hot tears clawing at the back of my eyes as I read the byline printed at the bottom.

Reporter Faye Musk.

She's stolen my story.

'Oh, Bea,' Emma whispers, putting her hand on my arm, 'are you okay? I thought you knew it was closing.'

'It's not true,' I manage, blinking the tears away, 'what she's written isn't true. They won't be homeless.' My eyes flick up to Emma's face. 'They'll see this. I don't want them to read this about themselves. I have to go and see them. I need to check they're okay.'

Emma takes her phone from me and for a horrible moment, I think she's going to tell me not to go.

'It's almost eight,' she says, looking back down at her phone. 'Is that too late?'

I shake my head, brushing the tears off my cheeks. 'No,' I say, 'they'll be up for another hour or so. I can't let them read this without me explaining. They know I'm writing a story, and I don't want them to think that I had anything to do with this.'

Emma looks at me, her eyes scanning my face. Suddenly, she reaches forward and pulls me into a hug. 'Okay,' she says, 'I'll stay here with Joy.'

She lets me go and I look at her. Emma never hugs me.

'Thank you,' I say, zipping my coat back up, 'I'll be home later.'

Emma nods, picking up two mugs of tea. 'I'll explain to Joy.'

I smile over my shoulder at Emma as I charge out of the

house. My heart races in my chest as I slam the front door, and the words swirl around my mind.

But where does this leave the three remaining, vulnerable residents with nowhere to turn?

Three residents homeless.

But with only a few days left, do they have any homes to go to?

I scrunch my eyes up as I taste bile at the back of my throat.

How could she write that about them? Making them the subject of some cheap news story. She doesn't even know them. They're human beings.

I need to see them. I need to make sure—

'Bea? Where are you going?'

I look over my shoulder at Priya, who is walking towards me. She has a long coat wrapped around her body and her eyes are wide. I keep walking, I don't have time to stop.

'Out,' I say, as I charge past her.

Priya turns to shout after me, 'Where?'

I keep walking, the wind whipping past me.

I don't have time for this.

'Wait!' I hear Priya scurry after me. 'Are you okay?'

She grabs my arm and I come to a halt by the bus stop. I feel my automatic smile limbering up, ready to spring on to my face, to tell her I'm fine, but as soon as I look into Priya's eyes the smile is washed away. Priya's grip on my arm loosens and she looks back at me, the icy wind whipping her ponytail.

'Bea,' she says, her voice stern, 'what's wrong?'

I look down at my feet, which become blurred as tears push their way into my eyes. I try to squash the emotion back down, like I always do, but this time it's stronger. As I raise my stinging eyes to look at Priya, I lose the fight entirely.

'They're closing the home,' I manage.

Priya takes my arm, but she doesn't speak.

'I'm about to lose everything again,' I say, tears now spilling down my face. 'I don't want to lose them. I don't want to go back to being on my own.'

The last words leave my mouth and I feel myself crumple. At this, Priya grabs my shoulders and pulls me into a hug. Her strong arms are wrapped around my body and she holds me tight, my weak body hanging limply in her arms.

'You will never be on your own,' she says fiercely, 'never.'

★

Priya yanks the handbrake up with a lurch and shoots me a grin.

'Whoops,' she says, 'don't tell Emma.'

I smile back, dabbing my eyes with the corner of my sleeve.

Priya twists her body round to face Sunfields and narrows her eyes.

'So this is the place?' she says. 'It must have been hell to get here by public transport. I would have driven you, you know?' She shoots me a grin. 'If you'd asked me.'

I laugh.

No she bloody wouldn't. Emma only added Priya to her insurance so she could drive the car for 'emergencies'. I dread to think what she'll say when she finds out about this little road trip.

Priya looks back at me. 'Are you going to be okay? If you call me later, I can pick you up. I don't mind. Or I can come in?'

I take a deep breath and unclip my seat belt. 'I'm fine,' I say, 'but thank you.' I turn back to face her and wrap my arms around her neck. 'Thank you so much.'

Priya squeezes me back. 'Course,' she mumbles through a faceful of hair.

I let her go and pick up my bag, before pushing open the car door and walking into Sunfields.

As I walk into the living room, my heart pounding in my chest, I spot Sylvia and Gus, sitting in their normal seats. Sylvia is reading a book with a different cover and I notice the newspaper is lying open on Gus's lap. He looks up at the sound of my footsteps.

'Hello, Bea,' he says, 'it's a bit late for you to be here, isn't it?'

Sylvia looks up from her book, a small frown playing across her face. I grab a chair and drop down into it, catching Nina's eye. She is sitting across the room watching the television.

'I know,' I say, my heart beating in time with my breath, 'I just needed to see you all.'

Nina makes her way over. 'Has something happened?'

I look back at Nina, and then down at the newspaper.

'Something was published today,' I gabble, emotion clawing its way up my body, 'but it's not the story I wrote, you have to ignore it. I didn't know she—'

I break off, the words tumbling out of my mouth.

Gus sighs.

'Ah,' he says, 'you mean this one?'

He flicks the newspaper open and I see Faye's story, printed in a small corner. To my alarm, I notice Nathan's face printed on the page opposite.

'Yeah,' I say, my body sinking into the chair. 'I didn't write it. Ignore it. It isn't true,' I say again.

Sylvia leans over to look at the paper, and then looks back up at me.

'We know you didn't write it, dear,' she says, 'but it is true. This place closes next week.'

I stare at Sylvia, my heart racing as her words sink in.

I don't want it to be true. I can't let this place close. I look back at Nina, who has settled herself on a small stool, and to my alarm I feel tears prick in my eyes again.

'But,' I say, my voice thick with emotion, 'where will you go?'

Gus puts his hands on the newspaper and looks at Sylvia, who has lifted her book up to hide her face.

'Well,' he says slowly, 'I think I'm moving into a lovely new home in Surrey.'

My heart sinks.

Surrey? That's miles away.

'Sam doesn't have the space, with his boys,' Gus chuckles, 'and I think Sylvie is off to somewhere nearby, aren't you?' He nudges her with his arm, but Sylvia doesn't respond. 'Was it Surbiton, Sylv?'

I feel my eyes well up again.

They're being separated?

'What about you, Nina?' I ask, barely daring to say the question aloud.

I don't want to know. I can't bear the thought of Nina being sent hundreds of miles away from me.

Nina cocks her head, her plait swinging across her shoulder.

'Oh,' she says, 'I'm not sure. Somewhere nice, I suppose.'

I look back at her, my mouth dry.

She doesn't even know?

'And I guess Jakub will be going back to Poland,' Gus chips in.

I look back at Gus. I hadn't even thought about what Jakub would do.

'He always said that he wouldn't want to live with anyone else,' Gus continues, 'although maybe he was just being nice.'

Gus smiles, and I feel a hot tear escape from my swollen eyes. Nina leans forward and places her hand on mine.

'It's okay,' she says. 'You've had a hard day, haven't you? What with that news about our Nathan too?'

I nod, almost numb to the hot feeling that bites whenever someone reminds me of my lie.

'Do you think you'll go and see him?' Nina asks. 'I'm sure he'd like that.'

I brush the tears off my face and try to smile at Nina's kind face. Nina's dark eyes look back at me.

'Maybe I'll go with you.'

I stare at Nina. I can't let her go. I need her.

'Live with me.'

The words fly out of my mouth and I stare at Nina, my face hot.

'I have the space,' I say quickly, my heart pounding in my ears. 'My housemate is moving out. There's room for everyone.' I turn to Sylvia and Gus, who are both blinking up at me from their chairs. 'That way, we can stay together and—'

'No.'

Nina's cold voice cuts across me and I whip my head back round to look at her.

No?

'It's fine,' I say, my smile fixing onto my face. 'I want to, and

I don't live that far away. So it wouldn't be that different for you and—'

'No,' Nina says again, 'we are not going to live with you.'

I stare back at her, my chest tightening.

'You are a young girl,' Nina says, her voice stern. 'You don't want to look after three old people.'

'Yes, I do!' I cry, getting up and moving closer to Nina. 'I really do, I—'

Nina lowers herself into a chair, her brow furrowed. 'You have your whole life ahead of you, Bea.'

I drop into the seat next to her and lean forward.

Why is she fighting this?

'But I love—'

'What happens when we get sick?'

My mouth hangs open as Nina's harsh voice strikes across me, her London accent thick. She catches my eye and her face softens.

'We're not your responsibility, Bea,' she says, 'we're not yours to look after.'

I feel my heart thud, heavy in my chest, as I look around at Gus and Sylvia. Gus gives me a lopsided smile and shrugs, and Sylvia stares back at me, her face taut, as always.

'But,' I turn back to Nina, my throat burning, 'where will you go?'

Nina meets my eyes and lifts her chin.

'That's not your problem,' she says.

My eyes start to burn as I stare back at her, and she turns her face away from me.

She doesn't know. She doesn't know where she'll go.

Why won't she let me help her?

I open my mouth to speak when I hear the bell ding from the reception desk. Instinctively, I look down at my phone. It's almost nine.

Who is that?

I clear my throat and get to my feet.

'I'll look,' I say.

I haven't seen Jakub since I arrived.

I walk into the corridor and spot a woman, a bit older than me. She has red hair that falls down to her shoulders and she is wearing a thick scarf. My eyes flit down and I notice that she's holding a newspaper.

'Hi,' I say, 'can I help you?'

The girl catches my eye and smiles back.

'Hi,' she says, holding up the newspaper, 'I'm looking for Nina Piletto? I used to know her grandson. My name is B.'

My stomach drops like a stone as I look at the girl.

No.

There, standing right before me, is my lie. I feel as if she's reached forward and wrapped her hands around my throat as anxiety storms through my body, ripping at my flesh and clawing at the backs of my eyes.

I step back, unable to speak as I feel my hand go instinctively towards the door that leads to the living room. I want to grab her, to tackle her to the floor or push her out of the front door. I want her to leave, I want her to disappear and never return.

'Hi . . .' Jakub walks into the reception, 'Who are you here to see?'

My entire body feels paralysed as I hear the woman say the words again.

'Nina Piletto.'

'Ah,' Jakub says, 'she's in here.'

I watch as the woman follows Jakub into the living room, taking my last ray of light with me, as I know I can never see Nina again.

And then I run.

CHAPTER THIRTY-TWO

'Hi, Mum,' I hold the phone close to my ear as I walk into the office, 'I'm sorry, I don't know what you must think of me, but I need your help. I've messed up and I don't know how to fix it. I don't even know if I can. I didn't mean to do any of it. I just . . .' I lower my voice as I reach my desk, 'I just don't know what to do now. I just need to talk to you, Mum.'

My voice breaks on the last words as tears burn in my eyes.

'I just need you to pick up.'

'Bea?'

I quickly brush the tears away with the back of my hand as Angela makes her way towards my desk.

I haven't allowed myself to properly think about everything that happened yesterday. If I think about it too much, I won't be able to breathe.

'Thank you for doing those press releases.'

I feel my face twitch.

Angela never thanks me.

'I think we should schedule in another meeting with Duncan

in a few weeks, to talk about your progress. I know he's been really happy with the stories you've been following up, even if you did share one with Faye.'

I feel a stab of anger.

I didn't share one with Faye. She stole one from me. Stole it, and changed it.

'Right,' I say, 'sure.'

Angela nods and walks back to her desk. I get to my feet and walk towards the kitchen, my clean mug gripped tightly in my hand. As I walk in, I spot Faye. She's hunched over her phone, which is shining brightly up at her. As she spots me, her body starts and a shadow flits across her face as if she's seen a ghost. I stare at her, and for the first time I don't feel my face pinging into a polite smile.

I just stare at her.

I slowly move towards the kettle and start to fill it up. Faye doesn't move.

'Hi Bea,' she says. 'How was your Christmas?'

I drop the kettle on to the stand and flick it on.

'Did you have a nice one?' Faye asks. 'Were you with family?'

I feel an icy shard lodge in my chest. Out of the corner of my eye, I see Faye watching me. The kettle begins to rattle.

'Listen,' Faye says, 'I know you're probably annoyed about the story I wrote, but it was a great piece.'

I feel a flash of anger.

A great piece?

'People love a sob story over Christmas,' she gabbles, as she scrolls through her phone.

'It wasn't a sob story,' I say tightly.

'Things like that happen all the time!' Faye says, her face

colouring. 'That's what happens when you work as a reporter, you have to find the angle. I saw an opportunity.'

My hands grip the kitchen counter as my eyes throb. I see a flash of colour as Duncan hovers by the kitchen door, but I don't care.

'They're human beings, Faye,' I say evenly. 'What you said about them exploited their vulnerability.'

'I checked my facts,' Faye snaps, 'I spoke to the council.'

'You didn't speak to the people the story was about!' I cry, my voice raised. 'It wasn't your story to tell! It had nothing to do with you, but it meant something to me—'

My voice cracks as I break off, my heart racing. Finally, Faye looks me in the eye. Her face is scarlet now and I notice tears welling up in her bright eyes.

'What's going on, girls?' Duncan says, clapping his hands together as if to break the tension. 'Have we run out of milk?'

I grab my tea and push my way past Duncan.

'Bea?' Duncan turns to me. 'Do you want to talk about it?'

'No,' I say, dropping into my chair and shaking my mouse roughly. As I do, I spot an email address I don't recognise at the top of my screen. I hear the muffled babble of Faye in the kitchen with Duncan, and I lean closer to my monitor as I click on the message.

Dear Ms Smyth,

I understand that you have been working with Sunfields Residential Home.

My name is Sandra and I work for the council. I would like to speak with you about the destinations of the current guests, as there may be some movement available.

I frown at the email.

Some movement? What does that—

'Bea!'

I look up at Faye, who has raced to my desk. Her eyes are now streaming and she glares at me, her eyes wide with fear. One look at her causes my heart to plummet.

'What?' I say.

'Quick!' she cries.

Without thinking, I stand up and race towards the kitchen. Duncan is leaning his body against the kitchen surface, short puffs of breath wheezing out of him.

Faye grips my arm and I feel the cold dawning of recognition sweep over me.

'Oh my God!' Faye cries. 'He's having a fit!'

'He's not having a fit,' I say calmly.

Faye stares at me. 'What?'

I look back at Duncan and take a step towards him.

I know exactly what's happening. I place my hand on Duncan's arm.

'He's having a panic attack.'

CHAPTER THIRTY-THREE

I hand Joy a steaming mug. She holds it in her hands and I notice that they're almost back to their normal size. I glance over at my house next door, sitting in darkness.

Priya is at work, and Emma will be out somewhere with Margot.

'Thanks, love,' she says.

Duncan's panic attack lasted about ten minutes, but by the time he came round his face was ashen. He tried to spring back into his animated self and laugh the whole thing off, but I could tell he didn't have the strength. Angela sent him home and for the first time since I met Duncan, he seemed relieved.

'You haven't had a letter in a while,' Joy says, glancing over to the pile of post on her coffee table.

I hold my own mug up to my lips and take a sip.

'I didn't write back,' I say.

Joy frowns at me. 'I thought you liked him?'

I take another sip of my tea.

'I don't know if I ever did,' I say quietly. 'A part of me thinks I just liked having someone to talk to.'

Heat pricks up my face as I hear the words aloud.

I had someone to talk to next door all along, I just didn't want it.

Joy tilts her head. 'Yes,' she says, 'I can understand that.'

She takes a sip of her tea and looks around the living room. I stare down at my hands, feeling my face burn.

'Have you been to see your mum recently?'

I feel a sharp pain in my chest as my eyes fly up to meet Joy's.

Joy is the only person who asks about Mum. She lived next door to her for thirty years. When Mum died, she almost took me in as her own.

I shake my head, feeling guilt wash over me.

'Why don't we go together?' Joy says, trying to hold my gaze. 'We could take some nice flowers, and then go for tea at that little cafe next door?'

I feel a zap of warmth spread through me as a small smile pulls at my mouth. Joy's smile softens as she places her mug on the coffee table.

'You know,' she says, 'although you heal, you never forget what life was like with your loved ones.' She raises her eyebrows at me. 'And you're not expected to.'

I stare back at her, my eyes glued to hers. Joy reaches forward and takes my hand.

'But I know that she'd be very proud of you, and all that you are doing.' She gives my hand a squeeze. 'You're just like her.'

I feel my chest ache. I never talk about Mum.

'It just feels so unfair,' I say in a small voice. 'She was only fifty-three. That's too young to die.' I wince as I hear the last few words fall out of my mouth

Joy's grip on my hand tightens. 'I know,' she says.

I wipe my eyes with my free hand and attempt to shoot Joy a smile.

'I'd really like to go see her together,' I say. 'I think she'd like that.'

Joy lets go of my hand, a broad smile spreading across her face. 'Yes,' she says, 'I think she would too.'

I take a sip of my tea and look around her living room. There are two plump sofas, upholstered in navy blue, and a large bookcase. My heart thuds as my eyes land on *Wuthering Heights*.

Sunfields closes in two days.

'And what about the care home?' Joy asks, as if she can read my thoughts. 'I read the story about that in the paper. So sad.'

I look down at my tea, feeling my heart swell.

'I know,' I say quietly, 'I've messed all that up.'

Joy frowns at me. 'Why?'

'Oh,' I shrug, 'it's a long story.'

I can't tell Joy what I've done. Telling Joy would mean reliving every detail. I can't bear to think of the looks on Gus and Sylvia's faces when they met the real B. I can't think of what it would have done to Nina.

They really let me into their lives, and I tricked them.

'*Argh!*'

I almost fall off my seat as Joy screams, staring out of the window.

'What?' I cry, reaching forward. 'What's wrong? Is it your knees? Do they hurt?'

I stare at Joy desperately, and then I realise she's looking behind me.

'What?' I cry, turning round. 'What is—'

My heart stops as I spot Jakub, glaring through the window.

317

His angular face is screwed up into a look of thunder and his icy eyes are locked on me.

He looks like he wants to kill me. Again.

Although I guess it's understandable, this time.

'Oh Christ,' I mutter, feeling my heart rate slow down. 'It's all right, Joy,' I say, trying to comfort her as she gawps out of the window. 'I know he looks like a serial killer but he is my friend.'

'Is that the man from prison?' Joy whispers, glancing around the room as if he's come to steal her collection of ceramic chickens.

'No!' I roll my eyes. 'He's a carer at the home.'

Jakub taps on the window. I glance back and notice he's still staring at me.

Good God, he's rude. I mean, he's literally standing on someone's front garden, trampling all over Joy's precious daisies with no regard whatsoever.

Can't he see I'm with someone? What does he want?

How does he know where I live?

'I'll be right back, Joy,' I say, placing my tea on the coffee table. 'He won't come in,' I add, as I notice a look of fear flash across her face.

I make my way through the hall and pull the door open. Jakub glowers at me.

'What are you doing?' he snaps, his Polish accent thicker than I've ever heard it.

I look back at him blankly.

'What?' I say, trying to keep my voice strong.

'Where have you been?' he says, his voice harsh. 'You said you'd help, and it's been days.'

His voice rises above the whir of traffic and I pull Joy's door shut behind me.

Bloody hell, it's cold. Why didn't I grab a coat?

'You've done exactly what you said you wouldn't do,' Jakub says, pointing a finger at me. 'You came and then left without saying goodbye. They need you. You're being selfish.'

I stare at him, bewildered.

What is he talking about? Doesn't he know?

'Jakub,' I say, exasperated, 'it's over. Didn't Nina tell you? B came to see her. They don't need me, they need her.'

Jakub blinks at me, his face unchanging.

'Who?'

I roll my eyes. 'B!' I say. 'I'm not Bea. It was all a lie, all right? It's over.'

Jakub looks at me like I'm speaking in Latin.

'Your name is not Bea?'

Oh, for God's sake.

'No!' I cry. 'Well, yes. It is Bea. But I'm not Nathan's ex-girlfriend. She turned up the other day. That's who Nina really wants. That's who should be there.'

Jakub stares at me, dumbfounded.

'That girl with the,' he moves his hand around his shoulders, 'with the red hair?'

'Yup,' I say, trying to ignore the anxiety swirling around inside me.

Jakub frowns. 'What about her?'

'She's who you want!' I cry, throwing my arms into the air in frustration. 'Not me. It's all a lie.'

Jakub looks behind him, as if B has followed him up the path.

'Her?' he says. 'Why would we want her? She came once and then left. She was there for five minutes.'

I blink at him.

She left?

'We don't care about her,' Jakub says, 'we want you. But you are too selfish, like I knew you would be.'

He tosses his arm at me, as if he's flicking a bug off his skin, and I feel myself snap.

'I'm not selfish!' I cry, stepping out on to the path and wincing as the icy cold penetrates my socks. 'I wanted to come back, I desperately wanted to see them, I—'

'Well, then, why didn't you?' Jakub says, cutting across me. 'Why have you been hiding here in your house?'

I flounder.

'I . . .' I stumble. 'I didn't think they'd want to see me.'

Jakub moves closer to me, and his icy eyes lock on to mine.

'Bea,' he says firmly, 'they need to see you.'

I stare up at him.

'You need to come back.'

I feel my heart pound in my ears. 'I don't know if I can,' I say.

At this, Jakub grips my shoulders with his large hands and leans forward so our faces are inches apart. I feel myself involuntarily hold my breath.

Oh my God, what's he doing?

'This isn't about you,' he says, his voice softening, 'it's about them.'

I blink as he lets me go, feeling as if I could melt into a puddle.

'We're going,' he says. 'Tell your friend.'

He gestures at Joy and turns to leave.

I grab his arm. 'Wait,' I say, 'there's something I need to do first.'

★

I turn the letters over between my hands, my heart pounding in my chest.

Is this a good idea? I don't even know any more.

'Are you sure this is where she lives?'

Jakub interrupts my thoughts and I look across at him. His long arms are draped over the steering wheel and he's looking at me from under a baseball cap.

Honestly, who wears a baseball cap on New Year's Eve?

'No,' I say, my insides squirming, 'but it's the only address I have for her. She left a forwarding address.'

I don't know how I didn't think of it sooner. Mum kept all of her tenants' forwarding addresses in a neat filing cabinet, which is still in our living room. I barely even notice it's there now, we use it as a DVD stand.

Me, Priya and Emma only moved into this house after Mum died. Her last tenant, a young mother with a baby, moved to Shropshire and suddenly the house was empty. The house was left to me, and living there almost felt like I had another piece of Mum with me.

But B moved out years ago.

I inch my body closer to the car window, focusing my eyes on the small house in front of me. The house is made of red brick, with a smart, shiny front door. It's a modern two-up-two-down, and I can see the lights on a skinny Christmas tree flickering through the front window.

As soon as I spoke to Mum, I knew what I had to do. It's funny, I've always been so desperate for Mum to answer her phone and speak to me that sometimes I don't even listen to what she has to say. I can still hear her voice. Even though she isn't here, I still know what she'd tell me to do.

'Are you okay?'

I look round at Jakub. He's stuffed into the driver's seat like a teenager crammed into a toy car. His back is arched over and his icy blue eyes are looking at me. My stomach twinges and I nod.

He is way too big for this car. He must be about six foot four.

Are all Polish men that tall?

'Do you know what you're going to do?'

I feel a stab of panic in my chest.

No. I have no idea. How can I say to a stranger that I've been pretending to be her for the past five weeks? That I've been writing letters to her ex-boyfriend, and signing her name at the bottom?

How do you say that to someone without sounding mad?

I hear a high-pitched ping and I look round at Jakub, who pulls out his phone. His expression flickers.

'What?' I say.

He shakes his head, unlocking his phone with a swipe of his finger.

'My flights,' he says. 'It's just check-in information.'

My stomach flips over.

'Flights?' I repeat.

He's going back. Of course he is.

Jakub looks up from his phone. 'Yeah,' he says.

I look away.

'You're really going, then?' I say, my face prickling as I force the words out.

I've been so focused on what's going to happen to Nina, Gus and Sylvia, I'd almost forgotten that Jakub would be leaving too.

I feel a strange tightness around my heart.

'Yeah,' Jakub says, 'tomorrow, just to look and see if I could move back there.'

He shoots me a half-hearted grin and shrugs, and I try to smile back.

I don't want him to go.

I look back at B's house, feeling heat ripple up through my body.

'Right,' Jakub says, pushing his phone back into his pocket, 'are you going in? I've left Sylvia in charge, but we need to go back.'

I feel a jolt of nerves shoot through my chest.

'Don't think about it too much,' Jakub says, folding his arms back against the steering wheel.

For a moment, we just look at each other. I reach forward and unclip my seat belt, my hands gripping Nathan's letters.

I step out of the car, raindrops splattering across my face as I walk down to the drive. I glance down at the stack of letters in my hand, all tied together with a piece of string, with the two most recent ones staring boldly up at me. One is addressed to Bea, the other to Nathan.

As I reach the front door, I tip the letters through the letter box and feel as though my heart has been posted with them.

The last letter I will ever write to him.

CHAPTER THIRTY-FOUR

I look down at my phone as a text from Jakub pops up on my screen.

Gus wants some brandy.

I laugh as I tap a reply and then click back on to Instagram as I walk towards Tesco. Immediately, a photo of Faye pops up on my screen. She's wearing a tiny green dress and has one arm pointed in the air, the other holding a fancy cocktail as she stands in a crowded bar. I look down at the bottom corner.

Uploaded five minutes ago.

137 likes.

I grab a trolley and push my way through the sliding doors, making my way straight to the alcohol section.

Well, I guess it is nearly 8 p.m. on New Year's Eve. I suppose everyone else is out, having a great time.

I reach the alcohol aisle and look around.

God, I can't believe I'm responsible for buying Gus's brandy when I know nothing about it. Which brandy is good? I don't even know where I'd find it. I mean, I know it's definitely not a beer, but, like, is it a spirit?

Why can't the alcohol aisle just be in alphabetical order?

I scan all of the posh bottles and feel my eyes widen.

Thirty pounds! Thirty pounds for a bottle of brandy!

I look around the rest of the aisle.

Is that the normal price of a bottle of brandy? Are they all that expensive? Or is this brand actually quite cheap?

I don't want to get Gus a really terrible bottle of brandy by mistake.

I reach out and grab a plump bottle, shining with oak-coloured liquid.

Thirty-five pounds. That'll do.

I drop it in my trolley and push it down the aisle.

It's a good thing I like Gus, there aren't many people I'd buy a thirty-five-pound bottle of alcohol for.

I turn the trolley into the crisps aisle.

Right. Snacks. Nina wants to share a bottle of red wine with Sylvia, Jakub will be having some beers and I'll probably stick to Baileys, but we'll all definitely want some snacks.

I start plucking large packets of crisps from the shelves.

And some dips too. Who doesn't love a dip with . . .

I pause as I notice a girl crouched by the bottom shelf. Her hair is piled up on top of her head and she's dressed in an old tracksuit. I step forward, my heart pulsing. I know that girl.

What is she doing here?

Before I can register any second thoughts, I step towards her. 'Faye?' I say, as I reach out.

Faye jerks up to standing, her wide eyes glaring at me. She

opens her mouth, as if she's preparing to lash out at me and I look back at her, realisation dawning.

'What?' Faye snaps, her voice thick with anger. 'What are you doing here? Did you follow me? What's wrong with you? What . . .' She trails off as the anger evaporates and, suddenly, with no warning, she bursts into tears.

All of the hatred I ever felt for her vanishes, and I reach forward and pull her into a hug.

She's not out with her friends tonight.

Maybe we have more in common than I thought.

*

I push a cup of coffee towards Faye, who presses the back of her hand against her bloodshot eyes.

'Thanks,' she grunts.

I smile, cradling my own cup between my hands as I look around the twenty-four-hour coffee shop. There are only three other people in here. One large man, with a big coffee and a panini, and two girls who keep whispering in the corner as though they're both undercover.

Maybe they are.

'Are you okay?' I ask, looking back at Faye. She's slumped against the back of her chair and is glaring out of the window. I see her eyes spark at my question.

'Yeah,' she snaps, 'of course I am.'

I look back down at my coffee.

Right. Of course she is.

I glance at the large wall clock and I feel a twitch of impatience: 8.32 p.m. I need to get going soon or they'll wonder where I am. This is the last night in Sunfields, and I want to be there for as long as possible.

This thought causes my throat to swell.

I don't want to ever leave.

I take a sip of my coffee, trying not to wince as it singes the back of my throat. Faye clocks me, and then looks straight back out of the window.

'Sorry,' she mutters, her face contorted.

I blink at her.

'Sorry?' I repeat.

'I shouldn't have taken your story,' she says. 'I shouldn't have done that.'

My hands tighten around my mug as I feel a stab of irritation.

'Well, then, why did you?' I ask evenly, keeping my eyes fixed on her.

Faye's eyes continue to glare out of the window, and for a second, I think she might ignore my question.

'I've said I'm sorry, all right?' she snaps.

I feel my body flinch.

Fine.

'Right,' I say, putting my coffee down on the table and my phone in my bag. 'Right, well, I'd better—'

'Wait,' Faye reaches across, her eyes finally looking directly at me.

I pause, waiting for her to say something else. She opens her mouth, as if the words are battling their way out, and then her mouth closes again.

My body sinks back into the seat and I let go of my phone. Faye links her fingers together, and although she's looking away from me again, I can see them shining.

'I'm not a good person,' she says quietly.

'What?' I say instinctively. 'Of course you are.'

Of course she's not.

'No,' Faye shakes her head, 'I'm not. I'm selfish. That's why I don't have any friends.'

I pause.

'You were so good with Duncan,' Faye mumbles, twisting her hands together. 'I didn't even know what to do.'

My heart pangs.

'Well,' I shrug, 'I knew what it was.'

We drop back into silence and I take another sip of coffee.

How can she say that she doesn't have any friends?

I watch Faye and notice how her shoulders cave into her body and her eyes, normally thick with make-up, are bare and raw.

Has she been like this the whole time? Have I just not noticed?

'Why don't you like me?'

My eyes fly up to Faye in shock.

'What?' I say, my face hot. 'Of course I like you.'

Faye shakes her head, her eyes still glued to her coffee. 'No,' she says, 'you don't. I can tell. You never want me to talk to you. You always want me to leave.'

I feel my mouth drop open, bewildered.

She actually wanted a conversation with me? That was her trying to be my friend?

'I didn't think you meant it,' I manage.

Faye cocks her head to the side, small red circles forming on her pale cheeks.

'Well, I do,' she says quietly.

'Right.'

I tighten my hands around my coffee, ignoring the heat against my skin as guilt brews inside me.

I can't believe I had her so wrong.

'I'm sorry I stole your story,' Faye says again, finally focusing her shining eyes on me.

I feel my eyes burn as I stare back at her.

'I'm sorry I wasn't your friend.'

CHAPTER THIRTY-FIVE

I push my way through the door, the hot, sweet scent filling my nostrils and forcing a wide smile on to my face.

I can't believe I used to hate that smell. My heart races as I walk through to the living room. I haven't seen any of them since I ran from the home.

'Bea?' I hear Gus call from the living room. 'Is that you?'

As I walk into the living room I spot Gus, sitting in his usual chair. Sylvia has her hand on his arm and Nina is by the table, a small glass of red wine next to her. I smile at Jakub, who is standing by the CD player. He walks straight up to me and wraps his arms around me in a hug.

I look around at their smiling faces.

They don't look angry. Why don't they look angry?

'Yeah,' I say, pulling the brandy out of the carrier bag, 'I've brought a peace offering.'

I put the brandy on the table and smile.

Gus frowns at me. 'Peace offering?' he repeats. 'What for?'

I feel the creature stir inside me, flexing its claws, as I look back at Gus's kind face.

'I lied to you,' I manage, forcing myself to look at Nina. 'You know, right?' I look back at Jakub, who nods. 'I'm sorry.'

I look around the room, feeling as if my body could crumple on the floor.

Please say something. Please, one of you, say something.

Nina reaches forward and touches my hand.

'Bea,' she says softly, 'we don't care how you came into our lives. We just care that you're here. We love you,' she says, her small hand tightening around mine, 'that's what's important.'

Tears strain at my eyes as I look at Nina's kind face.

They love me. They don't care. They still love me.

'Thank you,' I manage, as Nina pulls me into the chair next to her.

Sylvia shakes her head.

'Right,' she says, 'are we playing this game of bridge or what?'

Jakub leans forward, takes the brandy off the table and walks towards the kitchen. I feel myself laugh.

'You only want to play now that you're good,' Gus says, shooting Sylvia a smile.

Sylvia picks up the deck of cards and starts to shuffle.

'I think you'll find I was always good,' she says.

'Well,' Gus says, 'I hope someone in your new home knows how to play.'

I see a shadow pass across Sylvia's face and my heart turns over.

'Oh,' I say, looking around the room, 'I've got something for you both.'

I stick my hand in my bag and pull out the printed email. I feel my heart rate quicken as I hand it over. Sylvia starts reading immediately but Gus squints, holding the paper away from his face.

'Bloody hell, Bea,' he says, 'I wish you'd given this to me before I'd had a glass of wine.'

Nina looks at me, her brow furrowed, but I watch Sylvia, waiting for her to finish.

'Is this true?' Sylvia says, as her eyes scan the last line.

Gus looks at Sylvia. 'What?' he says. 'What does it say?'

Sylvia looks back at Gus. 'Bea has found us a home together,' she says, clasping Gus's hand in hers. 'She's found a home that can take us both, and it's by the sea. It's in Cornwall.'

I hear a sharp intake of breath from Nina and I see Gus's mouth drop.

'You don't have to,' I say quickly, 'but I've spoken to Sam, and he thought it was a good idea. He said that they could all come to stay in the holidays. I know you said that you used to like going there.'

My heart pounds in my chest as Jakub reappears, holding two glasses of brandy.

'That sounds lovely,' Nina says. 'How nice.'

I look at Nina and feel a sudden stab of emotion. I reach over to my bag and pull out a second piece of paper. As I step towards her, Nina meets my eye.

'Nina,' I say, 'I—'

'I'm not living with you,' Nina says firmly, narrowing her eyes at me as if I'm about to stuff her in my handbag. 'You're too young.'

I raise my eyebrows at her.

'I know,' I say, feeling myself laugh, 'but I thought you might be okay with living near me.'

I hand her the piece of paper. Nina takes it off me dubiously and scrunches up her face so that her eyes resemble two prunes.

Honestly, why doesn't she ever wear her glasses?

'It's for a home in Teddington,' I say. 'The lady from the council said they have a space. It's a nice home that's just up the road from me, so I can come and visit you all the time and we can get the train to Cornwall,' I look at Gus and Sylvia, 'so we can visit.' I turn back to Nina, feeling my heart pick up its pace. 'What do you think?'

Nina keeps her eyes fixed to the letter and rests her hand on my arm. She gives me a squeeze and her face breaks into a smile.

'Now that's more like it.'

CHAPTER THIRTY-SIX

I stagger down the garden path, struggling to carry the large box, which tilts towards my shoulder.

Bloody hell, what on earth is in this thing? How can Nina have so much stuff?

Priya sticks her hand out and holds the door open. I grin at her gratefully.

'Wow!' She laughs as I drop the box on our living-room floor. 'Be careful with that. It might be filled with valuables.'

I place my hands on my hips and look back at Jakub, as he fishes another box from his car. As he walks down the drive, a thought flits through my mind.

I don't want you to go.

Priya follows my gaze.

'Oh yeah?' she teases, nudging me. 'Is there something—'

'No,' I say quickly, rolling my eyes at her, 'we're just friends.'

Jakub walks through the door and carefully puts the box on the floor. He smiles at me.

'Only a few more,' he says, turning and walking straight back out of the door.

I shoot Priya a warning look as I follow him out.

She'd better not say anything to him.

'Bea?'

I look round and see Joy, leaning out of her door. I walk over, smiling.

'She's moving in, then?' Joy says, peering out at Jakub as he picks up another box.

I shake my head. 'No,' I say, 'but she's staying with me for a few days while the new home gets her room ready. I'm going to make a big roast tomorrow. Actually,' I add, 'you should come and meet Nina. You'll like her, she's really nice.'

Joy smiles at me, her eyes gleaming.

'Oh yes,' she says. 'That would be lovely.'

I smile back at Joy and turn to leave.

'Right,' I say, 'well, I'd better—'

'Oh, Bea,' Joy says, 'before you go . . .'

I turn round and, with a jolt, I notice what is in Joy's hand.

'. . . you've got another letter.'

I look down at the scrawled handwriting, my address written exactly as it has been for the last five weeks. But the stars have gone.

He's written back.

Why?

Joy looks up at me. 'Do you want to open it here?'

I glance back at Jakub as he enters my house.

I don't want him to see it. I don't want anyone to see it.

Without speaking, Joy steps back and gestures for me to come inside. I follow her into her living room and sink down on to the sofa, my heart thumping.

I don't know if I want to open this. What is he going to say? Why is he writing to me?

Slowly, I pull the letter open and as I read, my heart seems to stop.

Dear Bea,

B has just left, she gave me your letter and told me everything. I was so angry at first. I just can't understand why someone would do something like that. I thought that you might have done it for a joke, or to take the piss or something. But then I read your letter. I don't know you, and I know that now I never will, but I meant what I said. Your letters kept me afloat in this place and, more than anything, I want to thank you for that. I also want to thank you for looking after Nina. I know things haven't worked out the way I thought, but a part of me thinks this was how it was supposed to happen. B is grateful to you. She said that she wouldn't have written back if she'd got that first letter, so I guess that's something else I have to thank you for. She's the love of my life.

I hope you're okay. You've helped me a lot over these last few weeks, so let me just say one more thing to help you. If there's someone in your life that you can't live without, don't let them go.

Nathan

I stare at the letter, my heart thumping. I look up at Joy who is staring at me, her eyes thick with worry.

'What?' she says. 'What is it? Are you okay?'

Before I can register my action, I get to my feet and race towards the door. Jakub is standing by the car door, the last box in his hands.

'This is the last one,' he says, 'and then I—'

But his words are lost as I throw my arms around his neck. He stumbles backwards, dropping the box to the floor.

'Whoa!' he cries. 'What is it?'

'Don't go,' I gabble, letting go of him. 'Stay. Please. I don't want you to go. I don't think you should. I think you should stay. I want you to stay—'

I break off, staring into his icy eyes. He looks down at me, and my heart races.

Say something. Please say something. Say anything.

Finally, he reaches down and kisses me, and I realise he doesn't need to say anything at all.

Epilogue

I look down at my phone as a text from Jakub pops up.

Just picking Sylvia and Gus up from the station. Be with you in an hour.

I smile, my heart flipping over.

Jakub didn't get on his flight.

My heart skips again.

He's going to stay.

'Hi, Faye.' I walk past Faye's desk, holding my clean mug in my hand. 'I'm going to make a coffee, would you like one?'

Faye smiles at me. 'Yes, please,' she says. 'I'll come help in a second.'

'Okay,' I say. 'Oh,' I turn back to face her, 'are you still coming on Sunday?'

Faye smiles at me. 'If that's okay?' she says. 'I can bring something. I know how to make chocolate brownies?' she offers.

I grin. 'Sounds perfect,' I say, as I make my way around the office. I reach Duncan's door and knock firmly. He only came back to work yesterday, and for the first time since I've met him, his bravado has been dropped. He now seems like a real person, rather than a cartoon character. I actually like this Duncan.

'Hi, Duncan,' I say, pushing the door open, 'I'm making a coffee, would you like one?'

Duncan looks up from his computer and grins at me. 'Oh yes please, Bea,' he says.

I walk over to his desk and pick up his mug. I notice a framed photo on his desk that I haven't seen before. His two daughters are perched on the knees of a woman who is wearing big sunglasses, and they are all sitting on a picnic bench.

'That's a lovely photo,' I say, looking down.

Duncan beams at me.

'How are you?' I ask, dropping into a chair before I can convince myself otherwise.

Duncan smiles. 'I'm okay, thank you,' he says earnestly. 'I've learnt my lesson,' he adds, pointing his pen at me.

I raise my eyebrows. 'What's that?'

'To talk about things,' Duncan says, leaning back into his chair and giving me a look. 'Not to bottle everything up. That there's no shame . . .' I feel a flash of emotion run through me and he shoots me a grin. 'I could go on,' he says. 'Oh,' he adds, as I go to stand up, 'can I have a decaf?'

I hold his mug up in recognition and smile at Angela as I walk through the office into the kitchen. I'm finishing work an hour early today, to meet Sylvia and Gus. They've travelled up from Falmouth to stay with us for the weekend. Nina is staying with Joy, and Jakub is sleeping on the sofa to make room for them. Even Priya, Emma and Margot are coming over tomorrow, and they've said that they're 'very excited' at the prospect of my roast, which makes me feel a bit sick. Also, I haven't really thought about how I'm going to sit ten people around our dining-room table, but I can work that out tomorrow.

I pull my phone out of my pocket and hold it up to my ear.

The important thing is that everyone is going to be there, together. My weird, but perfect, mismatched family.

I hold my phone close to my ear as I hear the click of the call being answered.

'Hi, Nina.' I smile into the phone. 'It's me.'

I wouldn't have it any other way.

ACKNOWLEDGEMENTS

As always, I need to start by thanking my Super Agent, Sarah Hornsley, who believed in me right from the beginning and continues to champion me fiercely.

I also have an enormous amount of gratitude to my Editor, Jess Whitlum-Cooper, who is as kind as she is brilliant and always understands exactly what I'm trying to do, even if I can't work it out myself.

Thank you to my publicist, Jenni Leech, and everyone else who is part of the fantastic Headline team. I really appreciate all that you do to make my dream a reality.

Thank you to Gemma and Ziggie, who made me dinner on the countless times that I was too consumed by writing to remember to buy food, and to Kola for helping me bring Jakub to life.

Thank you to Arianna for always believing in me and laughing at my jokes (the good and the bad . . . especially the bad).

Thank you to Chris, for helping me through my writer's block and making me endless cups of tea.

Thank you to Catherine, Lynn and Ziggy for allowing me to run away to the seaside and making the last chunk of the novel seem much less scary.

Thank you to Lynsey, my ultimate author friend who is always at the other end of a whatsapp when I'm worried I've forgotten how to spell my own name.

Thank you to my soul sister Kiera, who always helps me see the funny side of writer's block in the time it takes to order another coffee.

Thank you to my cheerleaders for their endless support, Claire, Libby, Anna, Laura, James, Maynie, Luke, Andrew, Hayley, Katy, Georgia, Becca, Alice, Emily, Adam, Sharon, Kristie and Jamie.

Thank you to my Grandparents for sparking my imagination.

And finally, thank you to my family for everything you have always done for me. My sister Elle, who keeps me calm, my brothers Tom and Dominic, who always make me laugh, my Dad, who keeps me motivated and my Mum, who never lets anyone feel alone.

If you enjoyed *The Accidental Love Letter*
then you'll love *The List That Changed My Life. . .*

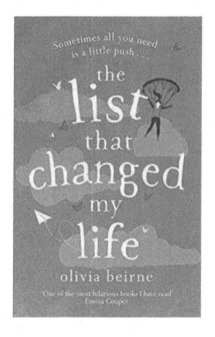

'One of the most hilarious books I have read for
a very long time'
Emma Cooper

Available now in eBook, audio and paperback
from Headline Review!

REVIEW

Keep in touch with Olivia Beirne!

www.oliviabeirne.co.uk
🐦 Olivia_Beirne
📷 olivia.beirne
📘 /Olivia-Beirne